"No, Richar...
I've never been in love."

Anna stared up at him with her heart beating like some muffled drum. "You wouldn't have married me if you'd known, would you?"

"No," Richard said with a wry twist to his lips. "I thought we were two people who'd suffered some...disillusionment that had left us ready to deal with realities. If you knew anything about me, you'd know that I didn't want to be burdened with a virgin bride," he said with sudden savagery. "Don't look like that!"

He pulled her into his arms, holding her close as her body shook in despair. "We'll make it work somehow," he said, not quite smiling. "Who knows, I might turn into a prince charming for you, after all." But there was a curious look of pain in his eyes.

Don't Call It Love

Lindsay Armstrong

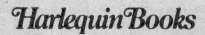

TORONTO • NEW YORK • LONDON
AMSTERDAM • PARIS • SYDNEY • HAMBURG
STOCKHOLM • ATHENS • TOKYO • MILAN

Original hardcover edition published in 1984
by Mills & Boon Limited

ISBN 0-373-02653-6

Harlequin Romance first edition November 1984

Printed in U.S.A.

CHAPTER ONE

ANNA HORTON picked herself up from the dusty roadway and brandished a clenched fist at the rear of a huge semi-trailer that was laboriously and noisily gathering speed as it moved away from her.

She had just climbed down from the cab of the same vehicle, seething with anger and distaste at what the driver had proposed to her, had had her bag pushed out after her, and had landed on the road in an undignified heap.

But what she didn't realise, as she stood in the middle of the road giving vent to her feelings, was that the driver of the semi-trailer, high up in his cab, had noticed a car approaching in his rear-view mirror that Anna was unaware of for several reasons—a bend in the road which she had her back to in any case and the noise of the giant engine of the semi-trailer itself being the two main reasons.

In fact the first intimation she had of the approaching car came when she lowered her fist, grimaced at the cloud of dust enveloping her and walked a few steps towards her bag. Then everything happened so quickly she had no time to take evasive action. The car swerved and she found herself unwittingly right in the path of that swerve. The next few minutes were a nightmare of squealing tyres, an even thicker cloud of dust and the heart-stopping conviction that she was going to be killed.

That she wasn't had to be a miracle, she knew not much later when an unnatural quiet descended and the boiling dust sank a little and she could see the car with its bonnet only inches from her and smell the burning rubber of the tyres as the body rocked on tortured springs.

She lifted her hands to her face and began to sink to her knees from sheer, shocked reaction, but the driver of the car took matters into his own hands then. He climbed out swiftly, strode up to her, jerked her upright by her shoulders and attempted to shake the life out of her.

'You bloody idiot!' he swore. 'I could have killed you!'

'I . . . I didn't see you,' she faltered, staring up into a pair of scorching grey-green eyes and receiving a confused impression of a tall, powerful presence and an arrogantly moulded face beneath thick, fairish hair.

'I'm not surprised!' the man blazed at her. 'You weren't damn well looking!'

'B-but you must have seen me,' she stammered.

'I came round that bend to see a swirl of dust and when I swerved you stepped out of it right under my wheels!'

'Perhaps you shouldn't drive so fast,' she countered, a faint spirit of rebellion coming over her. 'You . . .' But she stopped and gasped as he shook her again, so hard that her head flew back painfully. '*Don't!*' she pleaded. 'You're hurting me!'

He let her go abruptly and she reeled back against the bonnet of the car.

'Perhaps you'll think the next time you're tempted to dally in the middle of the road,' he said savagely.

He looked around then as if expecting to see something, but all his eyes alighted on was her bag lying almost under his wheels and his angry gaze came back to rest on her white, dust-streaked face.

'Just what the hell are you doing here anyway?' he demanded with an all-encompassing gesture that took in the virgin bush stretching limitlessly to the horizon on either side of the road. But almost immediately his face changed and she felt shrivelled by the look of withering scorn he cast her as he said contemptuously, 'Oh, don't tell me! You hitched a ride on that semi-trailer I was catching up on, didn't you?'

'I . . .' Anna bit her lip.

'So what went wrong, sweetheart?' he queried derisively. 'Was the price of the lift becoming a bit more than you thought you should pay? You know, you should always be strictly businesslike about these things, then these little misunderstandings wouldn't occur. Why don't you get a price list printed? Say, something like—up to a hundred miles, a kiss or two permitted; up to two hundred miles, some fondling allowed . . .'

'You . . .!' Anna snapped furiously, and slapped his face.

But no sooner had she done it than she found herself regretting it, for the retaliation that came was swift and brutal and humiliating. He jerked her into his arms and sought her lips unerringly with his own and kissed her mercilessly.

And when he'd done the job thoroughly, her lips were bruised and swollen and her legs shakier if anything, than they had been several minutes earlier, so that she had to bear the added humiliation of finding herself clinging to him helplessly as she stared up at him shocked and wide-eyed and breathless.

'Let that be a lesson to you to pick someone your own fighting weight next time, my friend,' he said softly but with so much mockery that a flood of colour came to her cheeks and she pushed herself away from him angrily.

He laughed then and she tensed anew, but something warned her not to cross swords with this man again, so with a toss of her head and her lips set defiantly, she lifted her bag off the road and walked away as steadily as she was able to. Which was none too steadily, unfortunately, and she stumbled almost immediately and felt his hand on her arm.

'Let go of me,' she said coldly.

'Then get in the car.'

'No! If you *think* . . .'

'I think, yes,' he interrupted, and swung her round.

Anna swallowed and said tightly, 'If you think I'd go anywhere with you, you're wrong! After having the gall to say to me what you did and then . . . and *then* . . .'

'Kissing you?' he supplied with one eyebrow raised quizzically.

'Yes!' she said hotly. 'I'd rather walk to Cape York!'

'Oh well,' he stepped back and for the first time there was a glint of genuine amusement in his eyes, 'it's up to you. I don't think you'll find yourself walking to Cape York, but you might have to walk to Innisfail. You see, what you might not know is that my car was the last one to cross the river on the ferry back there. It's now closed until tomorrow morning.'

Anna had been in the act of turning away again, but she stopped abruptly. 'So . . . I mean . . .' She trailed off uncertainly.

He nodded.

'But there'll be local traffic on the road, surely?' she said somewhat desperately.

'I doubt it. I know this road pretty well. There's no habitation on it for the next fifty miles, roughly.'

'Fifty miles?' she echoed faintly, and looked around. It would be dark soon, she knew. The swift velvet darkness of the tropics.

'And you'll be coming into cane country soon,' he added casually. 'That has its disadvantages for pedestrians. Cane is notorious for unpleasant things like snakes and rats.'

Anna closed her eyes briefly. 'How—how far is it to Innisfail?'

'It will take me a bit over two hours. I don't think you have much choice, my dear,' he said indifferently. 'Nor do I have all the time in the world to stand here while you deliberate,' he murmured coolly.

Anna licked her lips and gazed at her would-be rescuer, taking him in properly for the first time. He was tall with a body that was powerful, as she now well knew, but it was also elegantly streamlined and the khaki bush shirt and trousers he wore didn't hide it. But his face was what she concentrated on, and she thought he didn't look like a would-be rapist or seducer. I mean, she amended to herself, can you tell by just looking at someone? Yet that man's face was intelligent and his mouth well cut. Other things about him pierced her consciousness too—the fact that he had an air of confidence, that his car was powerful and foreign and obviously expensive as was the watch he wore. She stared at the watch and noticed absently the fine golden hairs on his arm and that his hands were slender yet powerful-looking too and faintly freckled on the backs.

Not a man, she thought with a sudden, curious awareness that made her skin prickle, not a man who would need to take anything by force, probably.

'Have you quite finished?' the object of her inspection drawled. He leant back against the car and glanced at his watch. 'You have two minutes,' he said evenly.

Anna's eyes narrowed. 'I'm sorry to keep bringing this up,' she said gently, 'but considering your earlier sentiments on the subject of hitch-hiking, I'm a little surprised that you should object to me weighing the odds.' She shrugged. 'After all, what are a few snakes— I'm told they're shy creatures anyway—compared to a fate worse than death?' she added.

There was a tense little silence during which his eyes roamed over her and left her in no doubt that he was mentally undressing her. And she began to regret her words and her impulsive nature which not infrequently led her into awkward situations.

Then he straightened up. 'Actually, I've revised my opinions,' he observed. 'Perhaps I was a little harsh on you.'

'What do you mean?' she asked after a moment. 'Because I prefer the thought of snakes and rats, have I suddenly become more respectable?'

'Oh, it's not that.' He smiled slightly. 'It's the fact that upon consideration, you kiss like a proper novice, my dear. Thus, you can banish all thoughts you might have been nurturing that I would try to take advantage of you in the way our late, unlamented semi-trailer driver did. So are you coming or not?' he finished impatiently.

Anna was so angry at that moment, she found she couldn't speak. And he took advantage of it to prise her bag from her fingers and sling it into the back seat of the car. Then he got in himself and leaned across to open the front passenger door for her.

She clenched her fists and thought of her brave words about snakes and rats. And she thought of trudging fifty miles in the dark and the fact that she was hungry and tired and filthy and considerably shaken up one way or another. The options seemed to be wildly overloaded.

'All right,' she said tautly as she slid into the car and looked at him, her face still pale with strain beneath its coating of dust, 'all right, you win—this time. But there are people expecting me in Innisfail so . . .'

'What other times are there likely to be?' he interrupted as he set the car in motion. 'Once we get to Innisfail we will part company most properly and I have no doubt you will go upon your merry way, hitch-hiking around Australia.'

'I—how did you know?' she asked, sinking back into the beautifully sprung seat.

'The signs are unmistakable,' he said. 'Even covered in dust you have a sort of—clean-cut, college girl air about you. Besides, the other kind of girl doesn't usually get herself turfed out on to a deserted stretch of roadway as you did.' He turned his head and their eyes clashed. 'I'm right, aren't I? You grew up in suburbia and you've saved for this ever since you left school? It's been the big dream of your life?'

Anna leant her head back and considered his words. 'You're more or less right. Although I'm working my way around rather than hitch-hiking, but I have hitched now and then. If you could work it all out, though, why were you so angry?'

'Perhaps because I don't often come so close to running someone down and splattering them on the roadway,' he said dryly.

'Well, I can understand that, and I'm sorry,' she said after a moment. 'But you were just as angry because I'd hitched a ride.'

'If I was,' he conceded grimly, 'it was because it's become an increasingly dangerous thing to do. You only have to read the papers to know that.'

Anna stirred. 'As a matter of fact I don't make a habit of it. But sometimes there are circumstances which . . .'

'Did you explain that to your semi driver?' His voice was taunting.

'Yes!' She sat up. 'I told him the whole sad story—how I'd been working on a station out from Georgetown and that I'd come into town to catch the bus to Innisfail, to find that it was their annual picnic race day,' she said bitterly. 'Which, to cut a long story short, I discovered to my cost is also their annual pickpockets' day. I was—relieved of all my money.'

'Go on,' he said tautly.

'I should have thought the rest was obvious,' she said shortly. 'I tracked down the lone policeman the town boasts, only to find him dead drunk because he'd backed the winner of the Cup for the first time in twenty years. There seemed to be no solution other than to hitch a ride to Innisfail where there's a branch of the bank I patronise in a small way. Do you know,' she grimaced, 'that driver was fifty if he was a day and he kept telling me about his grandchildren! He even showed me their pictures,' she added aggrievedly. 'To think that I deliberately bypassed several younger, more—well, virile-looking truck drivers and picked on a fatherly, homely-looking man, only to find . . .'

She stopped suddenly and turned her head. 'Which all goes to prove your point, doesn't it?' She smiled ruefully. 'I stand convicted,' she said quietly.

There was a brief silence. Then he smiled back at her and she caught her breath unexpectedly, because it was an amazingly attractive smile that lit his eyes with amusement and she found herself wondering, curiously, how old he was. Probably in his mid-thirties, she decided.

And as they drove on through the fast gathering dusk in an oddly companionable silence, she found herself thinking, rather strangely, of all the men she had dated since leaving college. All of them nice enough in their own way, she mused, but in comparison to this man . . . well, boys, not men would be an apt description, she thought, although they would be horrified to have me say so. Then again, they were all round about my age, and I'm only twenty-three—just, so perhaps I'm being unfair . . .

Her eyelids drooped at this point and although she

strove valiantly to keep them propped open, the fact that the headlights were now picking up an everlasting, serried sea of cane on either side of the road didn't help. Nor, probably, did the fact that it had been a totally traumatic day, and she fell asleep.

She woke with a jerk and sat up to stare round confusedly. The car had stopped.

'We're here,' her companion said a shade dryly.

Anna turned to him and blinked. 'Innisfail? How . . . I . . .' She trailed off awkwardly and peered out through the windows. But there was no doubt they were in the sugar town of Innisfail. She could see a sign to Johnson River bridge and also the tracks in the road for the cane trains. 'I'm sorry,' she said uncomfortably, 'I must have been asleep for ages! Not the most entertaining companion in return for . . . but thank you very . . .'

'Hang on,' he said, as she reached over to get her bag. 'You mentioned something about people expecting you. I'll take you there.'

'Oh no! No, this is fine, honestly. And you did say you didn't have much time . . .'

He regarded her thoughtfully for a moment before remarking, 'Another half hour won't make much difference. And having brought you this far I might as well complete the job.'

Anna winced and went faintly pink. 'That wasn't true, actually—what I said about people expecting me. I said it to . . . to . . .'

His lips twitched and then he started to laugh at her confusion. 'Did you really think that of me?' he asked finally and with a wicked glint in his green-flecked eyes.

She breathed deeply. 'How was I to know what to think?' she said stiffly. 'And you yourself . . .'

'Got hoist with my own petard,' he agreed, looking still amused. Then he sobered. 'But what will you do? You said you had no money, and the banks won't be open.'

'That's no problem,' she said hastily. 'A couple of months ago I worked at a hotel here—in fact it's only a block or so away,' she pointed down the road, 'so they know me and I'll have no trouble getting a room and a meal. And tomorrow I'll get to the bank.'

'Then I guess this is farewell, Miss Hitch-hiker, reformed,' he said gravely.

'Definitely reformed,' she agreed wryly.

'I'm glad to hear you say that,' he said softly, and she looked across at him, trying to formulate the correct words of gratitude, and was suddenly arrested by what she saw in his eyes—a mixture of devilish irony and something else that made her heart start to pound in a curious way.

'W-what do you mean?' she stammered.

'I suppose you could put it this way,' he drawled. 'It wouldn't take much on my part to start wondering how you'd look once you got rid of that layer of dirt. But I think I could guess. In fact I can just see you stepping out of a shower now.' He stared at her consideringly, 'Yes, dark hair, blue eyes and a faintly olive skin, an unusual combination but quite delightful, I'd say. And that smooth skin would gleam like satin and be damp and cool, and that figure you've rather unsuccessfully tried to hide under a man's shirt and jeans would catch the light in some places and be deliciously shadowed in others. I think it would be a thing of grace and beauty and lovely, curving symmetry, your body, and not at all hard to picture lying naked beside me.'

Anna stared at him, mesmerised, for a long moment, until he said, 'Perhaps you can visualise it too?'

Then she came out of her trance and was visited by a tremendous gust of anger. 'Oh . . . you . . .!' she breathed, but found she couldn't go on so she yanked her bag off the back seat, stumbled out of the car and slammed the door shut as violently as she could. But she heard his laughter all the same, and if she'd had a rock or a brick to hand, she would have thrown it at the car as it pulled away from the kerb smoothly and he had the gall to toot his horn in farewell. Then he turned a corner and was gone from sight.

'Of all the. . .!' She couldn't think of a suitable epithet and had to be content with venting her rage on an inanimate kerbstone with her boot, which hurt her more than the stone. 'I could die of mortification!'

A couple of hours later she was not dead though considerably cleaner, but not in any better frame of mind. Because in spite of herself, she had paused after stepping out of the bath. There were no showers in the rather antiquated hotel she was lodged in, in fact there was only one bathroom on each floor. All the same, she stepped out of the old-fashioned bath with its claw feet and found herself gazing into the uneven, mildewed mirror with her towel held in both hands in front of her.

The wavering reflection that stared back at her held no immediate surprises. Just a fairly tall girl with very dark, heavy hair which she usually wore brushed back loosely from her face to reveal a perfect widow's peak, and pinned behind her ears to fall in a smooth curve to her shoulders—well defined eyebrows, thick lashes and blue eyes that could look grey or bluer depending on what she wore, and a curving mouth that, although she didn't know it, revealed her generous, sometimes impulsive nature. And what she privately thought was her best feature, very clear smooth skin that was not precisely olive, as the man in the car had called it, but more like warm ivory that tanned easily.

But, as her hands hovered for a moment, it was not her face she was thinking of, nor her face that she studied as she dropped the towel to the floor. Nor was it that she had never thought about her body because she had wondered what it would be like to lie naked beside a man and she had received several offers to do it, two from men she had liked very much but not enough, it had seemed, on reflection, to take them up. She had also often been conscious of a feeling of gratitude that she had a slender waist, firm breasts that were neither too big nor too small, a trimly curved bottom and long shapely legs, because it was the kind of figure that was easy to dress and looked good in inexpensive clothes that she could make herself and not only save money—a thing she *had* been doing since she left school—but also give some rein to her own sense of style.

It was none of those things that she thought of as she

stared at her reflection—at least, it seemed like something very different to her as she heard those words again in her mind—a thing of lovely, curving symmetry, and saw a faint tinge of colour stain her cheeks, and felt again the undeniable magnetism that had kept her rooted to her seat for those moments. Only it got worse. For a fleeting instant her imagination took wings and with a sharply indrawn breath she found herself picturing her rescuer-cum-tormentor naked too, his long, streamlined body beside hers in some dim shadowy place, his hands on her . . .

She shivered and closed her eyes suddenly, and wondered how it could be that a man she barely knew and didn't even like should have had this effect on her. But almost immediately she got angry all over again and snatched the towel up and began to dry herself vigorously, resolving severely at the same time never to think of him again.

It was only later, when she was in bed, that she was finally able to relax and even laugh at herself a little in the darkness.

'I'm never liable to meet him again, thank goodness,' she told herself. 'But why couldn't I have thought of something cool and cutting to say to him? And why couldn't I have slid casually out of the car and waved to him after I'd verbally demolished him? Why do I always think of the right things to say two hours too late?'

But it occurred to her that in this instance, she still hadn't thought of anything cool and cutting she could have said, and she rolled over with a wry smile, punched her pillow and vowed to put the whole traumatic day out of her mind.

Two days later she was taking tea with Mrs Robertson who owned the Hotel Louis, on a side verandah. Mrs Robertson was a lively, elderly widow who was something of an institution in Innisfail, as was the equally elderly Hotel Louis. It was only ten-thirty in the morning, but already a heat haze was shimmering across the rooftops of the houses nearby and Bob

Wetherby, the hotel yardman, was raking and watering the gravel paths around the building which he did twice a day to cool them. The air was already heavy with humidity—an enervating fact of life about northern, coastal Queensland where, in summer, any activity after about eight o'clock in the morning left one drenched in sweat.

'Well, Anna love,' said Mrs Robertson, 'you know I'd only be too happy to have you back if you need a job.'

Anna glanced at her affectionately over the top of her cup.

She said, 'That's very kind of you, Mrs Robertson . . .' and hesitated.

'But you want to move on? Of course you do,' Mrs Robertson said briskly. 'So would I if I was your age. Just thought, having had all that money stolen, you might need a bit of a job to tide you over. Know what I mean?' She tilted her head with its crown of rigid curls to one side like a bright-eyed, enquiring bird.

'Yes, and I love you for it,' Anna said sincerely. 'But in fact I'm not broke. It's just that I was going to use the money that was stolen to give myself a little treat. I was going to take a proper holiday—just a week, seeing places like Bingal Bay and Mission Beach and all those romantic-sounding islands like Dunk and Hinchinbrook. But now,' she shrugged, 'I think I'll head for either Cairns or Cooktown and look for work there. Which isn't exactly a penance. They say it's lovely up there too.'

'Yes,' Mrs Robertson said slowly, 'it is. Still, it's a pity to miss out on Mission Beach and so on, because I doubt if even Cairns or Cooktown could beat it . . . Now what am I thinking?' she asked herself, and screwed up her eyes. 'That's it!' she cried suddenly. 'Yandilla! It would be perfect, and it's right there,' she added triumphantly, and went on to explain to Anna's look of enquiry, 'Mrs Lawson, my bowls partner, was telling me that Mrs Gillespie from Yandilla was in town only the other day, looking for someone to help her with the child. Not quite sure how old the child is now—round eight I think. Well, she didn't find anyone who suited and she said she was going to advertise in the Brisbane papers, see, for a governess. That's what you are, isn't it?' She looked at Anna expectantly. 'I mean, you're a qualified teacher, and that's what you were doing up round Georgetown, weren't you?'

'Yes,' said Anna, and thought of the job she had just left. It had been no easy task trying to governess five lusty boys on a truly outback property who would definitely have preferred to spend all their time on horseback anyway, and she'd thought sympathetically of their permanent governess who'd been taking well-earned, no doubt, leave. But if this was only one child . . .

'You said it was right there. Do you mean on that part of the coast? How would one get there?' Because if I'd have to hitch a ride, it's out, she added, but to herself.

'You'd take a bus and then a boat,' said Mrs Robertson.

Anna stared. 'A boat?'

'Yes. It's an island. Haven't you ever heard of Yandilla? It's somewhere near Dunk, off Mission Beach, but it's privately owned. The Gillespie family have owned it ever since I can remember—they have some enormous cane farms on the mainland.' Mrs Roberston sprang up energetically. 'Now why didn't I think of this earlier? Bob!' she called to her long-suffering yardman. 'It'd be as easy as falling off a log to get to Yandilla from here, wouldn't it?'

'I wouldn't say that,' Bob replied from over the verandah railing. He rested his broom and spat out a piece of matchstick. 'Who wants to go?'

'Anna here, and of course it's easy,' Mrs Robertson said crossly. 'All she'd have to do is take a coach from here to Mission Beach and then get on one of those boats that take day trippers round the islands. I know they stop at Yandilla if necessary, because Cynthia Lawson was telling me that's how they get their supplies and mail. Now you run over the road and find out when the next coach leaves, Bob Wetherby,' she

commanded. 'And don't take your time about it!' she
added.

Bob departed mumbling under his breath, and Anna
blinked.

Mrs Robertson turned back to her. 'Don't think I'm
trying to rush you, Anna, but this is a marvellous
opportunity. They've got scads of money, the Gillespies,
and they tell me the island is like a tropical paradise.
And it's right in the heart of the Great Barrier Reef—
have you ever seen the reef? No—well, it's incredible.
And I'll tell you something else—once Mrs Gillespie
advertises in the southern papers, there'll be a mort of
city slickers applying for the job!'

Anna laughed. 'I was one of those myself not so long
ago.'

'If you ever were, you got the worst of it out of your
system before you hit here, love. And you'd be perfect
for the job. What do you think?' Mrs Robertson asked
excitedly.

Anna frowned faintly. But it was hard not to be
affected by such enthusiasm. 'It sounds almost too good
to be true,' she confessed. 'But just to turn up?
Shouldn't I . . .?'

'Can't do any harm to be on the spot, can it? And
you can mention Cynthia Lawson's name—I'll square it
with her. See, she and Mrs Gillespie went to school
together. Also, I'll write you a reference. There aren't
many people in these parts who don't know my name—
and respect it, what's more!'

Anna didn't doubt this, but still she hesitated.

'The other thing is,' Mrs Robertson said persuasively,
'in the unlikely event that they don't take to you, there'd
be the opportunity for other jobs in the area. People come
from all over the world to see the Reef, you know. And
there's the resort on Dunk and motels on the mainland,
boats to work on . . . What time did you say, Bob?' she
called as Bob approached the verandah railing.

'I didn't yet,' he replied dourly. 'You never give me
half a chance to get a word in edgeways. But she'll have
to sprint,' he jerked a thumb at Anna, 'because it goes
in half an hour, and it's the last one today.'

CHAPTER TWO

'. . . IF Mrs Gillespie of Yandilla went to school with Mrs Lawson, who's a friend of Mrs Robertson's, wouldn't she be little old to have an eight-year-old child?'

Anna shook her head as she stared out of the window of a large tourist coach and found she was still a bit dazed by the speed with which events had occurred. Mind you, she mused, there's no saying how old Mrs Lawson is, because Mrs Robertson has friends of all shapes and sizes and ages. Look how she's befriended me! And they do say bowls is appealing more and more to younger people. But what if they want a permanent governess? For all that Yandilla might be a tropical paradise, I don't want to be tied down for ever. As it is, it's taken me nearly nine months to get this far, and I'm not even out of Queensland yet. Maybe two years is just not long enough to work your way around Australia!

She sighed lightly and decided that the deed was done now and there could be no harm in having a look at Yandilla, at least.

And it wasn't hard to turn her attention elsewhere after a while, as the coach threaded its way through the spectacular scenery between Innisfail and Mission Beach and they drove through glorious rain forest and the abundant fertility of an area that had the highest rainfall in Australia.

'They don't talk about how many inches of rain they had last night in this part of the world, folks,' the driver of the coach said into his microphone. 'Here the rain falls in feet. No, I'm not joking either,' he added as a surprised murmur ran down the length of the bus.

But none of the lush scenery they passed through prepared her for the beauty of Mission Beach. To the north, the high cliffs of Bingal Bay swept down to the beach and then the land flattened and the beautiful white sands curved away to the south almost as far as the eye could see, richly fringed with a variety of tropical vegetation—banana trees and coconut palms and many that she didn't know. Dunk Island dominated the sea, looking rocky and faintly forbidding but enticing at the same time. Other, smaller islands were visible and far away to the south, looking violet and insubstantial in the distance, lay Hinchinbrook Island, the largest of them all and separated from the mainland by a narrow strip of water known as the Hinchinbrook Channel.

Anna savoured all these names as she stood and drank in the sheer beauty of it all, and she wondered which island was Yandilla. And decided there was only one way to find out.

'Yandilla?' the captain of the pleasure boat, the *Lotus Lady*, said. 'Sure. We've got a cruise leaving in ten minutes and it'd be no sweat to stop off at Yandilla. You ... uh ... expected?' He looked her over thoroughly.

Anna smiled inwardly. The captain of the *Lotus Lady* looked to be in his late twenties and he had bright brown eyes in a pleasantly open face so it was hard to be insulted by that all-encompassing look.

'No, I'm not,' she said gravely. 'But I've heard they're thinking of engaging a governess and I thought I'd apply in person.' She stopped abruptly at a sudden thought. 'But perhaps you can't just go to Yandilla? Perhaps you need a pass or an invitation? Would you know?' she asked.

He shrugged. 'I take all their stuff over and if there's an embargo on people, no one's ever told me about it. So you're a governess?'

'Well, I'm a qualified teacher. Same thing, more or less.'

He grinned suddenly, an appealing grin that made his eyes twinkle. 'Maybe. All I can say is, things have changed since I was at school. Teachers didn't come put together quite the way you are, ma'am, if you don't mind me saying so, in those days.'

'Thank you,' Anna said politely, and was struck by another thought. She frowned faintly. 'I . . . I was just wondering how I could get off Yandilla. You see, they might not like me, and it would be—awkward to be stuck there. Do you . . . does the cruise come back that way, by any chance?'

'Can do! But there'd be worse places to be stuck than Yandilla. So they're engaging a governess now for Chrissy, eh?' he said thoughtfully. 'Seems only yesterday that she was a baby.' A shadow seemed to cross his face, then it was gone, and he straightened up from the post he had been leaning against. 'Time flies,' he said. 'I'm Mike Carmody, by the way. Do you have a handle, or are you just there to be looked at?'

Anna, having now had some experience with the jargon and customs of the north, interpreted his meaning correctly. In a subtle yet at the same time direct way, he was trying to establish whether she was available for, or averse to, being 'chatted up', as the time-honoured saying went. She had also established her own formula for dealing with this approach.

She put out her hand and said very seriously, 'I'm Anna Horton.'

They shook hands. And after a moment, Mike Carmody said with an amused look of resignation, 'Pleased to meet you, Anna Horton. You're still a sight for sore eyes, if you don't mind me saying so.'

Anna smiled at him, content that all communications had been received and decoded correctly.

But she had to admit a little later, as the *Lotus Lady* ploughed majestically through the quiet, inner reef waters with its happy load of tourists, that while Mike Carmody might have read everything loud and clear, there was something in the way his eyes lingered on her now and then which led her to think that he might not altogether have discarded the idea of slower approach.

Then someone mentioned Yandilla and she forgot everything else. Viewed from the sea, Yandilla wasn't very big. In fact all you could see of it was a white, elliptical beach topped by a fuzz of coconut palms and the only sign that it was inhabited was a long white wooden jetty upon which, presently, she found herself standing and accepting her bags from Mike Carmody and, at the same time, his assurances that he would be back three hours later to pick her up if necessary. Then the *Lotus Lady* pulled away with a powerful thrust of her engines and she lifted a hand to wave, but dropped it almost immediately as it tooted a deep, asthmatic-sounding horn.

'That's twice,' she murmured out loud. 'In three days I've been tooted at by two men!'

She thought of the other man who had saluted her in like manner and shivered for no reason at all—except, perhaps, that despite her resolution it hadn't been that easy to put him out of her mind, and she had even once thought suddenly, *hazel*—that's what you'd call those green-flecked eyes. Light hazel . . .

She stared out over the sea. 'Follow the path from the jetty, Mike Carmody said. It'll lead you to the homestead.' She sighed as she watched the *Lotus Lady* getting smaller. 'I can't help wishing I was still aboard you. This *is* a strange way to arrive! I wonder if I should have allowed myself to be stampeded into it?' She sighed again. Anyway, I'm here now, she thought as she bent to pick up her two bags, one of which Mrs Robertson had kept for her while she was up country. And how does the saying go? Nothing venture, nothing gained!

She took a deep breath and turned resolutely to start the long walk up the jetty, and immediately narrowed her eyes.

Because a wind-surfboard had suddenly appeared, complete with colourful sail, in the waters beside the jetty, and as she watched it skim across the water away from the beach, the small form clinging to it let out a faint cry of alarm which the playful breeze picked up. Then, quite suddenly, the breeze died and the sail went limp, and the would-be surfer let go of the bar and toppled into the water.

Anna dropped her bags and stared anxiously across the water to see the small figure—it had to be only a child, she thought—bob up beside the board, only to get solidly clouted on the head by it.

She didn't stop to think then. She pulled off her sandals and dived into the deep, clear water.

It was a tiring swim because the distance between the jetty and the board had been deceptive and she had to keep stopping to check her direction. But at least she could still see the bedraggled sail lying on the water and a blob of orange beside it. And when she finally made it, it was to realise that the blob of orange was a life-jacket, and she breathed a sigh of relief as she gathered the small limp form wearing it into her arms and flipped on to her back and changed strokes to a lifesaver's crawl.

The bump on the head must have knocked him—her, more likely, with such long hair—out, she thought breathlessly. If she hasn't swallowed too much water . . . oh, please God, she prayed, let her be all right!

Then her thoughts took a different turn as she realised she was nearly at the end of her strength and there was no sign of shallow water yet. The skirt she was wearing wasn't helping either, and she found herself grimly trying to remember all the life-saving techniques she'd ever learnt. Not to panic, that's it—golden rule number one. And I must be getting pretty close to the beach by now.

Yet it seemed like an intolerable age before her feet struck sand, and when it happened she barely had the strength to wade through the water and she found she had to crawl clear of the water mark, dragging the small, still lifeless body along.

Then she thought she must be dreaming or hallucinating, because out of nowhere, it seemed, a confused babble of voices surrounded her and many hands seemed to be tending her and the child. But it was no dream, she realised, as someone kept asking her urgently if she was all right, and finally she found the breath to say yes, she was, and not to worry about her, just to concentrate on the little girl—and she tried to explain about the bump on the head.

From that point on things became ever more confused, and all she could remember afterwards was seeing two dark people working on the child and then feeling herself being lifted into a pair of strong arms, and it wasn't until she felt herself being deposited on to something soft that the world began to make some sense again.

She sat up and realised she was on a broad, well-padded cane lounger on the verandah of a strange house and that there was an almost tangible air of urgency about the place. She looked around slowly, taking in the cool white walls and the stone floor of the wide verandah and the comfortably luxurious cane furniture with its bright lime-green cushions, and realised that the air of urgency was probably induced by the sound of fleet footsteps moving around inside and someone saying harshly, 'What the hell's going on?'

A confused murmur of several voices answered this query, but Anna couldn't make out what was said, and she gripped her hands in her sodden lap and found she was praying again.

Then, she didn't know how long afterwards it was, she heard a woman's voice saying distractedly, '*All* I know is, Chrissy was doing a jigsaw puzzle and I left her for a few minutes, only to find she'd *gone* when I got back. So I sent everyone off to look for her, and they all converged at Jetty Beach just in time to see a complete stranger dragging Chrissy out of the sea. The . . . *your* windsurfer was out in the water, capsized, and it seems Chrissy must have been on it . . .'

The person the woman was talking to swore then and it was obvious it was a man. Anna frowned.

'Quite so,' the woman said. 'But be that as it may, either we've been harbouring a stowaway or some phenomenon delivered a perfectly strange young woman on the scene, and she undoubtedly saved Chrissy's life.'

'If it's a strange young woman,' the man's voice said, 'you can bet your life she's a trespasser. It's happened before,' he added grimly. 'Where is she?'

'She's on the verandah,' the woman said agitatedly. 'I don't think she came to any harm, but she was quite exhausted, and even if she is one of *those*, you mustn't . . . after all . . . oh, come!'

Anna had tensed violently during this conversation. I

must be imagining this, she thought dazedly. It couldn't be! No . . .

She turned jerkily as a screen door opened and she stood up unsteadily with her lips formed to ask how the child was. But her mouth dropped open and her eyes widened incredulously, and she said foolishly instead, 'It *is* you! W-what are you doing here?'

A pair of hard, angry grey-green eyes swept over her—and narrowed. Then the man who only two days ago had so nearly knocked her over, rescued her from the consequences of her own folly and then propositioned her, said coolly, 'I happen to live here, Miss Hitch-hiker. More to the point, what are *you* doing here?'

'Richard!' The woman beside him looked shocked and anxious and harassed.

'I . . . I . . .' Anna began helplessly. 'Actually I . . .' She swallowed and found it amazingly hard to speak. But it didn't occur to her that her confusion would be taken for anything else than what it was—the shock of seeing him coming on top of her recent ordeal, until he ended the strangely tense little silence himself.

'Did you perhaps decide you weren't quite so averse to my thoughts on a certain subject?' he said meaningfully. 'I wonder what made you change your mind? Was it finding out who I was or, more importantly, what I represented that did it?'

'I . . . I had no idea who you were!' Anna stammered. 'How could I?'

He raised his eyebrows sardonically and shrugged. 'For one thing, my car is the only one of its kind in these parts. And I've long since realised that anything to do with Yandilla is not only a common source of gossip from here to Cairns, but it's also a rather powerful attraction to members of your sex. Is that why you're here?'

Anna stared up at him aghast. She tried to speak, but again found it impossible.

'Well, Miss Hitch-hiker, I'm waiting,' he drawled, and when she still couldn't produce anything intelligible, he laughed and remarked, 'You should have come better prepared, my dear.'

The woman beside him stared up at him open-mouthed and then glanced at Anna's white face. 'Richard!' she burst out. 'I don't believe what I'm hearing. You ... whatever ... you're still talking to the person who saved Chrissy's life—your own *daughter's* life!'

'Oh, I'm very grateful for that,' Richard Gillespie said coolly. 'And she'll be suitably rewarded. Most suitably. In fact, Samson can take her across to the mainland right now and he can see that she gets some medical attention in case she needs it. And I'll pay for her to spend a week wherever she chooses to ... recuperate. Now don't argue, Phil,' he commanded. 'I can do no less.'

'You'll do no such thing!' the woman called Phil exclaimed in outraged tones. 'And don't for one minute think you're fooling me with this so-called ... generosity!'

Oh, God, Anna thought distractedly as the two of them stared at each other belligerently. And she sank back because her legs would no longer support her and burst into tears—a thing she hadn't done for years.

Her bout of weeping proved unexpectedly difficult to bring under control. It must be reaction—to everything, she thought dimly, as she tried desperately to master the sobs that racked her body. And the fact that the two people with her on the verandah were still arguing fiercely over her head didn't seem to help.

Then Richard Gillespie said distinctly, 'Very well! No, I'll do it. You'd better get back to Chrissy.'

Anna found herself powerless to resist as she was again lifted into a strong pair of arms and carried a short way into the house, to be deposited on to a bed. For some reason, this filled her with a strange sense of fear and she struggled to sit upright, but was immediately pressed back against the pillows.

'Don't fight me,' Richard Gillespie said curtly. 'And stay there until I get back.'

Anna stayed, but only because she was quite sure her legs still wouldn't support her.

He reappeared a minute or two later with a glass in

his hand and sat down on the bed beside her. 'Here, drink this,' he said briefly. 'It's brandy.'

But all she could do was stare up at him, her face tear-streaked and flushed now and her damp hair clinging to her temples.

He made an impatient sound and slid an arm around her to lift her up a little, and put the glass to her lips as if she was a child. 'Drink it. And don't look like that, I'm not going to eat you.'

Anna drank some of the brandy and choked as it slid fierily down her throat. She tried to turn her head away but he made her take another mouthful. Then he put the glass down on the bedside table and let her lie back.

'I'm sorry,' he said abruptly. 'Phil's right—that was no way to repay you for an act of extreme bravery under . . . any circumstances. And there's no question of you leaving until you're fully recovered.'

Anna licked her lips and found herself saying huskily, 'That's all right.'

His lips quirked in a way she remembered. 'Is it? I guess if our positions were reversed, I'd think that a very tame apology.'

'Well,' she hesitated, 'when you get a shock like that—seeing someone you love half-drowned, you react strangely. I remember once when I was a child and I fell out of a tree and broke my arm my father, who loved me dearly, shouted at me first and then turned on my mother, although it was no fault of hers I was up the tree in the first place . . .' She trailed off uncertainly and wondered incredulously why she should be defending this arrogant, insufferable man to himself.

He said dryly, 'You have a point, although I haven't yet got stuck into Chrissy, but the urge was there.'

'How is she?' Anna asked quickly.

'She's fine. She came round almost as soon as they got her up here. She's got a bump on her head and may have some concussion, but she doesn't appear to have shipped any water. In fact, she's sitting up now and chatting, and I don't for one minute believe that this experience will keep her out of mischief for any longer than it takes for the bump to subside,' he added with a wry bitterness. 'How do you feel now, though? From what we've been able to piece together now, you must have seen her from the end of the jetty, which is a considerable distance to swim to where you both ended up on the beach.'

'I—I'm quite a good swimmer,' Anna confessed. 'At least, I used to get medals for it at school. I'm also still very wet,' she added wryly, 'and making a mess of this bed.' She fingered the pristine white cotton bed cover.

'Don't worry about it. How would you like to have a shower or a bath,' something in his eyes flickered, 'and to get into something dry and then have a long sleep? You look as if you could do with it.'

Anna stared up at him and felt her nerves tighten and her fleeting sense of good will towards him drain away. Because that look in his eyes at the mention of showering had not escaped her, and it had looked very much like sardonic amusement to her. And although she felt wearier than she had thought possible, it suddenly seemed supremely important to let him know just how much she disliked him.

'The last thing I'd want to do in any house of yours is take a shower, thank you all the same,' she said deliberately and dispassionately. 'If I could just have my bags brought up from the jetty so I could change into dry clothes and ... and have a rest somewhere until the *Lotus Lady* calls back for me, I'll be fine.'

The silence was complete for about a minute while she met his meditative gaze coolly and disdainfully and refused to look away.

'Your bags are already here,' he said finally. He stood up. 'And there's no question of you going back on the *Lotus Lady* today, so I'll send a message down when she comes in. Er ... further to the question of you relieving yourself of the liberal amount of sand you've acquired, if you thought I was offering to help you get rid of it personally, you were mistaken.' He smiled slightly. 'I find the half-formulated urge I once had to see you without your clothes has quite deserted me, Miss Hitch-hiker.'

Anna sat up and found herself speechless with anger.

Richard Gillespie waited for a moment, then shrugged and grinned. 'That upsets you too?' he said mildly. 'I can't win, can I? Would you have preferred it not to have had that assurance after all?'

'I . . . you . . .' she breathed.

He raised his eyebrows. 'You what?'

Anna's nostrils were pinched and white and her lips tight and she looked longingly at the glass of brandy on the bedside table because it was the only weapon to hand. But her lashes flew up when he laughed and said dryly, 'You'd be much better off finishing that, my dear, than throwing it at me. I'll send someone in to give you a hand.' And he strolled out of the room.

Many hours later Anna swam up out of a deep sleep of exhaustion and lay for a long time in the darkness, grappling with a frightening feeling of disorientation. Then it all came back to her and she knew where she was and sighed heavily, and reflected upon one of the stranger days of her life.

I was so sure I'd never meet him again, she thought, and how I wish I never had! But I still don't really understand why he should have so automatically jumped to the conclusion that I'd . . . pursued him here! Even though I never did get an opportunity to explain anything . . .

She frowned and her mind wandered back to the confused events after Richard Gillespie had walked out of the room leaving her shivering with sheer, furious frustration.

The lady he had called Phil had arrived precipitously a few moments later and been immediately consumed with concern.

'My dear child!' she had exclaimed, anxiety again written all over her face which, although she looked to be in her fifties, was still beautiful on account of the delicate bone structure and luminous blue eyes. 'I'm so sorry to have had to leave you alone when you're feeling so awful! But it did seem at first as if Chrissy was the one we had to worry about. Yet she seems to be quite fine and in the manner of small children is actually lapping up all the attention. She's in fact quite proud of herself, the naughty child! And I'm so glad to see her alive I haven't the heart to point out to her the error of her ways. But then Richard has always maintained that I indulge her too, too much. By the way, I'm Philadelphia Gillespie, Richard's aunt and Chrissy's great-aunt,' she had added. 'But everyone calls me Phil.'

Anna had blinked under this onslaught and been able to think of only one thing to say. 'How do you do? I'm Anna Horton . . .'

But her voice had trembled and of all things she had started to cry again. Not the awful sobs which had racked her earlier so much as a helpless welling of tears which had trickled slowly down her cheeks. She had wiped her nose on the back of her hand and said, 'You were right to concentrate on Chrissy. There's nothing wrong with me. I was just so afraid she'd . . . but she hasn't, has she? And I'm so very glad . . . so . . .'

'You poor thing!' Philadelphia Gillespie had exclaimed, and crossed to the bed swiftly to take Anna into her arms. 'There, there, my dear, don't cry. I can't imagine what got into Richard earlier—well, I can, I suppose—but all the same, to carry on like that! I'm not surprised you feel dreadful, coming as it did on top of everything else. There are times when I quite despair of him, and so I shall tell him! The only excuse I can offer is that it came as an awful shock to *all* of us, but more so to him, I suppose, to see her . . . to think she'd drowned too. Then, when she sat up and said brightly, "But I was wearing a life-jacket"—well, you know how it is . . .'

'Yes, I do,' Anna had sobbed. 'I do! I told him . . .'

'Come, sweetheart,' another voice had interjected, and Anna had looked up to see a broad brown face with very white teeth grinning down at her. 'I got you a bath runned, pet. You'll feel one helluva lot better with all that sand washed off. Come with me and Phil.'

'Letty's right,' Philadelphia Gillespie had said. 'There's *no* way you could be comfortable like that. And unless you make a habit of swimming a couple of miles a day you might end up very stiff.'

'I put some herbs in the bath water,' the woman called Letty had said, and Anna had seen hazily that she was almost as broad as she was tall and that she had grizzled grey hair and a round face with not a wrinkle on it and the laughingest eyes she ever seen. Then, between the two of them, they had undressed her as if she was a child and tenderly helped her into the bath and commanded her to lie for a while. After which they had helped her out, put on one of her nightgowns and put her back into the freshly made bed.

'Letty will stay with you until you fall asleep,' Phil had said. 'And we shall look in on you every so often, but if you wake up and don't know where you are . . .'

But the warm bath or the herbs or something had done the trick, and she had fallen asleep.

Now, lying in the darkness, she thought—stiff, and moved warily. Only a little, she conceded, and wondered what herbs Letty had used. She also wondered what the time was. Her room was in darkness, but there was a faint glimmer of light coming through the partly open doorway as if a dim night light was on somewhere. This, and the fact that the house was very silent made her think it was very late.

Her thoughts moved on as she lay quietly in the comfortable bed, and it struck her that she had met Chrissy Gillespie's father, her great-aunt, and someone called Letty, but not her mother. Was she away? she wondered. Perhaps she was down south interviewing prospective governesses? She smiled a little grimly. Unless . . . unless Philadelphia Gillespie was the Mrs Gillespie of Mrs Lawson's acquaintance?

Almost immediately something else niggled at the back of Anna's mind. Something Phil had said . . . to think she'd drowned too . . . yes, that was it. She frowned. Had someone actually drowned at Yandilla? she wondered.

Two things disturbed her thoughts. Some faintly heard birdsong which made her wonder incredulously if she had slept from mid-afternoon to dawn; and a movement beside the bed which nearly made her die of fright.

CHAPTER THREE

'WHO's there?' Anna whispered after a moment, with her heart still pounding uncomfortably.

'It's me,' a whisper came back. 'Chrissy Gillespie. Did I wake you? Can I put the lamp on? I'm *dying* to see you because Aunt Phil and Letty and everyone says you saved my life!'

'Well . . .oh!' Anna blinked as a soft rosy glow flooded the room and she found herself staring into a dark lashed pair of grey-green eyes in a pointed little face, that were regarding her with the utmost solemnity. 'Hello, Chrissy,' she said gravely. 'I'm very happy to meet you.'

'Me too,' the child answered, and flung her arms around Anna's neck in a sudden movement that took Anna completely by surprise. 'I'm very, very grateful to you, Anna—may I call you Anna? Aunt Phil said that was your name. And seeing as you saved my life, I'm yours to command for ever,' Chrissy Gillespie added dramatically, and went on, 'I read that in a book once and thought it sounded awfully silly, but now I see that it's not. Er . . . would you mind if I slipped in with you? You see,' she pulled a face, 'I'm not supposed to be out of bed on pain of death. But I wouldn't actually be out of bed if I was in bed with you, would I?'

'Well,' Anna temporised, 'technically no. I suspect you were not meant to get *up* in the first place. But seeing that you're already up, we'll waive the small print. Hop in,' she invited, and moved over.

Chrissy needed no second invitation. She hopped in and settled down beside Anna with a contented sigh. 'Shall I turn the lamp off?' she asked. 'There's something about talking in the dark that makes it special, don't you think?' She reached out and switched off the light. 'See what I mean?'

Anna smiled in the darkness. 'I do. What shall we talk about?'

There was a short, pregnant silence, then Chrissy said, 'Could we talk about you? Because there seems to be a bit of a mystery about you. I think you must be the new governess, only I can't ask because . . . well, I can't.'

Anna started to speak, but was struck by the coincidence of this artless revelation and changed tack. 'Why can't you ask? And what makes you think that anyway, Chrissy?'

'I heard Daddy and Aunt Phil talking about getting a governess for me a few days ago, but they didn't know I was listening,' Chrissy confessed. 'You'd think they'd at least discuss it with me, though, wouldn't you? After all, I'm the one directly involved. But Daddy's like that. Much as I love him, he can be exasperating sometimes. Aunt Phil says it runs in the family,' she added in a quaintly unconscious but perfect imitation of her great-aunt's intonations.

'I see. Chrissy . . .'

But Chrissy chatted on, 'Did you know my great-great-grandfather bought Yandilla for fifty guineas and we Gillespies have lived here ever since?' she said proudly. 'We made all our money out of sugar—still do,' she added matter-of-factly. 'Only Letty says the family's running out now, because I'm the only one in my generation and I'm a girl. She didn't know I was listening when she said that,' she said hastily. 'But it's sad, don't you think?'

'But you might one day have a brother or a sister,' Anna suggested.

'No.' Chrissy sighed heavily. 'My mother's dead, you see. She died when I was nearly two. I can just remember her—she was very beautiful. She was drowned—that's why they were all in such a tizz yesterday. It would have been ghastly if I'd been drowned too, you have to admit.'

Anna was silent for a moment, suddenly seeing things more clearly. She said finally, 'Yes. But why did you do what you did then?'

'I . . . I'm not quite sure,' Chrissy Gillespie answered honestly. 'Sometimes you just do things you know you shouldn't. Don't you ever?'

'Sometimes,' Anna admitted wryly.

'Of course, if I had a governess I probably wouldn't . . . well, not so often.'

'Have you never had one?' Anna asked curiously.

Chrissy sighed dolefully. 'No. Not a proper one. But I've had dozens of nannies.'

'Really?' Anna queried sceptically.

The little girl shrugged. 'Four, actually. But they never stayed long. And I haven't had anyone for ages.'

'Why was that? I mean why didn't they stay long?'

Chrissy sighed again and said in a voice heavy with drama, 'They all fell in love with Daddy and he had to send them away.'

Anna stirred and nobly refrained from laughing at the thought of a succession of nannies falling in love with Richard Gillespie. Surely not all four? she thought with an inward grin. She said gently, 'I think you're having me on, Chrissy.'

'No!' Chrissy sat up indignantly. 'They did! And two of them were really nice – they'd have made super mums and I even told them so, but he just didn't fall in love back. I don't think he understands how much I want a mother, otherwise . . .' She trailed off, then turned to Anna urgently. 'Did you have a mother?'

'. . . Yes.'

'Then how would you have felt if she'd died when you were just a baby?'

Anna was silent for a minute, because despite a certain unreality about this conversation, she couldn't help feeling unwittingly touched by the ring of desperation in the child's voice.

'I wouldn't have liked it much,' she said eventually. 'But sometimes these things happen, and finding a new mother isn't such a simple matter. She'd have to be a special person for both you and your father.'

'I know that,' Chrissy said broodingly. 'It means he'd have to fall in love with her. That's the big problem—at least it is for him,' she added almost accusingly.

'Well,' Anna thought for a moment, 'you see, falling in love is a strange thing. It's not something you can . . . tell yourself to do. It just happens.'

'I know that too,' Chrissy said despondently. 'I heard Miss Sawyers—she was the last one—say to Aunt Phil, that she hadn't wanted it to happen. That's what she said and she was crying and angry. What I don't understand is, why it's so easy for them and not for him? Why does he find it so hard to fall in love back? Have you ever been in love, Anna? You sound as if you know something about it.'

Anna grimaced and felt some pity for whoever it was who did end up as Chrissy Gillespie's governess—for more reasons than one, she thought.

She said, 'No. I've never been in love. But there's probably more written about it than any other subject and as you grow up, you see it in other people.'

'Then, seeing as you're grown up, Anna, why do you think my father's so hard to please?'

Anna bit her lip and wondered if she was imagining this conversation.

'Anna . . .?'

'Honey, I barely know your father so it would be impossible to say.' She grimaced in the darkness and thought, actually not hard at all, Chrissy. From what I've seen of your father so far, he's an arrogant, over-bearing bastard who'd find it hard to fall in love with anyone but himself. How he managed to have such an appealing child is . . .

Then something occurred to her and she turned to the child and said gently, 'Chrissy, there's another thing. When someone you love dies, it can take time before you can even begin to think of loving someone else in the same way.'

There was a long silence until Chrissy said, 'It's been nearly six years now. And I think he's really lonely sometimes, you know.'

Anna moved and put her arm round the child. 'But he's got you. And you've got him. I . . . in a way, you're luckier than I am. Because although I had a mother and father all the time I was growing up, they were both killed in a car crash three years ago, so . . .'

Chrissy sucked in a breath and turned to embrace Anna fervently. 'Oh, you poor thing!' she whispered.

'How terrible you must feel! Why didn't you say so before, then I wouldn't have carried on like that. How do you manage on your own?'

Anna couldn't help feeling warmed. 'I've got ... more used to it now. And I've got my job and I'm at present ...'

'What do you do?' Chrissy interrupted.

'I ... I'm a teacher, but ...'

'Well, now you're here,' Chrissy interrupted again, and patted Anna's face tenderly, 'I'll look after you. And so will Aunt Phil and Letty—you'll see! It'll be just like having a family again.'

'Chrissy,' Anna said urgently, 'I—thank you, you're very sweet, but ...'

She stopped as Chrissy tensed and tensed herself as she heard someone moving about. 'Chrissy,' she said in a lower voice, 'I'm not ...'

'Well, blame me!' Letty's voice wafted into the room quite distinctly. 'Drat that child! She gone again!'

'That's Letty,' Chrissy said unnecessarily. 'She was sleeping in my room ...'

'Chrissy!'

But Chrissy wasn't listening as more voices became audible and footsteps came down the passageway, then there was the sound of doors opening and closing and Philadelphia Gillespie saying, 'She's not anywhere! I've looked in every room. Unless—no, surely not ...'

Surely yes, Anna thought, and knew with a curious certainty what was going to happen. And it did. The bedroom door swung fully open and the room was flooded with light. And she found herself staring into three pairs of eyes, Aunt Phil's, Letty's and Richard Gillespie's.

Chrissy said, 'Don't be angry, Daddy. I just wanted to thank Anna for saving my life. And anyway, seeing she's going to be my new governess, the sooner I get to know her the better.'

Anna froze and could never remember when she'd felt more at a disadvantage than she did at that precise moment. Or more helpless, as Phil's mouth dropped open and Letty blinked incredulously.

No one said a word.

Then Richard Gillespie, who had neither gaped or blinked but merely narrowed his eyes as he took in the two of them lying side by side in the bed, sent Anna a look of such cold, murderous anger that she shivered involuntarily.

He said tersely, 'Back to your own bed, Chrissy. I'll talk to you later. As for you,' that he meant Anna was abundantly plain, 'I'll see you in my study in half an hour. In the meantime,' his lips twisted sardonically, 'can you fix up some breakfast for our guest, Phil? She's going to need it.' He turned on his heel and walked out.

'Oh dear,' Phil said nervously. 'I don't understand . . . anything!'

'Why is Daddy so angry?' Chrissy asked tearfully. 'What have I done that was so bad?'

Letty sprang to life. 'We didn't know where you'd gone, you naughty girl, that's all,' she scolded in such loving tones that Anna would have been moved to smile in any other circumstances. 'Now you come back to bed and Letty will make you comfortable.' And so saying she lifted the child from the bed and hurried out of the room with her.

Which left Anna and Philadelphia Gillespie confronting each other awkwardly.

'I . . . Chrissy just assumed that,' Anna stammered finally. 'I didn't . . . I . . . oh, what's the use!' she said wearily. 'Look, can I just get off this island as soon as possible? Please don't worry about breakfast, I *just* would like to leave. There must be some way—someone who could take me off.' Her voice had risen slightly and she fought to control the feeling of hysteria that was claiming her and was quite out of character for Anna Horton. But then Anna Horton has never had anything as insane as this ever happen to her, she thought grimly, and managed to say, equally grimly, 'And there must be some way that I don't ever have to see *him* again!'

Phil looked intensely embarrassed and twisted her thin, elegant hands. 'I'm afraid no one would take you off without Richard's permission.' She hesitated.

'Anyway, don't you think it would be better to have it out with him for once and for all?' she went on.

'. . . Have what out?' Anna asked ominously. 'I can tell you categorically that Chrissy assumed I was the new governess because she'd overheard you and her father discussing hiring someone. As a matter of fact, you'd all probably be quite amazed at the number of things Chrissie overhears which she probably shouldn't. However, that's beside the point . . .'

'No, no,' Phil interrupted, looking troubled. 'I meant—well, it's obvious you and he have——' she took a breath, 'known each other,' she said in a rush, and smiled apologetically. 'Please don't think I'm being inquisitive or that I'm condemning you—I'm not, because I've known for years exactly the kind of effect Richard has on members of our sex. In fact I've occasionally thanked my lucky stars that I'm years too old for him and was very happily married to his uncle! But I still think,' she went on gently, 'you'd be better to . . . to have it out with him.'

Anna stared at her incredulously. 'I . . . it's not that way at all!'

'Then, forgive me, but why did you come to Yandilla?' Phil asked bewilderedly.

'I . . .' Oh hell, Anna thought hollowly, I knew I shouldn't have come here like this. Why did I let myself be stampeded into it?

'Although I for one will be eternally grateful to you,' Phil added, looking sympathetic as she observed Anna's confusion. 'My dear, men have a horrible habit of tying you in knots, don't they? But anyone with eyes in their heads could see that you're not the common run of sharp-clawed huntresses who have, I can't deny it, pursued him from time to time. And I sometimes think he treats all women as if they are, like some sort of . . . acid test! Which isn't right even if it is—perhaps understandable from his point of view. Look, I'll make some breakfast for you and some coffee, and that might make it easier for you. I don't know why it should be, but when your body's fortified, your soul seems to be too, have you noticed? Goodness me,' she glanced out of the window, 'the sun's come up! That's another thing that helps, I've found. Daylight always improves things. I'll leave you to get dressed,' she went on confidentially, 'and then when you've had some breakfast, you might feel like going in and telling Richard exactly what you think of him! You see if I'm not right,' she added over her shoulder, and actually winked.

Then she closed the door softly and Anna was left staring at it, quite bereft of any powers of speech.

Forty-five minutes later, nevertheless, she was sitting in Richard Gillespie's study.

She had breakfasted and she was dressed in a lemon-coloured crinkle cotton blouse, a full cream cotton skirt and yellow sandals. Her dark hair was loose and smooth, just brushing her shoulders. She wore no make-up other than a light moisturiser and some lip-gloss because when her skin was lightly tanned as it was now after six weeks in the outback, it had a silky bloom that needed no adornment.

Yet, despite having had breakfast and presumably fortified her soul, and despite the daylight and Aunt Phil's strangely fighting advice, she felt, as she sat with her hands lying loosely in her lap, that somehow her ire had lost its momentum. Or, put another way, that she didn't precisely feel like telling the tall, still coldly angry-looking man across the desk what she thought of him. I wonder why? she mused. Because he has a habit of always coming out on top? Perhaps, she thought. And perhaps I'm just a little afraid of him, but I don't know why. She looked down at her hands and then lifted her eyes to meet his green-grey gaze squarely, and to wince inwardly at the look of contempt she saw.

'So we meet yet again, Miss . . .'

'Just a minute,' Anna interrupted, knowing full well what he was going to call her and finding the thought of it returning the keener edge of her anger to her. 'My name is Anna Horton,' she said deliberately. 'And while we're on that subject, would you kindly inform your family—and everyone else—that we know so little about each other that you didn't, until now, even know my name.'

'Why the hell should I do that?' he asked after a moment.

'Because,' Anna said caustically, 'they're labouring under the delusion, at least your Aunt Phil is, that we have some . . . prior knowledge of each other.'

'But we do,' he drawled.

'No, we don't. Not the kind she's thinking of,' Anna retorted. 'She imagines we've had some kind of an affair, or something, and that's why I've mistakenly pursued you here. Perhaps you make a habit of abandoning your lovers or mistresses or whatever, which is why the thought naturally sprang to her mind?' She looked at him enquiringly.

'Or perhaps there just seemed to be no other explanation,' he remarked blandly. 'We don't seem to have got to the bottom of why you are here, do we?'

'I can tell you one thing,' Anna said softly, 'if you were the last man on earth, I'd die rather than pursue you even across this room. I don't think I've ever met a man I detested more—or, for that matter, a more presumptuous one,' she added with gritted teeth.

Richard Gillespie smiled, but it didn't reach his eyes. 'Brave words, lady,' he said casually. He sat back and folded his arms across his chest and studied her coolly. 'How old are you?' he asked abruptly, at last.

'Twenty-three. What's that got to do with it?' she demanded. 'Look, this is wasting my time just as much as it's wasting yours, so could we discuss something constructive for a change? For example, how I'm to get off this island.'

He raised his eyebrows. 'Certainly. As soon as you tell me why you came here in the first place and why Chrissy seems to think you're the new governess, we can discuss anything you like.'

Anna took a deep breath, and to give herself time to think, looked round the room.

She had thought it austere when she had first come in. Now, in spite of herself, she saw it was austerely beautiful like the other parts of the house she had seen. Built for the tropics, its ceilings were high and the walls thick and white-painted and the deep verandah ran

right round the house, adding to the coolness. But the
beauty lay too in the woodwork of the floors with only
the occasional Persian rug to show up jewel-bright
against the polished surfaces, and the carved doors with
their brass handles. It was also an uncluttered house, as
typified by this room which contained only the
mahogany desk and two chairs, a built-in bookcase that
took up one whole wall, an exquisite oval walnut table
in the corner that bore a crystal vase of violet blue
agapanthas, and one painting on the wall—an original
Namatjira of the red, dusty heart of Australia. Across
the room from where she sat, french windows opened on
to the verandah and through them she could see in the
still, early morning light, a sweep of green lawn that led
to a gap in the coconut-palm-studded shrubbery and
beyond, a tantalising glimpse of white beach and pale
blue sea.

'Very well,' she said suddenly. 'You have a right to
know, so I'll tell you why I came. You can believe it or
not, that's up to you. But one thing you must believe,'
she raised her eyes to his at last and stared at him
levelly, 'is that I never led Chrissy to think I was the
new governess. She *first* thought it because she'd heard
you and her aunt talking about it some days ago. Then
when I mentioned that I was a teacher—she, well I
suppose it seemed to follow. That's the truth, and the
fact that the rest is,' she shrugged, 'an amazing
coincidence I suppose you could say, is not my fault
excepting for one thing—I should have made an
appointment to come here first. But I don't intend to go
on defending myself about the rest of it.' Her gaze
didn't falter and a stubborn light entered her blue eyes.

'Go on,' he drawled, his eyes never leaving hers. 'Tell
me about this amazing coincidence.'

Anna did as best she could. And when she'd finished,
she pulled Mrs Robertson's letter from her pocket and
slid it across the desk to him. 'You're very welcome to
check that out, by the way,' she said coolly. 'In fact I
wish you would. Not because of the job, but because if
you do, Mrs Robertson will be able to tell you that
until she brought the subject up, I'd never heard of the

Gillespies or Yandilla, or connected them with a certain person who gave me a lift into Innisfail, and one who I rather devoutly hoped I'd never meet again. You see,' she added dryly, 'I'm not in the least flattered by everyone's assumption, not the least *yours*, that I was so devastated by you personally, or what you represent, or both, that I came here on that account. And while I hope never to see you again after this, I'd just like to set the record straight.'

There was a curiously tension-laden silence as their eyes clashed. Then Richard Gillespie picked up the letter and opened it. 'I know of Mrs Robertson, as it happens,' he observed.

'Then you might find this quite believable after all.' Anna looked at him coldly.

'Mmm.' He scanned the letter briefly and as he did a wry grin twisted his lips. 'She has a way with words, Mrs Robertson. So,' he lay back in his chair and regarded her with a detached sort of interest, 'she recommends your character highly and, quote, thinks you'd make a fine governess, unquote. Would she know?'

Anna hesitated. 'No,' she said honestly. 'But she liked me and thought I was honest and trustworthy. And she knows I'm a qualified primary school teacher and that I've been governessing in fact I've just . . . oh!' She stood up and paced across the room. 'What are we getting into this for?' She threw him an irate look over her shoulder. 'There's no question of me being Chrissy's governess now, that's not the point, is it? All I'm trying to establish, in the hope that you might *some time* let me off Yandilla,' she said bitterly, 'is that I came here with a legitimate purpose! But I can assure you, if I'd had the least idea who you were, I'd never have allowed Mrs Robertson to talk me into it. And I'll tell you something else,' she added tautly, 'if there's no other way, I'll swim off your precious island!'

He laughed softly. 'That reminds me of something else you once threatened me with. Something about walking to Cape York rather than go anywhere with me.'

Anna bit her lip unseen to him and castigated herself for letting her anger and indignation trap her into making wild statements.

'Mind you,' he went on pensively, 'it would probably have been less dangerous to walk to Cape York than to swim off Yandilla, so I wouldn't advise you to try it.' His voice was suddenly steely. Then he went on in more normal tones, 'But there's an alternative. I think you'd make an excellent governess for Chrissy.'

Anna stopped pacing as if she'd been shot and swung round. 'You don't mean that!' she said at last, taken utterly by surprise.

Richard Gillespie looked up at her thoughtfully. 'I said it. Don't you want the job now?'

Anna shook her head as if to clear it. 'No! I thought I made that clear. But I don't understand you! Why such an about-face? Ten—no, *two* minutes ago you were convinced I was a conniving adventuress or something worse. I'm afraid you go too fast for me, Mr Gillespie,' she said somewhat grimly, and sank down into her chair.

He looked amused. 'I thought the fact that I could revise my opinions would make you see me in a better light. But I've noticed before that you don't seem to appreciate this quality I have of being flexible. Would you rather I'd stubbornly refused to believe a word you've said?' he asked gently, tauntingly, his eyes alive with devilish amusement.

Anna's lips parted but no sound came and she found herself choking on her rage most ignominiously, while Richard Gillespie grinned faintly, then offered politely to get her a glass of water.

She shook her head and thought to herself, that's it! That's the last time I cross swords with this detestable man. That's the last time I ... even talk to him, she thought incoherently, and set her lips in a tight line and stared defiantly at him.

But he only shrugged and stood up and walked across to the french windows to gaze out over the garden. Then turned almost immediately and leant his wide shoulders against the frame.

And with a twinge of surprise Anna saw that all the mockery and amusement had gone from his eyes and what was left was complete, businesslike gravity.

'I apologise,' he said quietly. 'I haven't treated you very well and I'd like to be able to make amends. If you really want to leave, I'll arrange it immediately.' He paused, but she was too stunned to speak. He went on, 'However, I'd—we'd all be very happy for you to spend some time with us, as our guest. And while you did, you might like to reconsider the position of governess to Chrissy, but if you do spend some time with us please don't feel obligated to accept the post. The one's not contingent on the other in the least.'

Anna blinked and rubbed her brow. Is this some kind of extended dream? she wondered dazedly, and knew it was not. Then just how does one deal with a man like this? She gazed up at him blankly. In such a short space of time I've seen him violently angry, I've seen him coldly and cruelly angry, I've seen him sardonic and mocking and wickedly, cynically teasing at my expense. He's kissed me, propositioned me, all but denounced me to his family as the lowest of the low . . . and proved less than easy to get out of my mind. Not that I've had much time to do it, but now he's offering me a job or a holiday or both . . .

She licked her lips and thought, if I had any sense I'd get up out of this chair and run for my life. Which of course I will! At least, I'll say no—no, thank you to everything!

And all I did to get myself into this crazy situation, she marvelled, as she still gazed blankly up at him, was accept a lift from a lecherous semi-trailer driver, happen to be on hand when Mrs Robertson had a brainwave and rescue one small girl from drowning. Life's very odd . . .

'What are you thinking?'

Anna blinked again. 'I was thinking how strange life is,' she said huskily. 'I really didn't think I'd ever see you again, let alone in these peculiar circumstances.'

Richard Gillespie said nothing for a moment. Then he smiled at her, genuinely and she saw with a sudden clarity what she had seen on the dusty roadside two days ago—a man to whom many woman would be attracted even without the knowledge of his wealth or Yandilla. Yes, it's all there, she thought, and wondered how best to sum it up. I suppose it's a combination of many things, an obvious though often cutting intelligence, a sort of worldliness and sophistication and a feeling that if you came up to his expectations as a woman it would be something to be proud of, and it would be heady and intoxicating and as if you were flying too high . . . Dear God, what am I thinking? she asked herself. A faint smile curved her lips at her next thought. Perhaps Chrissy was right after all—maybe they did all fall for him and have to be sent away lovelorn and desperate . . .

'I was thinking the same thing,' he said, cutting into her thoughts and with a curious inflection that she couldn't decipher. 'But you haven't given me an answer.'

Anna looked away and for no real reason felt a faint heat come to her cheeks. Be careful, she thought, don't let it happen to you . . . and almost immediately felt like laughing, for that would be crazier than anything else that had happened so far. She stood up and said with decision, 'Thank you very much, and I mean that, but I'd like to go as soon as possible.

He regarded her silently until she began to feel unnerved again, although she was determined not to show it.

Then he said dryly, 'You haven't forgiven me, have you? And you're not prepared to let me make amends either.'

She rubbed her hands together awkwardly. 'There's nothing to forgive I . . . it was a misunderstanding. As for Chrissy, I'm only glad I was on the spot in spite of the . . . misunderstandings that came about.' She looked at him steadily.

He straightened up and said the most surprising thing. 'You so often speak with the maturity and good sense of someone much older. How come?'

Anna thought for a moment, very conscious that he

was looking at her over assessingly but this time not in the least insolently. Yet she still found it strangely disturbing. She said finally, 'Twenty-three isn't so young really. And I've been on my own for a few years now, so perhaps that's why I sound older, if I do.' She smiled suddenly and added wryly, 'But then I often do things which ... well, land me in trouble, very much like someone much younger—as you must know.'

His eyes narrowed. 'Do you mean you have no parents?'

'No.' She explained as she had to Chrissy.

'I see. Look,' he said abruptly, 'the more I get to know you, the more convinced I am that you'd be just what Chrissy needs. No,' he lifted a hand as she started to speak, 'please just let me explain. Chrissy lost her mother when she was nearly two—she no doubt told you?' He looked resigned as Anna nodded. 'She never loses an opportunity to tell people that. But anyway, since then she's had to make do with Phil and Letty who both adore her and spoil her rotten, and a succession of unsuitable nannies. Believe me, it's terribly hard to find someone, the right person for a motherless child. But I think you might be right for her. If—say if none of the .. misunderstandings, as you call them, had occurred, would you have taken the job on?'

'I ... maybe Chrissy doesn't need anyone. I mean anyone *employed*,' Anna said confusedly. 'Even if your aunt spoils her, and Letty, at least they love her and they're permanent.'

A fleeting hint of weariness touched Richard Gillespie's eyes. 'But she needs more. You see, Phil didn't have any children of her own and she treats Chrissy like an adult—which she readily admits, just as she admits that the child is becoming precocious because of it. Besides, Phil has her own career and she's not getting any younger. And Chrissy needs someone younger, not only to ... balance the influences in her life but also someone who could cope with and channel all her energy more productively. That's why she's so everlastingly up to mischief.'

Anna swallowed. 'Chrissy ... needs a mother,' she

said quietly. 'I know,' she added as he moved impatiently, 'I know you can't produce one to order, but that's one reason why I'd be ... very wary of taking on this job, why I'm not at all sure a governess, a young governess, is the answer for Chrissy. You see, she spilt her heart to me this morning. At first I thought she was romanticising, but I don't honestly think so.' She stopped and took a breath. 'You may not realise this, but every nanny she's ever had, she's weighed up as mother material, and two of them came through with flying colours, apparently. So much so, she let them know how she felt.'

Richard Gillespie frowned. 'What do you mean?'

'I mean she desperately wanted you to fall in love with them and marry them ...'

'God!' he said reverently. 'Are you sure?'

'Well, she asked me why I thought you were so hard to please. She said they fell in love with you ...' She stopped abruptly and coloured as his eyebrows shot up. 'Then she *was* making it up? They didn't ...?'

'They ... well ...' he looked briefly uncomfortable, which Anna would have got some enjoyment out of in other circumstances but, oddly, didn't in these. 'Hell!' he muttered at last. 'I had no idea, believe me, that Chrissy was egging them on. I mean ...' he sat down suddenly, 'can you imagine ... it?'

They stared at each other and then both began to smile reluctantly and then to laugh.

'It's not funny, really,' Anna said at last.

'No,' he agreed. 'It must have been bloody unfunny for them,' he added, suddenly sombre. He looked at her. 'Does she really want a mother as badly as all that?'

Anna nodded. 'She ... thinks you're lonely too, and that you need a wife. Also, that as a family the Gillespies are ... running out ...'

'Oh, Chrissy!' he sighed, and for a long time stared broodingly across the desk at nothing in particular. Then he looked up at Anna and smiled a twisted, self-mocking smile. 'I don't suppose you'd like to marry me, Anna Horton? No, don't answer that, but seeing that you've unwittingly become the recipient of all these confidences, Chrissy's and now mine, can you see a solution? I . . . she's terribly precious to me, for all that she drives me mad sometimes.'

Anna sat quiet for a few minutes, thinking and concentrating carefully. And she thought, after all, what have I got to lose? She said slowly, 'If—we were to make it very clear to her that it would be quite useless for her to entertain any dreams of matchmaking between us, I . . . would stay a while and be her governess. Although it wouldn't be the best arrangement, because I couldn't stay for ever. But then that's a risk you'd take with anyone, I suppose, and at least I understand . . . some things, and I might be able to help after all.'

His eyes searched her face probingly. 'Thank you,' he said at last. 'I'm doubly grateful to you now.'

Anna bit her lip and found herself entertaining some second thoughts. It certainly wasn't what I meant to do, she reminded herself.

'Then you'll explain to her?' she said awkwardly.

'Of course. Unless you'd rather do it?'

'I . . . no. I've already tried to do a bit of explaining about love and how it happens and how it can't be engineered.' She smiled ruefully.

'No, it can't, can it? Have you ever been in love, Anna?'

'No. I thought I might be—you know how it is.' She grimaced. 'Now I've decided there are many variables, and perhaps the most important is not to go looking for it.'

'I'm surprised it hasn't come looking for you,' he commented. 'There must be plenty of young men who've been attracted to you.' He looked at her quizzically.

Anna frowned and found herself feeling curiously nettled. 'Some not so young too,' she replied. 'Although you can't always believe what they say—particularly when they have a habit of revising their opinions,' she added dryly.

He grinned at her appreciatively. 'Point taken,' he murmured meekly, but his eyes danced with devilry.

Anna stared at him frustratedly. 'But that is the point, isn't it? You have to learn to distinguish between that kind of thing and the real thing. Then, too, you have to consider that not everyone is cut out for a grand, hit-you-on-the-head kind of passion. Sometimes it's more like a slow sort of warmth that takes time to grow.' She smiled suddenly. 'I think that's what my parents had. It certainly took time to grow. They claimed they knew each other for ten years before they married and that their love grew out of a mutual interest in rats and mice—they were both biology teachers. I think that's how it might happen for me.'

'Because of the way it happened for them?'

She hesitated. 'Not necessarily. But, although you might not believe this, having somehow always contrived to catch me at a disadvantage, I'm really quite a sane, down-to-earth kind of person. And not—normally—given to wild excesses of any kind.'

His eyes travelled over her slowly and she felt her nerve ends flicker uncomfortably. 'Strange,' he said at last. 'You don't look to be a passive, stoical kind of person. You don't think it might only need the right man to come along for you to feel as wild and wanton as everything about you promises?'

A bright little flame of anger began to burn in Anna's eyes. 'I've no doubt that's a peculiarly male philosophy,' she retorted.

Richard Gillespie smiled slightly, a cool, faintly derisive twisting of his lips which angered Anna even more so that she tilted her chin defiantly. 'I've discovered that's not a very reliable guide either I'm afraid,' she added cuttingly.

'Oh? How?'

I've discovered you can feel that way, fleetingly, about someone you don't even know and don't even like . . . The words popped into her mind unbidden and for a horrified moment, she wondered if she'd said them and went hot and cold with relief that she hadn't. But she couldn't control the faint colour that came to her cheeks as she stared at him hostilely.

'How?' she said at last, suddenly uneasily conscious

that his eyes had narrowed as he watched her. 'I . . .'
She broke off and bit her lip.

'I'm sorry,' he said abruptly. 'I have no wish to pry
into your personal life. Except to say that to sleep with
a man in good faith isn't such a momentous thing to do
these days, even if it doesn't end in wedding bells and
all the trimmings. So, if you have any regrets, or feel
you have good cause to distrust men who make you feel
that way, I should try to put it all behind you.'

Anna's eyes widened. 'I . . .'

He waited, but the shock of what he had said, of
what he had implied, made it impossible for her to
think very coherently, let alone speak. And to make
matters worse, the extreme discomfort she was
displaying, she knew, could only be cementing his
impressions. But at the same time, two things did occur
to her—that to explain what she had in fact meant was
not something she cared to get into particularly; and
that he should have come to such a conclusion so
easily—although I suppose I did lay myself open to it a
little, but not *wittingly*, she thought—is insulting in the
extreme.

At least enough, she discovered, to make her say
finally and bitterly, 'I don't make a habit of it, so *if* . . .'

'I didn't think you did,' he interrupted smoothly.

She eyed him angrily and thought, oh *hell*! What have
I done now? Why don't you think before you speak,
Anna? Mind you, wouldn't it be more to the point to
wonder why you accepted this insufferable man's job
after all? And what does it matter—does it *really* matter
if he thinks you're a virgin or not? It's not as if you're
about to marry him . . . In fact, it might even get you
off the hook! He might not think you're suitable any
more . . .

She took a breath and hoped that none of what she
was thinking was betrayed in her face as she said, 'I
don't quite know how we got on to this in the first
place, but if you'd like to change your mind on account
of it, I'd understand.' She tried to look amused.

'It seems to be a topical subject in this house, I guess,'
he murmured wryly, his eyes dwelling on her

thoughtfully. Then he looked away and employed the same technique he had used earlier, so that when he looked back his expression was only businesslike. 'No,' he said definitely, 'I don't want to change my mind. However, if you'd care to reconsider, I'd understand, because I wouldn't want you to feel I'd played on your sympathy for Chrissy unfairly. It is, after all, not your problem.'

Oh, you clever, infuriating man, Anna thought acidly as she gazed at him. If I say no now, I'll look and feel a fool. She set her lips for a moment, then a stubborn light entered her blue eyes. 'I said I'd do it and I will. If *you're* sure?'

There was a little silence, then Richard Gillespie said briskly, 'Quite sure. And Chrissy will be thrilled, I've no doubt. By the way, welcome to Yandilla, Anna—may I call you that? We're quite informal around here, you'll find, and I'm sorry the welcome's a bit belated.' He grimaced slightly. 'My fault,' he apologised. 'Oh, one thing, I'm leaving for America tomorrow—I'll be gone for a few weeks, but you might appreciate that. It will give you a chance to get settled without me breathing down your neck.' He grinned at her just a touch maliciously, she thought.

And because on top of it, she was still feeling irritated and confused and altogether caught on the wrong foot, she was prompted to say sweetly—and unwisely, as it turned out, 'Ah! A holiday? How nice.'

He observed her speculatively for a moment before remarking dryly, 'If you're implying that I'm going away to waste my time in the manner of the idle rich, I'm not this time, as it happens. I'm attending a seminar on the Box Jellyfish which infests tropical waters and is a particular menace in this part of the world.'

'Oh,' she said feebly. 'Then you're a biologist?'

He nodded, his face quite grave but his eyes laughing wickedly. 'A marine biologist—in my spare time.'

'Oh . . .' was all Anna could find to say.

Welcome to Yandilla . . .

Anna grimaced drowsily many hours later. I ought to

pinch myself to find out if I'm real, because here I am, back in the same bed again, only this time, contrary to all expectations and sworn vows and all that kind of thing, I'm here to stay . . . for a time.

Well, not always in this bed, precisely, she mused, but to inhabit this pretty room, this house, this island for a time. How strange, how very curious, Anna. You have to admit that. You also have to admit you got outweighed this morning, overruled, outsmarted *and*, in the process, acquired a murky past! Quite a dubious achievement, wouldn't you say?

She sighed sleepily and her thoughts drifted back over the rest of the day. Chrissy Gillespie had been thrilled, of that there was no doubt. And Philadelphia Gillespie had been intensely relieved by the explanations her nephew had given her—not that Anna had been privy to those explanations, but Phil's relief had been obvious when she had said to Anna, 'I'm so very glad it was just a silly misunderstanding, my dear, and I do hope you'll forgive us. Unfortunately, from time to time we do get trespassers on Yandilla. And I'm afraid over the years—well, it hasn't been unknown for girls to try and scrape an acquaintance with Richard. It's one of the penalties of being wealthy,' she had said humorously, but gone on immediately, 'Though I didn't honestly think that about you, Anna. Strange to say, I got the impression that Richard knew you rather well! But then I often get things wrong . . . And you've no idea how happy I am to have the question of a governess for Chrissy settled so easily. So you could say we were doubly blessed that you came to Yandilla!'

Then in the afternoon Chrissy had taken Anna on a tour of the island instructing her knowledgeably as they went.

'Daddy's mad about the reef,' Chrissy had also confided to her. 'He loves it. Letty says even when he was a little boy he was fascinated by it and everything to do with it. She says she was always finding bottles hidden under his bed with strange fish and things in them . . .'

An unexpected side to Daddy, Anna mused in the darkness, still smarting from the way her unruly tongue had led her into discovering this side of Chrissy Gillespie's father. But then all round, not quite the common run of daddy, Chrissy ... Or to put it better, not quite your common or garden male of the species. More like a sleek, dangerous golden panther.

She thought of Richard Gillespie at dinner that night. He had been friendly and seemingly unaware that she wasn't quite at ease in his company. And she had found herself watching him unobtrusively with a kind of irate perplexity and thinking, it's strange that he hasn't married again. Six years is a long time. Or is it? Perhaps not. Then again, he doesn't give the impression of being bereft. Not that it's any of my business ...

'Exactly, Anna,' she muttered to herself, feeling rather wide awake now and correspondingly annoyed again. 'And for your information, Richard Gillespie, what I was trying to say when you somehow or other got me trapped into that peculiar ... fiction, is that even while you may remind me of a Greek god, albeit a rather impatient, haughty, fallen kind of Greek god, I'm not so foolish as to imagine it meant anything more than a passing physical attraction, here today, gone tomorrow. Nor ... oh, damn! For heaven's sake, just admit that you got carried away today, Anna! That you let one superior man taunt you into telling a lie—no, going along with it for the sake of pride or something. Just admit that, and get to sleep.'

CHAPTER FOUR

ANNA looked up from the letter she was writing, and thought incredulously, I've only been here for three weeks now, yet some days it feels like three months. How the time's flown—and despite my misgivings, I can only say I've enjoyed it. Although, she grimaced wryly, that could be mostly due to the fact that my boss hasn't been here.

She put down her pen and stood up and wandered over to her bedroom window. It was that lovely hour between daylight and dark when normally the heat of the day was waning and the promise of cool breezes and dew on the grass was an intoxicating, reviving thought, although this particular day had been hotter than any day she'd spent on Yandilla so far, and she wondered idly if the evening breezes ever failed.

'And I've grown into the lifestyle here so very easily. At least, they've accepted me warmly—so warmly, all of them, I sometimes feel embarrassed. But at least they weren't suspicious of the way I arrived here, only touchingly grateful that I did.'

She winced as she thought back to that day, not sure why it still had the power to disturb her. She dropped her hand in a sudden restless movement. Probably because *he*'s due home tonight, she thought ruefully. And I can't help wondering how that will change things.

A light knock interrupted her thoughts. 'You there, Anna?'

'Yes. Come in, Letty.'

'Your laundry,' said Letty as she advanced into the room. 'Didn't get a chance to bring it in earlier. Phew, it's pretty damn hot, isn't it?'

'You mustn't wait on me, Letty,' said Anna. 'I'm quite capable of collecting my own laundry.' She had said this before, but it hadn't taken long to discover that anything to do with the running of the house was something Letty preferred to do herself, and did magnificently, with the help of her young niece, who was called Sunshine.

'Remind me to tell you about Letty one day, Anna,' Phil had said to her not long after she had arrived. 'But one thing you'll soon find out for yourself—if Letty ever left us, Yandilla would fall apart.' And she had gone out to her studio looking vague and anxious, which was something Anna had now got used to, for one of the great surprises she had had on coming to Yandilla was to discover that Philadelphia Gillespie was none other than Eunice

Thurby, whose detective stories were known and loved world-wide.

'There,' said Letty as she sorted Anna's washing into the drawers of her dressing table. She sank down on to the bed. 'Mind if I take a breather? Chrissy's safe in her bath, that's one place she is safe—she loves her bath. Mind you, since you've been here that child's pretty well reformed, and thank the Lord for it! I tell you, Chrissy Gillespie's put ten years on me, I reckon. Me and Phil both,' she added ruefully. 'How'd you do it?'

Anna grinned. 'I'm not sure. I think she looks on me as a sort of guardian angel after what happened.'

'That'd be right too. Every day I give thanks that you were there! Mr Richard should be home soon,' she added, apropos of nothing, and glanced at Anna keenly. 'You don't like him much, do you, Anna?'

Anna was caught totally off guard. 'I . . .' She bit her lip and remembered something else Phil had said about Letty—to the effect that Letty was devoted to Richard and Chrissy.

'You can tell me,' Letty said kindly.

'Well, I think we just rub each other up the wrong way. If . . . if it wasn't for Chrissy, I wouldn't be here,' Anna said quietly.

'Thought so,' Letty said wryly. 'But I reckon you oughta give him a chance. Sure, men get on your nerves sometimes! They act as if they're God, but he's not a bad man. I know, because I've known him since he was born. He's got a helluva temper sometimes—like his daddy, he is, but his mother used to cope—did you know I first came here to work for his mother?'

Anna shook her head.

'Yes,' Letty went on, 'I'm a Thursday Island girl—T.I., we call it up there in Torres Strait, and Mr Richard's mother was a teacher like you and she came up to T.I. when she was twenty—we were the same age. I didn't get a chance to go to school before that, but she didn't mind how old you were in her school. She stayed with us for two years and we got to be good friends. Then she met Mr Richard's father—swept her clean off her feet, he did!' Letty smiled reminiscently and went on ruefully, 'All the same, when she found out about Yandilla and everything,' she waved an expressive hand, 'she said to me, I'm scared, Letty, they're very different people to what I'm used to. And I said to her, I'll come with you! You don't need to be scared of no one, but all the same I'll come with you if you want me to! I was a bit of a savage in those days, learnt a lot since, but she wanted me to come, so I did. And I brought my baby, Samson, and we've been here ever since. Oh, I go back once a year and check on the family and sometimes I bring one back with me, like Sunshine's here now, getting trained. But to get back to what I was saying, I've known Mr Richard all his life, and he's not a bad man.'

They gazed at each other and Anna was seized by an amazing thought. But she found herself rejecting it almost immediately. No, I'm really imagining this. Letty wouldn't be so foolish as to think I would be ... mother material for Chrissy? No, she's only trying to ease a potentially awkward situation.

'You're right, Letty,' she said quietly. 'I took on the job because I couldn't resist Chrissy. And now that I've taken it on, it would be foolish to carry on a sort of silent feud with her father. But I ... did feel ... I'm sorry I made it so obvious I was a little tense about him coming home.'

'That's all right,' Letty said with a smile. 'And you didn't make it so obvious.—it's just that I'm a bit sensitive about anything to do with Mr Richard or Chrissy, I reckon. And that's why I took it upon meself to try and explain. You see, I'd do anything for them.' She hesitated. 'Something else—when something happens the way it did with Chrissy's mother, it can make you bitter and twisted about *everything*.' She looked at Anna searchingly. 'Even though it was a long time ago now. You ... don't mind me butting in like this, do you, Anna?'

'No, of course not, Letty,' Anna said warmly. 'I only wish I had someone who cares for me the way you do for them. And I will try, I promise.'

Letty got up off the bed and hugged Anna. 'I knew you would,' she said. Then she looked up at her and grinned mischievously. 'All the same, you don't need to let him walk all over you. While I'm all for doing the right thing by a man if he does the right thing by you, it don't do any of 'em any good to think you've got no backbone. You gotta steer a middle course, but it helps if you understand some things. There now, I better go and see if Chrissy hasn't washed herself away ...' And she took herself off.

Anna stared at the closed door for a minute or so, but again she rejected the strange thought that had occurred to her earlier. No ... She shook her head impatiently and started to dress for dinner. And she found she felt oddly warmed, because although there was no doubt where Letty's devotion lay, at least she understood that her boss was not the easiest person to deal with. And she must like me enough to want to try and help, she mused.

But Richard Gillespie did not arrive as expected, and Chrissy grew fractious and tearful, and nothing Anna did helped much.

'She's worried about him,' Phil said quietly. 'She misses him when he's away. But I'm sure it's only a delayed flight, otherwise he'd have let us know. Also, it's turned so hot and muggy, hasn't it? Never improves people's tempers I've found.'

'It is hot,' Anna agreed, wiping her brow. 'Not that I can complain, it's the first really hot night I've had since coming here. It's usually so lovely and cool and breezy after dark.'

'It's bound to rain,' Phil said knowledgeably. 'It always does when the humidity gets this high. By the way, I've found the best thing for Chrissy when she gets this way is to put her to bed and read her a few stories until she falls asleep. But I must warn you, it can take quite a few!' she smiled ruefully.

Anna thought for a minute.

'You have a better idea?' Phil queried perceptively.

'I ... no, not necessarily,' Anna said hastily. 'But I do have a little portable tape-recorder and a cassette of *Peter and the Wolf*. I've found most kids love it, but I usually keep it for special occasions. Then again, she might already know it?'

'No. What a good idea!'

As it turned out, it was. Chrissy began to relax as they listened to *Peter and the Wolf* together and finally fell asleep trying to imitate the duck.

Anna pulled the sheet over her and smoothed her fair hair off her forehead, feeling her heart contract as she watched the child's face lose its tension in sleep and saw the absurdly long shadows her eyelashes cast on her cheeks. For in all honesty, she found that Chrissy Gillespie touched some deep, inner part of her heart that had never been touched before.

Maybe it's because I'm an orphan now and you're a part orphan, Chrissy, she mused with a half smile. Whatever it is, despite your reputation, you've treated me with so much care and consideration—just like you said you would—I'd have to have had a heart of stone not to be charmed and warmed . . .

She took a breath as Chrissy stirred, not wanting her to wake and worry about her father again. But she settled, and Anna stared down at her and thought, how sad for your mother to have missed out on you, Chrissy. No wonder . . . if I had a little girl I'd like her to be just like you, bright, sometimes impetuous, sometimes mischievous, a real tomboy sometimes, yet quaintly feminine other times . . . no wonder your father is bitter and twisted often! I think your mother might have been rather special too. I think that's what Letty was trying to tell me earlier. To—make allowances for him because he lost her . . .

The long hot night felt as if it would never end. Anna twisted and turned uncomfortably and finally decided she wasn't going to sleep, so she climbed out of bed, slipped on her pale blue silk robe and slid noiselessly out on to the verandah on bare feet.

But it was just as hot and stifling outside—as if a great blanket impregnated with moisture lay overhead only waiting for some giant hand to squeeze it. And an eerie silence seemed to have the world in its grip. There were no cicadas trilling, no frogs croaking, not a sound. She decided to walk round the garden nonetheless, in the hope that it might make her sleepy. Then, when she was at the farthest garden boundary from the house, it started to rain. But it didn't begin with a few spots and gradually gain momentum—that wasn't how it happened in this part of the world, she recalled ruefully, as it simply started to pour and within moments she was drenched to the skin and gasping as the water ran off her in rivulets.

Yet it was such a relief from the hot, breathless stillness, and seeing she was drenched anyway, she stood there for an age, enjoying it. Then she turned regretfully to retrace her steps through the grey, strangely insulating downpour, and bumped heavily into something that bowled her right over.

She gasped again and lay winded and confused as she felt a pair of hands run over her and heard someone mutter something unintelligible. But the voice was recognisable even if the words were not, and she thought, oh no!

Then that voice swore briefly in an exclamation of surprise and Richard Gillespie said, 'Whoever the hell you are, would you mind telling me what you're doing in the middle of the lawn at this time of night just where I could trip over you?'

Anna sat up. 'You didn't trip over me! You bumped into me and *knocked* me over!'

There was a tiny silence, then he said wearily, 'Oh, not again! I should have known it would be you. Are you by any chance going to make it a habit to be where I can knock you down?' he demanded.

Anna bit back an angry retort and tried to scramble up and found she had to accept his help. 'No, of course not,' she said coolly, and as suddenly as it had started the rain stopped and a much overdue breeze got up playfully, the clouds parted overhead and a clear white moon shone down on them.

'Then what, Miss Anna Horton, are you doing out here, may I enquire?' he asked, taking in her sodden robe and the smear of mud on her legs. His eyes came back to rest on her face and they were as mocking as she'd ever seen them.

She stared at him, conscious of feeling the peculiar tension and irritability he seemed to be so adept at arousing in her. He was wearing a beautifully tailored grey suit that was damp too, although not quite in the soaked condition her clothes were in. 'I . . . nothing in particular,' she said haughtily, and almost immediately knew she had made a mistake as he raised his eyebrows.

'Oh, I see,' he drawled. 'Just another example of the sane, level-headed person you are, is that it?'

'No!' she said crossly.

'Then perhaps you came out to meet me?'

'Why would I do that? I didn't even . . .'

'You tell me,' he interrupted, and his eyes glinted challengingly at her, and she caught her breath because she had seen that look before and had felt before that he could hardly have undressed her more effectively with his hands.

But as she followed his gaze downwards, she flinched and bit her lip because the thin silk of her robe and the equally thin cotton of her nightgown beneath it had fused together wetly and were plastered to her body like a second skin, so that the curve of her breasts and the outline of her nipples were clearly visible and her hips and thighs were moulded unmistakably.

A torrent of colour poured into her cheeks and her hands clenched and unclenched as Richard Gillespie laughed softly and said, 'You're a funny girl, Anna. Sometimes you quite take me in and I'm convinced you're a little different from the great majority of the fair sex.' He lifted a hand and fiddled with a strand of her wet hair. 'All the same, I don't think I'm proof against this kind of an invitation.' His hand slid down her arm and crossed to the small of her back.

She moved jerkily and brought her hands up to push him away, but he smiled slightly and his other arm came up to encircle her shoulders. 'It's O.K., I get the picture,' he murmured. 'You don't want to appear *too* willing. That would never do, would it? So why don't you just stand there and let me do it all? Just to . . . preserve the illusion, shall we say?'

To say that his words stunned Anna was to put it

mildly. She felt as if she was turned to stone, and it was only the feel of his lips on hers that brought her to life. She twisted her head away and fought dementedly, but she might just as well not have bothered, because he only laughed at her quietly and easily resisted all her efforts. Then when she lay panting with frustration in his arms, he started to kiss her again, not brutally as he had done once before but quite gently, and not her lips which she kept clamped shut but the corners of her mouth and her throat and the soft hollows where her neck met her shoulders, and she shivered suddenly and was conscious of the curious feeling of her bones melting and her skin tingling as if it was on fire where his lips had been.

He lifted his head at last and their eyes met, hers wide and shocked but with a different kind of shock registering now, and his dark and strangely sombre. And in the stark white moonlight and with the tantalizing fragrance of damp earth all about them, he said softly, 'I'm not going to hurt you, don't be afraid.' He bent his head again and this time he teased her lips apart—and what followed was something that Anna knew with a strange certainty she would never forget for the rest of her life.

For two reasons—because she offered no resistance, and because although she had been kissed before, it had never been like this, and she had never known it could be an experience so intensely intimate or so devastatingly sensuous, so that every other time she had been kissed faded by comparison almost as if it had never happened. In fact everything faded, the moonlight, the fact that the cicadas had come to life refreshed by the brief, heavy rain, and the frogs and all sorts of night creatures including two wallabies that hopped cautiously out into the open only feet from them and stood for a minute with ears twitching and nostrils quivering before bounding away into the bushes.

It all might not have been there, because the only thing she was burningly, achingly conscious of was Richard Gillespie and the feel of his tall, hard body against the softness of her own and the way she trembled at his touch as he moved his hands lingeringly, tracing the curve of her waist. And that to be kissed as he was kissing her was strangely and unbelievably intoxicating, and it made her heart beat heavily to think that she was surrendering to it willingly as if she had choice.

Then she moaned, a slight despairing sound, as much at the beauty of it as at the sheer inexplicability of it, and his lips left hers slowly and once again found herself clinging helplessly to him, afraid that if he let her go, her legs wouldn't support her.

But he didn't let her go. He held her loosely in his arms and his grey-green gaze played over her quivering lips and took in the shimmer of tears in her eyes. Then he said quizzically, 'Whoever he was, either he didn't teach you much or he didn't know much. You look just about as shocked as someone who's never been kissed properly before.'

She took a ragged breath and coloured painfully.

'Anna?' His eyebrows were raised enquiringly.

'Perhaps it was the shock of ... being taken advantage of like that,' she said shakily, desperately trying to summon a sense of outrage into her voice. 'You shouldn't have done it.' Her voice cracked unfairly, and a fresh wave of colour crept into her cheeks.

He watched that tide of colour in the pitiless moonlight and his lips twitched faintly. 'Perhaps not,' he said at last. 'But I wanted to.'

'W-why?' she stammered. 'You don't really believe I came out here to waylay you, do you? I had no idea you'd arrived! I only decided to walk in the garden because it was so hot I couldn't sleep. And it could have rained any time in the last few hours, it's been so muggy.'

He stared down at her consideringly. 'No,' he said slowly. 'I think I might have wanted to, because of something we discussed once. You remarked that you weren't given to—wild excesses, and—with a certain amount of disdain—gave me to understand that you'd been turned right off men ... and this.' He touched her mouth gently. 'Which at the time made me wish I could be a fly on the wall when some man cut through that so sane, no-nonsense, slightly superior façade and kissed you into submission so that you begged for more ...'

Anna wrenched herself from his grasp and had no trouble in projecting a furiously, genuinely outraged image.

'Then you thought you'd appoint yourself to the task? Well, you've miscalculated,' she spat at him. 'I'm certainly not going to beg you for more! And if you ever lay a hand on me again ... oh, *look!*' she said angrily. 'I can't stay on here if you ... if you ... God knows why I agreed to in the first place!' she stuttered.

'Not the first place,' Richard murmured. 'You knocked me back the first time.' His eyes glinted in the moonlight. 'Perhaps, although you might not have admitted it to yourself, because you were just a little afraid of the effect we have on each other. I can understand why, now ...'

'I ... you ... oh!' Anna gasped. 'You effect me like a hole in the head!'

'So I noticed—just now,' he commented, and his lips twitched again.

'If you laugh at me once more,' she said in a low, choking voice, 'I'll *hit* you, I swear. As for us affecting each other, I think it would be fairer to say that for some inconceivable reason, you feel you have the right to kiss me whenever you feel like it! And I can't help wondering if you aren't a little disappointed that I didn't pursue you here, after all!'

She stared up a him bitterly and was incensed to see him take his time before answering.

'I have to admit,' he said at last, 'that in certain respects you leave the other ... nannies we've had here for dead.' He glanced fleetingly down the length of her and she flinched visibly, and tried to drag her sodden robe into a less revealing mould for her body.

'There should be a law about the kind of man you are, Mr Gillespie!' she snapped furiously, and bit her lip in silent but blazing frustration at the look of outright laughter she saw in his eyes. *All right*, she thought, all right, I'll just show you that I can be as cool about it as you can. She said coldly, 'Anyway, I thought we had an agreement about this kind of thing?'

'Chrissy and I have an agreement,' he said gravely.

The mention of Chrissy made Anna move restlessly. 'I . . .' She stopped abruptly, suddenly less sure of herself and conscious of a feeling of pain around her heart as she pictured Chrissy distraught and tearful as she had been during the evening. She sighed inwardly. 'Then if you want me to stay,' she said bleakly, 'you'll have to include me in that agreement.'

'If that's the way you want it,' he said after a moment, quite seriously, but she could see the amusement still lurking in his eyes.

'That's the way I want it,' Anna said flatly. 'Can you doubt it?' she added, suddenly hotly angry again despite her resolution. 'Do you really think I'd enjoy being,' her voice shook, 'treated like some sort of an experiment? Like someone in need of therapy, even *if* I . . . I mean,' she changed tack effortlessly, thinking swiftly, the principle's the same even if the circumstances are not! Take a man, it'll cure everything . . . 'as if I was a stone statue that could be brought to life by any man? And say, just say I had begged for *more*, as you so insultingly phrased it, what would you have taunted me with then? Oh, you don't have to tell me,' she said ironically. 'Sooner or later, probably sooner, we'd have got back to that old question—why did I come here in the first place! And wasn't it after all to pursue you and your wealth and your p-precious island? But I can tell you, *either* I stay here as Chrissy's governess and *nothing* else, or I go.' She realised for the first time that she was crying and brushed the tears away impatiently.

'All right,' Richard said meditatively, 'I stand corrected, Miss Horton—as you once said to me. But I must add, in the interests of honesty, that while I did kiss you more or less,' he smiled suddenly, 'as an exercise in therapy—to see if I couldn't breathe life again into a stone statue, I can't say I didn't enjoy the results. And when you've calmed down and all your natural indignation at being so shockingly treated subsides, you might find you don't feel so badly about these things now. Yoy see, you're really so lovely, it's a crime to think of you all bitter and twisted about it. By the way,' he looked upwards and Anna followed his gaze to see that the moon was about to be eclipsed by a bank of lowering, threatening looking clouds, 'if you don't want to be drenched again, it might be an idea to get back to bed. See you in the morning.' He looked at her wryly.

'The Box Jellyfish,' Samson said measuredly, 'is a mean creature who don't pay no attention to the colour of your skin. He just wraps these'm long tentacles round you and if he gets holda enough of you, the pain's so bad you're dead in minutes.'

Chrissy shivered. 'Put it down, Samson,' she begged. 'Anyway, I've seen hundreds of them.'

Samson lowered the transparent, ghostly-looking 'creature' he was holding, into a tank. 'I got gloves on, Chrissy. Can't hurt me through them. And I thought Anna might be interested.'

Anna came back to the present at the mention of her name. 'Oh! Yes, I am, Samson.' She looked down at the round dome of the jellyfish and its frilly beard and long, delicate tentacles. 'A serpent in Paradise,' she murmured, and looked up.

'You could say so,' Samson answered, and she detected a ghost of a smile in his eyes. Letty's baby was in fact a tall sinewy man with none of his mother's roundness nor much evidence of her boundless good humour. Yet Anna had noticed before that his eyes smiled often, though not a trace of hilarity ever creased his face.

'You don't want to take any chances. Specially not now,' he said more to Anna than Chrissy, 'at this time of the year when it gets really hot and we can get storms. That's when they seek out more sheltered waters like round Yandilla. Really, you shouldn't swim outside the enclosure now unless you wear pantyhose and a long-sleeved shirt.'

Anna grimaced, then had to smile. 'Sounds like taking a bath with your clothes on,' she said, and winced, thinking of last night.

'But it works,' Samson assured her.

'I will be careful,' she promised. 'Well, Chrissy, we've had a long break, what say we get back to lessons?'

Chrissy pouted. 'I don't really see why I have to do school work today. I think I should have a holiday because Daddy's back.'

'I think that's a good idea,' a voice said from behind them, and Chrissy spun round ecstatically and ran to her father.

Anna turned more slowly. So far, although it was only mid-morning, she'd managed to avoid Richard. She had deliberately stayed out of the way while he and Chrissy had been reunited and had been surprised to find that Letty had for once accepted her offer of help in the kitchen, and they had breakfasted out there together, while Phil and Chrissy could be heard discussing his trip animatedly with him in the dining room. But not long afterwards Chrissy had come to look for her, to show her the presents her father had brought home for her, and Richard had repaired to his study and closed the door. She had started lessons with Chrissy mostly because she could see the child was in a fever of impatience to be with him and becoming more disappointed by the minute as the study door remained firmly closed.

Now, she looked across the boatshed at the man who had taken such incredible liberties with her last night, and hoped that she didn't look as wan and heavy-eyed as she felt. For the truth of the matter was, she had found it even harder to get to sleep after her encounter in the rain with him than before, and no amount of sane, logical discussion with herself, nor any calling upon Letty's wisdom, which she had only remembered once back in the safety of her room, had helped to ease the turmoil of her mind.

Not anything, she had thought bitterly, not even the fact that *you are* bitter and twisted about life in general because you lost a wife you loved, is an excuse to treat me like that. In fact I don't believe that's got anything to do with it—sorry, Letty, she had found herself thinking torturously. I'm sure the real reason is that he's simply a male chauvinist of the highest order who thinks he can treat women as . . . mindless dolls, and I could *die* because for a little while that's rather how I felt . . .

'I . . . hello,' she said helplessly, knowing she was

making heavy weather of hiding the conflict she felt but not able to do anything about it.

'Hello, Anna,' he said quietly, and slid his fingers absentmindedly through Chrissy's silky hair as he scanned Anna's face and took in the faint shadows beneath her troubled blue eyes. 'I'm sorry about what happened last night,' he added in the same quiet way.

Anna's lips parted with surprise.

'What happened last night?' Chrissy asked curiously.

Let him explain this, Anna thought fleetingly, and tensed anew. No, surely he won't ... But then why bring it up in front of her ...?

Richard looked down at Chrissy. 'I was rather rude to Anna last night. She was walking in the garden because she couldn't sleep when I got home, and we both got caught in the rain—in fact we bumped into each other and I knocked her over ...'

'Told you you'd get soaked,' Samson interjected. 'Told you, if you waited a while after we got across from the mainland it might ease off. It did,' he said laconically.

'Remind me to take more notice of what you tell me, Samson,' Richard said wryly. 'But after a twenty-four-hour flight and a delay in Brisbane, and then having to drive up from Townsville, all I wanted to do was get to bed. Not,' he looked across at Anna, 'that *any* of that is an excuse for anything that happened last night.'

There was a strangely tense little silence and Chrissy looked from her father to Anna with wide eyes, and back again.

'But you're not still ... cross, are you, Daddy?' she said with a slight break in her voice. 'Anna wouldn't ...'

'Oh no,' he said to her, then smiled and put a finger to her lips. 'It's more a case of—is Anna still cross with me? Because I was the one who was in the wrong last night.'

Anna stared at him, not quite believing what she'd just heard and not in the least able, she found, to interpret it correctly. Either he's diabolically clever or ... but what! 'I ...' she said huskily, and stopped. Is Letty right after all? she wondered shakily. She must be, or why do I get the feeling this is a genuine apology, a genuine attempt to wipe the slate clean? But I've thought that before. . .

'Anna?' queried Chrissy, and her own turmoil was clearly visible.

Oh God, Anna thought, it isn't fair to bring her into this. 'No, sweetheart,' she said gently, 'I'm not cross.' She looked away and encountered Samson's gaze, of all things, which said as clearly as if he had mouthed words—you don't say! She caught her breath and blinked in astonishment, then looked back at Richard incredulously. He said immediately, 'Far be it for me to want to laugh again, Anna. But that no man is an island is particularly apt on Yandilla.' And his eyes *were* laughing but not at her so much as at her astonishment.

'That's true,' Samson remarked lugubriously. Then his expression brightened fractionally, but only so that he no longer looked as if he was going to meet a hangman's noose, just a life sentence instead, and he went on to say, 'The breeze is right, the cutter's all rigged up, and seeing as the boss has declared a public holiday, what say we head out for the reef? Ever seen the reef proper, Anna?'

'Oh, Daddy!' Chrissy exclaimed delightedly. 'Did you have this planned?'

'Not at all,' her father said.

'But . . . why, there's a picnic basket here!' she said, darting just outside the door. 'And my togs—and Anna's . . . you did, you did!' she accused lovingly as she danced back inside, her face alight with joy. 'I thought you'd forgotten all about me!'

'Not so, honey—I've found that's very hard to do.' His eyes teased her. 'But I did have some overdue business to attend to this morning. Now that it's all out of the way, though, there's no reason why we shouldn't declare a week of holiday. What say you, Anna?'

He looked across at Anna and caught her off guard. She had been about to suggest that he and Chrissy might like to spend the day on their own, but something stopped her. She thought later it might have been the way Chrissy was looking at her, expectantly and happily, so that she knew she would only be putting a damper on her day if she opted out.

She said weakly, 'Sounds fine! No, I've never seen the reef proper, Samson.' But she thought, oddly, be careful, Anna. Don't get trapped . . . trapped? How could I do that?

CHAPTER FIVE

THE holiday week passed surprisingly quickly and pleasantly, in fact. So pleasantly that Anna found herself reviewing each day in some perplexity.

She even wondered once if she had imagined what had occurred in the rain-soaked garden the night Richard had come home from America. But of course not, she had assured herself immediately. And what he did was unforgivable. What's more, to be as he's been since, as if it had never happened, could be construed as unforgiveable too. Not that I'm complaining about that! Only . . . well, I suppose in all honesty I can't help feeling that to be kissed so passionately, and then to have that kiss dismissed as if it was a non-event, is just a little galling.

Now, Anna, she chided herself with a wry smile, what an utterly female way of thinking! You know very well you'd have hopped on to your high horse if he'd given you so much as a questionable look in these past few days. Yes, I would, she agreed with herself. And if I'm a little piqued, I guess it's because I haven't been able to dismiss it so completely from my mind. But that's obviously because it's a surprisingly new experience for me—whereas for him—ah, I'd say not new, nor was his technique even a little rusty, she thought somewhat sardonically, for all that everyone around here thinks that you're an inconsolable widower, Mr Gillespie. At least if it was, I'd hate to think what you could do when you were 'in practice' again!

Then she sighed suddenly, conscious of feeling faintly bitchy and not liking it. I suppose I did ask for it in a way, she mused. And he wasn't to know I was being deliberately disdainful, was he, when I said what I did? Yet is it really any wonder I got on the defensive and tried to put him in his place, in the circumstances? Besides, when you're twenty-three, you're entitled to wonder if you're ever going to fall in love . . . but I've been through that before! I just wish I'd been able to act as anything other than . . . Galatea personified when he did kiss me!

She grimaced ruefully as she thought of the Ancient Greek legend, but had to smile almost immediately. 'I might have given a good impression of it at the time, though,' she murmured, and winced.

Then she set her teeth and thought, well, if he can do it, I certainly can!

And she carried this thought with her through the leisurely days that followed although something else began to niggle at her, for the most part subconsciously, and only crystallised in the vague thought that not all governesses were as fortunate as she was. For every time she tried to fade gracefully into the background so that Chrissy and her father wouldn't feel as if she was playing gooseberry, Chrissy objected strongly and Anna found herself included in every expedition they made, in fact everything they did virtually, which was plenty.

They made several trips to the 'reef proper', as Samson called it, where they fished and swam and Anna found herself being instructed on this phenomenon—the eighth wonder of the world, as some people called the Great Barrier Reef.

'Like all living things,' Richard said to her, 'it's vulnerable. A lot of people think of all coral as hard and dead, the kind you see in souvenir shops, and of course it dies like all living things. But that's not its natural state. And like most other living things on this planet, it needs to be conserved.'

'Is it in any danger?' Anna asked curiously. 'It's . . . there's so much of it.'

He hesitated, then grinned at her ruefully. 'That's a loaded question to ask me, lady. I'm surprised someone hasn't warned you about my pet hobbyhorse, because I

tend to become a bit demented on that subject. But yes,'
he said more seriously, 'it could be in danger from lack of
thought. Some people would like to drill for oil out here,
which could do untold damage. It also appears to have
natural enemies, like the Crown of Thorns starfish. Then,
a lot of people don't realise what a world-wide attraction
it is and how many tourist dollars it earns for Queensland,
but there are problems inherent in that too, people
tramping on it, pollution problems from boats as well as
humans . . . I could rave on.'

'Do you . . . you sound a little as if you'd like to bar
everyone from it?' Anna looked at him questioningly.

He shrugged. 'Sometimes when I see the wilful acts of
destruction that go on—yes, I do feel like that.'

'That wouldn't be very fair.'

'No.' He glinted a grey-green glance at her. 'But it's
often hard not to be possessive about the things you
care for.'

'I suppose so,' she said quietly.

'Do you . . . have anything you feel that way about?'

The question took her by surprise. The boat was
anchored and they were sitting in the shade of the blue
and white striped awning. Samson was fishing over the
stern and Chrissy was curled up asleep on a cushion
beside Anna, replete with a large lunch and the
inevitable excitement of a trip to the reef. The sky was a
limitless pale blue and there was no other craft in sight.
'I think I feel that way mostly towards people,' she said
slowly. 'Not possessive so much, but I like to think—to
feel that I've understood them. I like to . . . get
through to them. I think that's more important to me
than anything else. I mean, I agree with you that it
would be awful to lose this,' she waved a hand, 'but I've
not yet become burningly militant about it.'

'That's perhaps the tallest order of all,' he said.
'Human relations. By comparison, what I feel for this
reef is so simple. I know what's good for it and what's
not. I know that it will grow and flourish under certain
conditions and wither under others. I can go in and
fight for it without a qualm. Your . . . chosen sphere is
much harder.'

'You make it sound as if you've given up human relations,' she said with a tinge of surprise. 'Yet if you go to battle for this reef it's people you have to do battle with.'

'That's true,' he said idly. 'And no, I haven't given up on people. I just find it hard to combat a natural cynicism, I suppose you could say.' He moved and clasped his hands behind his head. He was wearing only a navy blue pair of board shorts and his tall strong body was evenly and goldenly tanned. By comparison, Anna was more conservatively dressed—she had on a short white towelling dress over her swimming costume, and she had noted that although she was not normally shy or prudish about being seen in a bathing costume, it had become a habit to don this towelling dress whenever she got out of the water—whenever she was in Richard Gillespie's company. She also knew why she did this. Because she couldn't quite get out of her mind the awful embarrassment of that night when the rain had plastered her clothing to her body so that she might as well not have been wearing any. And something about the way he was lying sprawled back so easily made her think of it again, and she felt a slight prickle run along her nerve ends that could have been apprehension.

She said, to cover it, the first thing that came to mind, 'Mind you, I don't know how you'd do battle with the Crown of Thorns starfish. It might be hard to get through to them!'

Richard grinned. 'You're not wrong.'

For a time there was a companionable silence. Then Chrissy stirred and Anna quite naturally gathered her into her lap and smoothed her tangled hair. 'I'm here, poppet,' she murmured, and Chrissy relaxed.

She looked up to see that Richard was staring at her with a curious intentness. 'What is it?' she asked, feeling suddenly awkward. Maybe I'm exceeding my duties towards Chrissy—when he's around at least, she wondered. After all, he is her father. Perhaps he thinks he should be the one to comfort her . . .

'It's . . . no,' he said, and looked away. Then he shrugged slightly. 'I was just thinking that Chrissy is

generally less highly-strung these days. Thanks to you.'
His eyes came back to rest on her face. 'And indirectly,
I suppose, I was thinking that you're right to stick to
human relations, because you seem to have a definite
knack for it. You've proved it with her.'

'Oh, I think I might still be a sort of nine-day wonder
with Chrissy,' Anna said uncomfortably.

'And Phil? And Letty and Samson?' he queried with a
faint smile. 'They've gone overboard too, in case you
hadn't noticed. And they've always been ... rather
particular.'

'Which Chrissy hasn't?' The words were out before
she could stop them.

'I didn't say that.'

She looked up to see if he was laughing at her, but he
wasn't. Yet they both began to smile ruefully. 'Did ...
no,' said Anna, her grin fading and a faint colour
coming to her cheeks.

'Did I explain to her about matchmaking?' he queried
perceptively, his smile still lingering. 'Yes, I did. I told
her to make the best of you while she had you and not
to entertain any other foolish notions. In a simplified
form.'

'Oh.'

'Has she ...?'

'No,' Anna said hastily, 'she hasn't.' She took a
breath. 'And yes, she does tend to be highly-strung at
times. But she's also one of the brightest eight-year-olds
I've encountered, and I've met a few. So I think, as you
said once, if that intelligence can be properly channelled
and ... and she has a ...' She stopped and bit her lip.

'Go on.'

'Well, stability is important to any child,' she said
quietly.

'You don't think she has that?'

'Yes, she does.' She hesitated. 'Not the best form of
it, perhaps, because, amongst other things, not having a
mother makes her more than normally anxious about
you. I saw that the night you came home. When you
were delayed, she was terribly worried and for the first
time since I've been here, wouldn't let me soothe her.

Although we did finally work something out.' She told him about *Peter and the Wolf*. 'But she does have Letty and Phil. She could be a lot worse off.'

'And now she has you,' he commented, and his gaze lingered sombrely and broodingly on the sleeping child.

'Yes,' Anna said uncertainly, 'but . . .'

'Wha-a-a!' Samson's voice interrupted and the boat lurched so that Chrissy woke up. 'Holy mackerel! That's the biggest damn fish that's ever got away from me. Holy Moses! That was a marlin, I reckon, and I tell you what! Just lucky I wasn't strapped into no chair, otherwise he'da towed the boat away!'

Saved by the bell, Anna thought later, and felt a further prickle of uneasiness. It's going to be hard to leave here . . . But then I did make that plain, that I couldn't stay for ever . . .

The lazy days of the week continued uneventfully. They sailed and, swam and fished, went bush-walking and played Monopoly at night, Chrissy's favourite game. Sometimes Phil joined them when her book was going badly, but she could never be depended upon to stay, because whenever an idea seized her, she dashed off to her studio, which was separated from the main house, and anyone passing by could hear the typewriter keys being pounded furiously.

'Murder and mayhem—it never ceases to amaze me that Phil has a fascination for such gruesome subjects,' Richard said once when they had been arbitrarily deserted in the middle of a game of lawn croquet— another of Chrissy's favourite games.

But there was affection in his voice, and indeed, Anna couldn't help but realise that he was very fond of his aunt by marriage, and she of him. In fact they shared a bond of humour and understanding that it was hard not to envy. But then Richard Gillespie was surprisingly human, Anna discovered more and more. Human and amusing and stimulating, mentally, and very nice to be with—now. As for Philadelphia Gillespie, she mused once—well, you could only call her a honey. Genuinely unbelievably vague some days, but

so sweet with it you could only chuckle at her. And she
was always worrying about something. If it wasn't
Richard or Chrissy or anyone on Yandilla, it was the
state of the world or nuclear disarmament, one of her
pet hobbyhorses. But one of the nicest things about
Phil, Anna thought, is how she's gone out of her way to
make me feel like one of the family. And I'd like to
think it's not only because I saved Chrissy's life.

The highlight of the holiday week came on the last day
of it, in the form of a beach barbecue to which the
occupants of Yandilla's nearest neighbouring island,
Bedrock, were invited.

Bedrock was leased from its owners by a Colonel
Jackson who, Anna discovered, had been a great friend
of Richard's father and who also ran three-monthly
seminars on the island for people interested in
alternative lifestyles and an increased self-awareness.

'How—unusual,' Anna remarked to Phil.

'It's not really,' Phil replied. 'I mean, he's not into
any particular creed or philosophy, just his own
conviction that more and more people ... are ... how
can I put it ... are interested in getting back to nature,
being more independent and creative and that going
back to the basics of life can help to achieve this.
They're entirely self-supporting on Bedrock. They grow
their food—everything's homemade, buildings—the
lot. The only form of entertainment they have is what
they themselves provide. They weave and make carpets,
paint, make pottery. And the amazing thing is that
when he first started this ten years ago, he only got a
trickle of people, but now there's a waiting list for each
course. And I think the beauty of them is that they
attract such widely different people. At any one time on
Bedrock of the twenty or so people in the seminar you
can find business executives, out-of-work plumbers—
the cost of it's not much more than what it would cost
you to live for three months anyway—airline pilots,
grandmothers—it's quite incredible. And they sing—I
must warn you the Colonel's very strong on community
singing!'

'What's the Colonel really like, Letty?' Anna asked curiously that afternoon as they put the final touches to the salads.

'Mad,' Letty said laconically. 'But nice,' she added affectionately.

'Like ... Phil?'

'Exactly,' Letty replied, and snorted for no apparent reason.

However, as the barbecue progressed, Anna was able to judge for herself. And she decided that Colonel Jackson, who bore the indelible stamp of the British Army and was, she judged, in his late fifties, was really a honey too. Strangely shy when you considered he had the fiercest blue eyes, and with courtly, old-world manners. Really, the last person you would imagine to be into alternative lifestyles, she mused, and caught her breath unexpectedly as she saw the Colonel's eyes rest briefly, on Phil, who was looking flushed and attractive, and then move away with an expression of something like pain in them. He's in love with her, unless I'm imagining things? I wonder ...

But she didn't get much chance to wonder further, because the barbecue got livelier and livelier. Someone brought out a guitar and they had a sing-song as the sun set, turning the sea from blue to a living rose pink. Then they ate, which Anna did in the company of the guitarist, who told her he had been a used-car dealer, but since coming to Bedrock he had discovered that the moon inspired him to write poetry, which gave him more satisfaction than he had ever believed possible.

And when he was called upon to play again so they could dance, Anna confessed to Phil that she had never seen food disappear so fast or with so much appreciation.

'It's the meat,' Phil said laughingly. 'A lot of them are trying to be vegetarians. Yes, thank you, Colonel, I'd like to dance,' she added gracefully, and went away with the Colonel without the least hesitation.

Doesn't look too good for the Colonel, Anna mused. That's a pity—I think. With no children of her own ...

but then she's got Chrissy, and it's not for me to wonder why. And she joined in the gaiety and was much in demand as a dancing partner as the night wore on.

It was inevitable that after a week off, it took some doing to get back to a working routine. But Chrissy did settle down after a few days.

As for Richard, he and Anna didn't have a great deal to do with each other, but what they did passed peacefully enough. In fact Anna even began to think that she was approaching the kind of relationship Phil had with him. A sort of laughing camaraderie and she wasn't at all prepared for the chain of events that disrupted it. Especially after the episode of the spider.

That happened late one evening when the house was quiet and Anna was sitting in her room working on a tapestry she'd been working on for a good six months without notably coming a great deal closer to finishing it.

When I do, though, she thought as she stitched neatly, I'll frame it and hang it in pride of place—no, I won't. I don't really like framed tapestries. Then why are you doing it? she asked herself. You've carted it around Queensland with you and worked on it in some highly unlikely places.

Because I've run out of books to read and ... well, it soothes me, when there's nothing else to do. And that's the truth. I ...

Something caught her eye at that moment, in the middle of this dissertation she was conducting with herself on the soothing aspect of handiwork, and she froze. For it was the largest, most hairy-looking spider she had ever seen, and it was advancing across the white rug beside her bed, towards her with a horrible military-like precision, not hurrying but purposefully as if it was not to be deflected.

She swallowed and cleared her throat and thought, stay calm, and threw her tapestry at it—only to see it emerge from beneath the khaki-coloured canvas unharmed, still marching purposefully towards her feet.

She took flight then, through the french windows on to
the verandah, and immediately thought, how stupid!
Because if it's gone when I go back in, I'll never be able
to sleep. I'll keep thinking it's lurking there somewhere.
It has to be killed! How do people kill giant spiders?

'With their shoes, idiot,' she told herself, and bent
down to take off her sandal, which was a pretty flimsy
affair. 'I need a boot,' she muttered, and glanced
around. But there was no boot in sight—not
surprisingly, she thought. Her eyes alighted on a heavy
cast iron ashtray 'That'll do it!' She picked it up and
peered around her verandah door—to see that the
spider had stopped in the middle of the rug. And her
eyes widened because it was all of three inches in
circumference including its legs, and horribly hairy.

My God, she thought, I've never seen one this big.
It'll make a mess on the rug. All the same, if it thinks
it's going to share my bedroom with me, it's mistaken!

She raised the ashtray to shoulder height and
prepared to hurl it—and nearly died of fright as
someone tapped her on the shoulder.

'Oh!' she gasped, and turned to see Richard Gillespie
regarding her quizzically. 'Oh . . .! You scared the living
daylights out of me,' she added breathlessly.

'I'm sorry.' His eyes glinted with laughter. 'But I
couldn't imagine what you were doing. You shot out of
your room like a bat out of hell. Then you started to
move around with such a great deal of stealth I was
reminded of someone who'd found a body under the
bed!'

'Nothing like that,' she said with a feeble grin. 'Only
the biggest spider I've ever seen.' Her grin broadened.
'To tell the truth, I was sitting in there sewing at the
time and . . . and well, I feel a bit like Little Miss
Muffet, only she was eating. Do you—seeing that
you're here, would you mind?' She looked up at him
ruefully. 'I'm not normally scared of spiders and things,
but this one I *am* scared of.'

'With pleasure,' he said promptly, and stepped into
her room. 'Ah yes. He's quite harmless, actually, just a
Huntsman, but he's one of the bigger ones I've seen.

There,' he said, coming out again with the spider clinging to his handkerchief.

'What ... what are you going to do with it?' asked Anna, backing away warily.

'Deposit in the shrubbery,' he answered, and did so at the edge of the verandah. 'They're very useful, as I'm sure you've taught a few kids.' He looked at her amusedly. 'Don't worry, we don't often get them in the house.'

'I'm relieved to hear you say so,' she said wryly. 'Even if they are harmless—well,' she shivered suddenly, 'it's not nice to think of them crawling all over you.'

He gazed at her thoughtfully, then surprised her by saying, 'Come and have a nightcap with me. It might help to put it out of your mind before you go to bed and lie awake imagining things.'

'I ... thanks.'

'What were you sewing?' he asked a little later when they were both sipping long cool drinks in the lounge.

'I'm working on a tapestry,' she said, and added ruefully, 'I expect I'll be working on it for years to come too, at the rate I'm going.'

'You don't sound terribly enthusiastic. Why do you persevere?'

'Strange you should ask that. I was asking myself the same question when I looked up and saw the spider. I ...' she leant her chin on her hand, 'I bought it not long after I left home. I found that being away from home—you know, living in other people's houses or rented rooms ... Well, put it this way, back home I was never at a loss for anything to do. I had my own flat that I always seemed to be decorating, or I was making clothes or I was expecting people and cooking,' she grimaced ruefully, 'or cleaning up. And I always had plenty to read and I had my own record player when I felt in the mood for music. But you can't carry sewing machines and record players and libraries round with you, and ... and sometimes I wish I had just a single pot plant to water and talk to! But you can't carry them around either. So I hit on the idea of the tapestry. But it's not quite my creative line, I think.'

He didn't answer for a while and Anna looked around the room. It was lit by two tall Chinese lamps with turquoise shades that matched the raw silk coverings on the long settees, between which was the most magnificent Chinese carpet in delicate shades of turquoise and rose pink.

Then he said idly, 'How long do you plan to continue in this . . . homeless state?'

Anna raised her eyebrows and shrugged. 'I'd planned on two years. It's lately begun to occur to me that I might not last the distance . . .' She stopped abruptly, surprised to discover that this was an insidious thought that had really only surfaced as she had spoken the words, and she found herself feeling suddenly awkward. I wouldn't want him to think . . . read anything into it that isn't there. 'At least,' she amended with a smile, 'that it could take me two years to see Queensland this way, let alone the rest of it.'

'Is that such a bad thing, Anna? Do you have any special plans for when the two years is up?'

She sipped her drink. 'No. It's hard to plan that far ahead. I did think I'd like to teach . . . well, in a different kind of school from what I'm used to. Like . . . the one your mother taught at on Thursday Island. Letty was telling me about it,' she added hastily as his eyes narrowed.

'I think that would be a good idea. I think you have a gift for teaching.'

'I do love it,' she said honestly.

'And have you never thought of a more—lively kind of life?' Richard asked curiously.

'What do you mean?'

'Perhaps I shouldn't get into this with my record,' he murmured, 'but wealth and riches, and being able to go where the whim takes you, but in style. Being able to . . . have your clothes made for you. That kind of thing.'

She looked at him with a faint smile. 'With *my* record I hesitate to answer that honestly,' she told him.

'Why?'

'You might think I'm being disdainful . . .' Anna set her teeth and felt a faint colour come to her cheeks. Why ever did I get on to that? she wondered, and looked away.

He laughed softly and his grey-green eyes glinted appreciatively. He said, still sounding amused, 'I promise I won't.' Anna looked across at him in the soft blue light and he added gravely, 'Scout's honour.'

She relented a fraction. 'I guess everyone thinks about it and dreams about it. I do too.' She grimaced. 'I have to confess to a secret weakness as well. I take a ticket in the casket whenever I'm in the vicinity of a casket agency. Sometimes I take two. But to be serious,' she grinned, 'I don't think about it that much. I . . . don't really have much cause to. All I have to support is myself. It could be different if I had a family and so on, then I might hanker after it much more. But . . .' she stopped, 'I . . . when we had that barbecue, we were lively and I think we all enjoyed it tremendously. But it wasn't an essentially wealthy thing to do.'

'No,' Richard said slowly. He drained his glass and set it down.

'You don't sound so sure,' she said uncertainly after a minute or two. '*Did* I sound smug and disdainful? I didn't mean to.'

He had been looking away from her at nothing in particular yet with a strange fixity. But as she spoke his eyes came back to rest on her face swiftly and his expression softened. 'No, you didn't. Just very earnest and rather solemn, and I know—now—you mean every word you say. I'm sorry,' he stood up as he spoke in one lithe movement and reached out a hand to draw her to her feet, 'I'm sorry for what happened the night I got back, Anna. And every other time we've . . . I haven't understood. But you're wrong about one thing,' he said very quietly as she stared up at him bemused. 'That *was* an essentially wealthy thing to do, that barbecue. It was wealthy because Phil is a little nicely mad and Letty and Samson are two of the nicest people I know and Colonel Jackson is actually very sane, though not pretty,' his lips twitched, 'and for some strange reason likes to surround himself with nicely mad people, some nicer than others. And you. You remind me of the Colonel in a way, so sane yet touched with an understanding of these things. But more than pretty . . . Then there was Chrissy, and Chrissy is . . . well, we all know the kind of enchanted web she weaves. That's an amazing array of wealth of spirit, don't you think?'

They stared at each other until Anna said, 'That puts it in a nutshell. But,' her voice was husky and her eyes searched his face, 'what about you? You were there too?'

He grimaced. 'I might be the poor relation.'

'Why?' she whispered, conscious of a sudden, compelling urge to get to the bottom of this man who puzzled her immensely, she found.

'It's a long story, Anna,' he said dryly. 'But it's a long time since I felt much wealth of spirit.'

'I know,' she said involuntarily, and winced at her own temerity. But I do know, she thought. How could I not know when I've seen the other side of him? The cold, cruel side. 'You . . . but when you're with Chrissy, and the others, you're . . . transformed,' she said haltingly.

'I guess Chrissy's my saving grace.' He shrugged. 'Who would have thought . . .' He stopped abruptly and it was as if he deliberately changed the direction of his thoughts. He smiled down at her, that devastating smile that always seemed to make her heart beat a little faster. 'You don't have to worry about me, though. Phil and Letty and Samson do enough of that.' His eyes glinted devilishly. 'By the way, I'm quite sure there must be a sewing machine on Yandilla, and I know there's a record player,' he pointed to the magnificent hi-fi set in the corner of the room. 'As for books, I know there are plenty of them too. Please feel free to borrow them and play the records. I'll also speak to Letty about letting you potter around her kitchen and . . .'

'Oh—thank you,' Anna said confusedly, 'but I'd rather you didn't speak to Letty. She's . . . well, she's accepting me more and more into her kitchen and so on, really she is. And I'd rather it came naturally.'

'All right,' said Richard after a moment, and looked at her thoughtfully. 'Maybe you're right. The other thing is, you haven't had any time off—I mean off Yandilla—since you came here. Part of the arrangement was . . .'

'Yes, I know,' she interrupted hurriedly. 'That I have a weekend off every month. But I really haven't felt the need to get away yet.'

He lifted his eyebrows. 'I'm sure it will come,' he told her. 'You can get island claustrophobia too, you know. But it's up to you. Well, think you can get to sleep now without worrying about spiders?'

'Oh yes,' she said wryly. 'You must think I'm a bit of an idiot.'

'Not at all. In fact I was beginning to think you were the most terrifyingly . . . competent person I've ever known. So it's a relief to find you're human after all. Goodnight, Anna,' he added with a wickedly amused look, and held the heavy double lounge doors open for her.

'I . . . goodnight,' she said uncertainly, not sure whether to be cross or gratified or what. Here we go again, she thought. He's *done* it again. Turned the tables on me somehow . . . but no, I won't be cross. He's been so nice tonight. She looked up at him as she passed through the doors and smiled. 'Thanks,' she said quietly, and walked unhurriedly in the direction of her bedroom.

But she didn't get to sleep immediately, though not on account of spiders.

And she was struck by a strange thought the next morning. That there was absolutely no reminder of Chrissy's mother in the house at all. At least, no photos, framed or otherwise. And nothing amongst Chrissy's personal possessions that she treasured particularly because it had belonged to her mother. It was almost as if she had never existed, Anna thought with an inward shiver. Except that she was undoubtedly still there in the heart of the man who had lost her.

Perhaps he can't bear the pain of seeing her face even in a photo, she mused.

I wonder what she was like? If one had known her, you might have a better idea of ... at least it would be easier than wondering how you measured up to a ghost ...

She closed her eyes abruptly and found herself feeling hot and cold at the same time. Whatever was she thinking? And she resolutely pushed the thought out of her mind.

CHAPTER SIX

'*Lotus Lady* just called,' Samson announced, and deposited a canvas bag on the verandah table. It was mid-afternoon and Letty had just served tea.

'Oh, good!' enthused Phil. 'I'm running short of carbon paper and I ordered some ages ago—perhaps it's come.' She untied the string of the bag and delved into it and withdrew a bundle of mail. 'Who's going to play postman? If my carbon paper still hasn't arrived ...'

'I will,' Richard said, and took the bundle of letters out of her hand as she started to looked distracted. He leafed through them. 'Two—no, three for you, Phil, one for Sunshine, a whole lot of ominous-looking bills for me,' he said wryly, 'and ...' His voice trailed off in a way that made most of them look at him enquiringly.

'Whatsa matter?' asked Letty. 'You look as if you've seen a ghost.'

'No,' he said slowly, but his voice was oddly grim as he studied the letter in his hands. Then he raised his eyes and looked straight at Anna. 'But perhaps I didn't make one thing clear to you, Anna. Nobody on Yandilla has anything whatsoever to do with Mike Carmody. And if you wish to stay here, you'd be wise to make it plain to him that that includes you.'

Anna gaped at him. 'I don't know what you're talking about!' she said at last.

He looked at her coldly. 'You might when you've read this,' he said, and tossed the letter he was holding on to the table in front of her. Then he stood up and walked inside abruptly and a moment later, for all to hear, the study door was closed ungently.

Anna stared at the letter and noted that it wasn't postmarked and was simply addressed to Miss Anna Horton, Yandilla. She reached for it and opened it with fingers that weren't quite steady. And her eyes widened incredulously as she scanned the letter, not taking in the contents because the big bold signature seemed to leap at her—Mike Carmody.

She looked up to see four pairs of eyes resting anxiously on her. 'I think somebody ought to explain,' she said helplessly. 'How did he know who it was from? And why would that make him so angry?'

Letty was the first to break the silence. 'Er . . . why, Chrissy love, I think our pavlova for dinner might be ready. Going to help me whip the cream and make the filling?' She held out her hand.

Chrissy looked at Anna and for a moment it seemed as if she was going to refuse. Then she slipped her hand into Letty's and went with her surprisingly docilely.

Phil sighed audibly and Anna looked at her bewilderedly as Samson too departed, but in the opposite direction and with a rueful shake of his head at Anna.

'Please tell me what's going on, Phil?' Anna begged.

'I . . . think it's up to Richard to tell you,' Phil said at last.

'Oh, that's all very well!' Anna exclaimed angrily. 'But if the way he looked at me is anything to go by, I don't particularly feel like asking him! And anyway, he can't dictate what I do with my free time or who I see. Can he?'

Phil wrung her hands—an indication she was deeply troubled. 'I suppose not. But he can make your life hell on account of it,' she said candidly. 'Does . . . do . . . I mean, is it important to you to . . . keep in contact with Mike Carmody?' she added delicately and a touch curiously. 'Because I can tell you he and Richard are—well, don't get on.' She pulled a face.

'No. At least, not particularly. Oh,' Anna sighed exasperatedly, 'that's not the point! The point is I'm legally of age, as the saying goes, in fact I'm more, and I'm employed here as a governess, but that doesn't mean he owns me body and soul and can dictate to me who I may or may not see!' She took a breath, her face flushed and her eyes bright and angry. 'And to do it that way too,' she went on furiously. 'So that I felt like a child being reprimanded! But for something I didn't even know about! Nor am I likely to, by the sound of things,' she added caustically.

Phil winced visibly. 'My dear, some things are hard to explain. And of course you're right! There was no need for him to do it like that. Oh, I'd be a little angry with him for doing it like that, certainly!' she conceded. 'But . . .'

'A little angry?' Anna fumed. 'The trouble with Richard Gillespie—I'm sorry, Phil—but the trouble with him is that he gets away with murder! And,' her gaze fell on the letter and she read the brief contents swiftly, 'all it says here,' she lifted her eyes to Phil, 'is that if I have any free time, he'd be happy to show me the Hinchinbrook Channel. Now I can't see how that could affect . . . my *boss* in any way or that it's any concern of his. And furthermore,' she stood up, 'I'm going in there to tell him that right now, and to arrange to take a day off as soon as I can!' She set her lips in a stubborn line and stalked inside, leaving Phil staring after her dazedly.

Five minutes later Anna had relieved herself of these same sentiments in no uncertain terms and she stared at Richard Gillespie across the broad expanse of his desk, undaunted and unshaken by the coldly unmoved look she was on the receiving end of.

'You can be as angry as you like,' she said furiously. 'And if I have to resign to prove my point, I'll do it. But you seem to think you can get away with murder where I'm concerned so long as you apologise afterwards!'

'I have no intention of apologising to anybody on the subject of Mike Carmody,' he said violently. 'Nor do I have any intention of allowing myself to be dictated to on my affairs by anyone, but least of all *you*.' He looked at her contemptuously, his eyes smouldering.

'But this isn't your affair,' she pointed out hotly. 'That's what I'm trying to say! And I'm also trying to say that I object to the way you handled the whole business out there. I don't have to take that from anyone. And you've now treated me that way just once too often, Richard Gillespie,' she stormed.

'If that's the way you feel, then it is better if you go. In any case it's better that you go, Anna,' he added curtly, and his eyes glittered strangely.

'I . . . *why*?' she demanded, not sure she was hearing right and totally taken aback by this unexpected twist.

'Because you were right,' he said tightly. 'Chrissy needs a mother, not someone who'll be here today, gone tomorrow or in a few weeks or a couple of months or whenever the whim takes you. It's going to break her heart to see you go if you go today, as it is.'

'I . . . I . . .' Anna whispered, and sank down into a chair as if she'd received a body blow.

'I thought you might get some satisfaction from being able to say I told you so,' Richard said grimly, his grey-green eyes raking her face mercilessly.

Anna licked her lips. 'If you did think that,' she said in a low choking voice, 'then you're more of a bastard than even I thought.'

'Then that's another reason why we should—part company, don't you think?' he said evenly. 'Although I'm quite sure one of the reasons you feel that way is because you can't forget that I kissed you once and you enjoyed it. But you won't allow yourself to admit it, despite the fact that you can't help thinking about it still.'

This was so true, yet so unfair, Anna could do nothing but stare at him disbelievingly. Then she found her voice, although it was strangely husky, and she said with a world of angry contempt, 'I've made allowances for you, you know. I've tried to convince myself that you are the way you are because of losing Chrissy's mother. Because you can't find anyone to measure up to her. But I always felt it didn't quite ring true. And now, despite the fact that everyone here thinks you're an inconsolable widower, I don't think it's that way at all. Oh no,' she said, 'and they might change their opinions if they'd seen the side of you I have. You're nothing but a . . . a . . .' she searched for the right word, only to find there was no other than one she'd already used, although she embellished it, 'an arrogant bastard, and you deserve to be pursued by fortune-huntresses and all the rest, because you don't have a heart!'

But to her astonishment he only raised his eyebrows at this outpouring and looked, if anything, faintly amused. 'Who told you I was an inconsolable widower?'

'It doesn't matter,' she gritted through her teeth.

'But I'd like to know. Because I can't imagine anyone here telling you that.'

Anna frowned. 'Well, indirectly they . . .' She tailed off uncertainly.

'How very loyal of them,' he commented. 'But you see, Julie was a faithless, treacherous woman, and the only reason we weren't divorced was because she died before it could happen.'

For the second time that afternoon she stared at him with her mouth open and a look of supreme shock and stunned disbelief in her eyes. 'But . . .' she whispered at last, 'this . . . you're talking about Chrissy's mother!'

'Do you think I don't know that?' he said angrily. 'Do you realise that not a day goes by that I don't look at Chrissy and wonder how she could be such a perfect little girl when she had two such mismatched parents? Do you think that prevented her *mother* from using her as some kind of a bargaining tool?'

Anna winced.

'Yes, she did,' he said coldly. 'That's the kind of woman Chrissy's mother was. And that's why I'm not exactly an inconsolable widower. And no, I don't think I have a heart. At least, what I have left tells me that if I ever do remarry, this time it will be to someone who's prepared to be a good wife and mother in the old-fashioned sense of the word. Someone who cares about

her home and her children and values and non-material
things I can give her more than the material ones.
That's the yardstick I'd use now. *Look*,' he said
savagely, 'for what it's worth, I don't . . . didn't blame
Julie so much for the fact that we cooled off towards
each other. Or to put it another way, I blamed myself
equally, because it was a violent mutual attraction that
didn't take into account the basic differences between
us until it was too late. But when that became apparent,
there should have been a civilised way of dealing with it
for Chrissy's sake. In fact I offered her one which she
declined although she *knew* I was going to fight her
every inch of the way over custody of Chrissy.'

Anna stared at him. 'I didn't know,' she said
shakenly.

'Well, now you do,' he said shortly. 'And since we're
being so beautifully frank, in case you're wondering
what Mike Carmody has to do with all this, I'll tell you
that too. The last words Julie said to me before she died
were that she was going to Mike, who really loved her.
Not that I needed telling that he was infatuated with
her. Most men she came in contact with were. Nor did I
need telling that they'd become lovers . . .'

Anna closed her eyes, still trying to take in what she
had just learnt. And she found that a lot of little things
suddenly fell into place, things Phil had said, and Letty,
things she had not understood at the time or
misinterpreted. If only someone had just told me the
truth, she thought despairingly. It explains so much.
Why he treats women the way he does . . .

She looked up at him at last, her eyes clearly
expressing some of the turmoil she felt. 'I . . . I'm
truly sorry,' she said haltingly. 'I had no idea—if I had,
I wouldn't have said some of the things I did.'

'Oh, I think you would,' he observed. 'I think you
have a habit of speaking your mind.'

'I might never again,' she murmured, still feeling
totally floored by what she had just learnt, and with an
effort she attempted to wrench her mind away from it.
'I . . . but to get back to Chrissy and what we were
saying earlier. I *can* see how fond she is getting of me.

And it's by no means a one-sided thing,' she added painfully. 'I just didn't realise it was possible to become so attached to someone else's child. I honestly don't know what to do. Maybe you're right, maybe it is better if I go now rather than later.'

There was a long silence. They didn't look at each other. Then Richard said abruptly, 'There's another solution, Anna. You could marry me.'

Anna felt suddenly as if she was suffocating and she flushed brightly. 'I don't think that's in very good taste,' she said stonily.

'I do,' he answered surprisingly. 'In fact I think it's the perfect solution—for both of us.'

She sprang up agitatedly. 'But you've just *told* me . . . how could you ask anyone to marry you after what you've just told me? But as for me, when you think of the number of times we've quarrelled I'm surprised— I'm really surprised you would even consider me. Particularly if you mean what I think you mean when you talk about an old-fashioned wife. Someone who'll meekly accept everything you choose to throw at her!'

He smiled slightly. 'I'm sure I'd have to learn to duck if I tried that with you!'

'If you think this is something to joke about . . .'

'No,' he interrupted, and came to stand beside her. 'Why don't you sit down and we can discuss this rationally?'

Anna trembled and thought distractedly, this can't be happening to me. Does he really think I can sit down and talk about this rationally? As if we're discussing the price of eggs? She took an uncertain breath and stared at him—and was unwittingly flooded with an acute sense of proximity so that every other time she had been physically conscious of him faded beneath this particular onslaught. It's almost as if I'm seeing him for the first time, she thought dazedly. But in an old context—as I could see him if I accepted this incredible offer, making love to me, stroking my body with those lean, strong hands, watching me with that clever, probing grey-green gaze, holding me against that tall, strong body . . .

She sat down abruptly amid a confusion of clamouring pulses and with a lurching heart in case he could read her thoughts.

But if he could, he gave no indication of it. He mearly waited with a polite, grave attentiveness until she said stiffly, 'All right. I suppose we can discuss it at least.'

'Good,' he drawled, and sat down on the corner of the desk. 'Anna, I've just told you how I feel about these things. And the reason I thought we'd . . . be right for each other is because you once told me how you felt. You said you didn't think you were made for a—quote—grand, hit-you-on-the-head kind of passion—unquote. You spoke of a slow sort of warmth that grows and feeds on a mutual interest. I think we have that. We have Chrissy, and you've fitted into the lifestyle of Yandilla so well, I can't believe we wouldn't have that in common too.'

Anna moved restlessly. If I'd had the slightest inkling how my own words were going to be used against me, she thought tormentedly, I'd have sealed my lips for ever. 'I . . .'

'No, hang on, let me finish. There's a lot more we have in common. You also told me once you're not particularly interested in a madly jet-setting existence. You like your pleasures to come more simply. That's how I like it too. She . . . Julie was bored to tears here after a while. Then too, we agree that children need stability and care and nurturing and they need to have time invested in them. We needn't, incidentally, confine ourselves to Chrissy either. We could have as many children as you liked, and I think you'd like that.' He looked at her probingly before he went on, 'So you see, in a sense we could make a better marriage than most because we have all these basic elements and perhaps, most importantly, we've each suffered our disillusionments and wouldn't be going into it with any . . . inflated expectations.'

'I . . . it sounds so sane when you say it like that. But I think you've twisted my words a little out of context,' Anna said with an effort. 'I didn't mean that my parents weren't in love when they married. I only meant that it ... didn't strike them like a bolt of lightning. And,' her voice shook a little, 'what you're suggesting is that we get married for a variety of very ... well, businesslike reasons, some of them ... or practical ones, put it that way, and *then* hope that it happens that way for us too.'

'You don't think it could?' Richard queried.

She looked away. 'I don't know. How could I?'

He waited for a moment, then he said, 'Anna, there's something else, from your point of view. If, and I don't know exactly what kind of an unhappy experience you had, but if it means you find it hard to contemplate marriage because of it, wouldn't this be a ... better way for you? At least you like me, I think. On my better days, of course.' He grinned faintly.

O, what a tangled web we weave ... She sighed. I should tell him now, she thought. I should set the record straight about this for once and for all. But is it so important? I can't—in all sanity, I can't marry him for these reasons. I couldn't marry anyone like that.

She took a deep breath and started to speak, but was stopped by a shaft of pain that struck her heart like an arrow. Least of all him, she thought dazedly. Because ...

'Anna?'

'I ... I'm sorry, Richard,' she said confusedly. 'I ... do you know that's the first time I've ever called you that, directly? Surely that demonstrates how crazy it is for us to even think of getting married?' she asked huskily with sudden tears in her eyes.

He looked at her steadily. 'Perhaps,' he said sombrely. 'If that's the way you feel ...'

'*Yes*. But what will we do?' she asked, brushing away the tears.

'You tell me, Anna.'

'Do you want me to go? For Chrissy's sake I will. But—oh God! I've ... all these weeks I've known that it was getting harder and harder to even think of leaving ...'

'Don't cry,' he said with an unexpected compassion

that, if anything, made it harder for her to stem the tears.

She stood clenching her fists and biting her lip. Then she whirled on her heel and ran from the room. And he didn't try to stop her.

It was Phil who found her lying on her bed, dry-eyed now but staring fixedly at the wall opposite.

'Anna?'

Anna didn't move. But she said tiredly, 'Come in.'

'Are you all right?'

'No.' Her eyes didn't leave the wall.

'I tried to warn you,' Phil said diffidently. She closed the door.

'Yes,' Anna answered bleakly.

'My dear . . .'

'But you didn't tell me,' Anna broke in, her eyes at last leaving the wall. 'No one told me about Chrissy's mother. And I've made the most awful fool of myself . . .'

Phil picked up one of her hands and massaged it gently, but there was a curiously alert look in her blue eyes as if she was pondering something unseen. Then she said quietly, 'We don't talk about it, for Chrissy's sake. We pretend it never happened that way.'

'What was she like?' Anna found herself asking after a minute or two.

'Julie was beautiful. She had the kind of beauty that could turn the worst day of your life into something worthwhile just to see her. And she was fearless and stimulating—in that respect she and Richard were well matched. She could surf and sail as well as he could, she loved to scuba-dive, but it was also a headstrong kind of fearlessness that was always seeking new challenges. She could never sit still unless she was planning what to do next. She was also stubborn to a fault, but I think a lot of that was due to a difficult childhood, a rather poor one, and a particularly repressive father who invoked authority as much for the sake of it as anything else. I think Julie grew up resenting authority similarly, for the sake of it, blindly and often mulishly.

'But in other respects,' Phil went on slowly, 'they weren't well matched. I don't think she ever realised just how much Yandilla means to Richard, as a lifestyle and not in the way that it's lovely to have your own island to retreat to now and then and bring your friends to. She was never happy for long here. And I don't think she ever understood that spending money in itself, more or less simply because it's there, buys you very little in the long run. Which led Richard to wonder often, I'm sure, what she enjoyed most about their marriage—him, or spending his money.'

'Oh,' Anna whispered, her eyes wide. 'Did she marry him for his money?'

Phil sighed. 'I don't honestly think so. I think the attraction was so strong, in the early days, she'd have married him if he'd been a pauper. But what she couldn't grasp was that if it was there, why not spend it? And while Richard isn't mean at all he . . . well, when you've always had it anyway, I think you find it in not very good taste to throw it about at whim. It's also harder, when you've always had it, to understand how it affects people who haven't. Some people anyway.'

'No . . . no wonder he's rather . . .'

'Wary?' Phil supplied, and smiled. 'I suppose so.'

'Is Chrissy like her at all?' Anna asked huskily.

'Oh yes,' said Phil. 'In lots of ways. Enchanting, fearless about some things, a little more highly-strung than most of us, but even though she's so young, I can see a much more *caring* personality developing in Chrissy.'

Anna lay still and listened to the faint, familiar sounds of the house as dusk approached. She said at last, 'If it hadn't happened, would they have divorced, do you think?'

'Who could say?' Phil answered thoughtfully. 'Things were bad and I can't deny that Richard can be . . . hard, very hard. But he did offer her a compromise which amounted to them virtually living their own lives but staying married for Chrissy's sake. I don't know if that kind of thing ever works very well, but anyway, one thing he was adamant about was parting with Chrissy.'

'She wanted Chrissy?'

'Yes. Stubbornly, furiously and determinedly too, although she left her to Letty's care most of the time. But Chrissy adored her—when she saw her. She adored them both.'

'She told me she can still remember her,' said Anna.

Phil smiled wistfully. 'I doubt it.'

'How . . . sad,' Anna said with an inward shiver.

'It was sad. These things always are,' Phil shrugged. 'But it got sadder in a curious way, unfortunately. No one in their right minds could have wished that kind of a solution to it. And I think Richard will always be a little haunted by it and experience a sense of guilt.'

'But it wasn't his fault that she died?'

'Oh no. The actual . . . the way it happened was typically Julie. She took a boat out on her own one night without even telling Samson, and got caught in a squall that blew up unexpectedly. It was the way she lived, and there was always the distinct possibility that one day she'd take up a challenge that was too great for her. But unfortunately, Richard wasn't here. He'd been at a sugar board conference in Cairns for two days when it happened. And they'd had a monumental row when he left.'

'And then she was dead,' Anna said slowly. 'I think I understand what you mean. Would—she have gone to Mike?' she asked involuntarily.

Phil shook her head sorrowfully. 'I don't think so. But there's no doubt she'd led Mike on to believe she would one day. He was very young then, Anna, and absolutely infatuated, and she was the kind of person who . . . used other people. But that too provided a further source of bitterness. Mike was so infatuated he was beyond much good sense for a while after she died. And he put it around the community that Richard had . . . that she'd been so desperately unhappy she'd taken her own life.'

Anna stared at Phil in horror.

'But that wasn't true, Anna. However unhappy, Julie would no more have dreamt of doing away with herself than I would imagine I could fly.'

'I'm surprised he still has the Yandilla contract . . .'

'Oh, that was my doing,' Phil said, brightening a little. 'I put my foot down there. Men do funny things when they imagine they're in love and I didn't like to see him penalised for her . . . well, I've known Mike since he was a baby too,' she said ruefully, 'and at that stage he only had one leaky old boat and the Yandilla contract was about his only sure form of income.'

'You're so very sweet, Phil,' said Anna with a break in her voice.

Phil contemplated her silently for a long time. Then she said, 'And you're more upset about this, Anna, than someone who has recently come into our midst need be. Would you like to tell me why?'

Anna sighed. 'Phil, you're not going to believe this— but Richard just asked me to marry him.'

To her astonishment, Phil didn't even look faintly surprised. She merely grimaced wryly and said, 'I was afraid of that.'

Anna sat up abruptly. 'What do you mean? Did you *know* he was going to?' she asked incredulously.

'I suspected. For two reasons—you and Chrissy get along so well. You have a rapport that makes it more than a governess-pupil relationship. And for some time now I've wondered whether he wasn't thinking of marrying again for Chrissy's sake.' She looked at Anna candidly. 'There's something else too. In lots of ways you're the antithesis of Julie, Anna.'

'So he told me,' Anna said dryly. 'None of which leaves me feeling much complimented or enthusiastic about his proposal.'

Phil sat forward. 'That's what I was afraid of. And you said no?'

'Of course I said no!' answered Anna, feeling angry tears welling. 'Would you have done any different? You don't marry for those reasons!'

Phil hesitated. Then she said carefully, 'You might do it for another reason, though. You might do it because you're attracted to him quite strongly.'

Anna closed her eyes and was silent. 'How did you

know?' she said finally. 'I haven't even let myself ... really admit that.'

'People often think I see a lot less than I do,' Phil remarked wryly. 'And I might have noticed it because you, in fact both of you, have been at great pains to hide it.'

'He ...' Anna stopped and bit her lip. But she thought almost immediately that it was obviously useless to try and hide much on Yandilla. 'He hasn't always tried to hide it. In fact it's given him great pleasure on occasions to—to take advantage of me quite unfairly. But the point is, Phil,' she said bitterly, 'he's done it in a way that's left me certain I could be any reasonably pretty girl—just a face and a figure, no more. In fact I think he can take me or leave me without a second thought, as he probably can all women. And if you must know, the thought that I might have joined a succession of ... of star-struck nannies fills me with a sense of humiliation and horror.' The tears trickled down her cheeks and fell on to her hands unheeded as she stared at Phil.

'Then you do think you might have fallen in love with him?' Phil asked gently.

'I ... I've no idea what it is,' Anna said wearily. She grimaced. 'What is this thing they call love? If it's this ... this mixture of uncertainty, of ... sometimes I'm sure I hate him! Quite sure and not without cause. In fact I think I hate him right now.'

'My dear!' Phil said concernedly.

'I shouldn't;' Anna sobbed. 'I've learnt so much today which I never knew that *explains* so much. But I can't help feeling as if I've had a slap in the face, somehow, all the same.'

'Anna, I think that one of the problems of this kind of situation is that it's hard not to have preconceived ideas about love.'

Anna stared at her. 'Oh, Phil,' she said grimly, 'don't let me get on to that subject. If I hadn't thought I was wise on these matters, and insisted on delivering myself of my wisdom to him, together with a whole lot of other rubbish, I might not be in this mess. Look, all I know now is that not so long ago I was happy and carefree. Then I met Richard Gillespie and I haven't known whether I've been on my head or my heels since. And I haven't been happy either, and if that's love, I think I'd rather live without it.'

'The thing is,' Phil said quietly, 'if it is, it's not something you can turn off like a tap. It's not something that you can say to yourself, now look, this is silly! I've got to stop this! It will still be there.'

'Then all the more reason to test it,' Anna said bleakly. 'I have to go in any case, Phil. The longer I stay, the harder it's going to be for Chrissy. And even if it does turn out to be ... true blue, as they say, there isn't a great future for it. Would you care to marry a man who doesn't love you in return?'

'Go?' Phil looked suddenly disconcerted.

'Yes. In fact, in lieu of marrying him, that's what Richard wants me to do—and he's right. And the sooner the better.'

'Oh, but you can't go just like that, Anna! You see, I ... I'm expected in London in a week's time.' Phil looked suddenly embarrassed. 'Believe it or not, they're making a series of television plays from some of my books and they want me there to consult with the scriptwriters. The letter came in the mail today, as a matter of fact,' she said breathlessly, and drew a crumpled airmail envelope from her pocket. 'At least, confirmation of the dates. It ... it ... well, I'd really love to do it, but of course I don't have to,' she said confusedly. 'It's not as if it's a contract thing, more of a courteous gesture to me, but—well, it's not that important! Certainly not as important as Chrissy ... I mean, if you and I both deserted her ... I mean ...' And she looked as flustered and remorseful as only Phil could.

Anna stared at her. 'How long for?'

'Oh, only six weeks to two months, but ...'

'Does Richard know?'

'Oh, yes! But he might have forgotten. He was rather surprised when I accepted. I'm generally such a stick-in-the-mud ... But that's neither here nor there. These

things can't be helped, can they? Now promise me
something, you're not to worry about this, not even to
give it a second thought.'

'Phil,' Anna said helplessly, 'there must be some
arrangement we could make!'

'Anna,' Phil smiled at her, 'it was only a little ego trip
really. Please, I don't want you to think about it any
more. You've got enough to worry about as it is.'

CHAPTER SEVEN

'CAN I talk to you?' Anna said hesitantly.

It was late, and if it hadn't been for Phil's revelation
earlier in the day about her trip to London, Anna
would not now be in the boatshed trying to talk to her
boss, she knew.

In fact, she had had to force herself to go to dinner,
although it hadn't turned out to be the ordeal she had
feared. But only because Richard had received a phone
call before the meal, a business call that had been a
lengthy one, and Letty had finally taken his dinner to
him in the study on a tray.

Yet it hadn't been a bed of roses either. Chrissy had
been visibly tense and Phil unsuccessfully trying to
project the image of not having a care in the world.
Only Letty had appeared normal.

Richard looked up from the bench he was working
at. He was still wearing the same jeans and khaki bush
shirt he had had on earlier—for that matter, Anna was
still wearing the simple lime green sundress she had
worn all day that showed off her smooth tanned
shoulders and went with the darkness of her hair. He
said, 'If you want to. Where's Chrissy?'

'She's asleep.'

He glanced at his watch and looked surprised. 'It's
later than I thought.' He stretched and stood up and
leant back against the bench, folding his arms across his
chest and regarding her impersonally.

'I . . . was waiting for you to come up,' Anna said
awkwardly. 'But perhaps this is a better spot anyway.
More,' she hesitated and looked round and up at the
exposed rafters and the shadows the light threw on the
whitewashed walls, 'private . . .'

He smiled, but without humour. 'I thought we'd dealt
with everything of a private nature between us, Anna,'
he said coolly. 'Not that it's possible to keep anything
private on Yandilla for long.'

'I had worked that out,' she answered dryly. 'But this
is about Phil. Has she said anything to you since we
talked this afternoon?'

'No. Nothing she wouldn't normally have said.
Why?' He sounded curious.

'I . . . this afternoon I told her I was leaving.' Anna
looked down at her hands, then she raised her eyes and
their gazes locked.

'You don't waste much time, do you, Anna?'

She flushed faintly, but said resolutely, 'I'd thought
we'd decided it would only make it harder if I did. But
something's come up which has made me wonder . . .
well,' she broke off helplessly, 'I think you should know
about it at least.'

He frowned. 'Like what?'

She told him about Phil's overseas trip.

'Hell,' he muttered. 'I'd forgotten about it. But I'm
sure it wasn't due just yet. She hasn't got the dates
mixed up, has she?'

'I don't think so,' Anna said slowly. 'No, she got the
letter today. Maybe she had the dates mixed up when
she first told you about it?'

'That's more than bloody likely,' he said impatiently.
'And she wants to go?'

'Very much, I think. But she said there was no
possibility of going if I was leaving too—that it
wouldn't be fair to Chrissy if we both deserted her at
the same time. But I think too she was really
disappointed, although she covered up as quickly as
she could, and I doubt if you'd get her to admit it
now.'

Richard stared past her for a moment. 'I see,' he said

at last. 'And how did she take your news otherwise? Was she surprised?'

'Oh yes,' Anna replied glibly, having anticipated this question, and she prayed that he would leave it at that.

He raised his eyebrows. 'What did you tell her?'

She looked at him uneasily and resolved never to utter futile prayers again. 'The truth,' she said baldly at last.

'Did you now,' he remarked with some irony. 'You surprise me.'

'I surprised myself,' she replied truthfully. In more ways than one, she thought but didn't say. Then, because just looking at him leaning negligently against the bench with his fair hair ruffled and his tall figure etched darkly on the wall behind him had the power to disturb her, she found, she added with a barely muted sort of hostility, 'As a matter of fact, she wasn't that surprised. It seems she's suspected all along that you would remarry for Chrissy's sake and that I might be a likely candidate because I get on so well with her.'

Richard laughed briefly. 'I'm quite demolished! I shall never scoff at feminine intuition again. But let's get one thing straight, Anna . . .' His eyes roamed over her in a way that was becoming familiar, and she tensed and vowed not to let herself be affected by it. 'That wasn't the only reason I wanted to marry you.'

'It was the main reason,' she forced herself to say unemotionally.

'It was *a* reason,' he countered. 'And one that I'd surely have to take into account—don't you see that?'

'Of course, but . . .'

'But so far we've only . . . skated over another vital element. I've always been intrigued at the thought of taking you to bed. In fact I told you about it when it first occurred to me, which was at our very first meeting—if you recall.' His lips quirked, although his words were deadly serious.

'Yes,' she said grimly. 'You did.'

'And you were very angry with me,' he supplied. 'Although for a brief moment I got the impression you were a little intrigued yourself even at that early stage of our relationship. Were you?'

Anna set her teeth. 'This is beside the point,' she said with an effort.

'It's not so far as I'm concerned,' he said quietly. 'And I've thought of it since.'

'You ... you told me once,' she said raggedly, 'that you'd quite lost your—half-formulated desire to see me without my clothes. Which I took to mean you'd lost interest in taking me to bed ...' She trailed off frustratedly, cursing herself inwardly in case her words had sounded piqued which was the last impression she wished to create.

'And you were very angry with me again.' His lips twitched. 'And rightly so. I do admit I can be a bastard sometimes. But I said that not because I meant it, but because you were so cross and so determined to put me in my place ... which I deserved at the time,' he added wryly. 'Then too, it was after that I kissed you despite the fact that I shouldn't have done that either. And for a little while you were soft and pliant in my arms and your mouth trembled under mine as if you were enjoying it as much as I was. So I think it's fair to say we're ... a little intrigued about each other.'

'And I ... I wonder if we should place too much importance on that,' she said shakily.

'You mean you don't think it has any place in a marriage?' he asked after a moment.

'No ... I mean, yes, obviously it does, but ... oh!' she sighed despairingly. 'Look, this isn't helping Phil!'

'Forget about Phil for a moment.' His voice was curt. 'I'm interested to get to the bottom of this. Are you trying to say that because of what happened to you once, you're not going to allow yourself to enjoy sex ever again?'

'No! I'm not trying to say anything of the kind,' she retorted angrily. 'But I am, as usual, a little confused about *you*. You were the one who ... mocked me when I said,' she hesitated briefly, then plunged on thinking, well, the principle's still the same again, 'when I said I didn't trust those kind of feelings. Then only this afternoon you basically agreed with me when you told me about Chrissy's mother. Now you're trying to say they mean something after all.'

'I think we're talking about two different things, Anna.' He surveyed her unsmilingly. 'You seem to want to pretend that you've been turned off the physical side of a relationship altogether, whereas I . . .'

'Obviously haven't been,' she muttered tautly, and thought, oh, why did I get myself into this in the first place?

'No. But I *can* put it in its proper perspective. If two people want to go to bed with each other and can enjoy it, that's fine. But don't call it love. Why call that love? There are other far more enduring things from my point of view—like trust and respect. But from your point of view,' he said compellingly, 'I think one of the reasons you're trying to pretend we don't feel this way about each other, that we could enjoy each other in bed too, is because I've never whispered a whole lot of drivel in your shell-like ear about undying admiration and love and God knows what! That's it, isn't it, Anna? Despite your brave words to me, you're as romantic at heart as the rest of them.' He smiled briefly.

She stared at him as he studied her sardonically, and thought with a shaft of pain that seemed to pierce her heart again, he's right. Oh God!

Then she forced herself to take a steadying breath and to think. He's also wrong about these things, surely? Otherwise why would I feel this way? But how to tell him?

'I,' she said huskily, and cleared her throat, 'I don't know what to think,' she confessed. 'I know I said a lot of things about love which might have led you to believe I——' she shrugged helplessly, 'well, that I knew what I was talking about. But if one thing is clear to me now, it's that I don't really have the slightest idea. Yet one thing I *do* know,' she said honestly, and couldn't help the note of bitterness that crept into her voice, 'I'm not sure about having a lot of drivel talked into my ear, but it seems it's just not acceptable to me to be made to feel "like that" by someone who with not much effort— perhaps an ad in the paper would do it—could find someone else just as suitable.'

'I advertised before,' said Richard with a sudden, dagger-like glance at her.

She winced. 'Now you're angry. I shouldn't . . .'

'You're damn right I am,' he said shortly.

'Well, I think I'm the one who should be angry!'

'Oh?'

'Yes,' she cried passionately—and found that she was angry and intolerably confused. And hurt, so inexplicably hurt, it made her angrier. So that she said precisely, 'And I've just worked it all out. I loathe and detest you. I'd be only too happy to never have to see you again. And if,' she went on, her anger now white-hot and past caring, 'you had the slightest regard for Chrissy, who is after all the cornerstone of this whole business, you'd see that a marriage of convenience isn't the answer . . . What are you doing?' she gasped as Richard reached across the intervening space and hauled her into his arms.

'This,' he said savagely. 'Try and talk your way out of this, Anna!'

'This' turned out to be a repeat of what had happened to her the night he had come home from America. Yet it wasn't quite the same, because he didn't deal with her frenzied struggles with the same kind of easy strength and tolerance he had used that night. This time he quelled her bruisingly and as if he didn't care. And he swept her up into his arms and crossed over to a pile of sails and lowered her on to them, imprisoning her, half lying, half sitting, with his own body.

Anna sobbed with frustration and despair and tried to wrench an arm free, although she knew she was fighting a losing battle.

Then it changed. He looked down at her hot face and agonised eyes and it all changed, but with a suddenness that took her completely by surprise. His arms were no longer like bands of steel around her and his eyes no longer violent but broodingly sombre.

'Richard?' she whispered his name pleadingly.

'No, Anna,' he said very quietly. 'We've both said too much. The time's come now to show you what can't be said. Don't,' he held her closer as she moved convulsively. 'I'm not going to do anything that will be regretted . . .'

But won't it? she thought fleetingly not much later as his fingers and lips traced a devastating path across her skin, discovering and exploring tender spots that she hadn't known existed in that sense. Places like behind her ears and the nape of her neck which he was stroking just gently, and the inside of her wrist which he was kissing at that moment. Can this be undone? Can I ever forget just this? Is there anything earth-shattering about having your wrist kissed, or your eyelids? Surely not . . .

Then she wasn't so sure, as her whole body trembled beneath his wandering touch and came alive as he slid his arm around her and drew her close to him and kissed her throat. And he moved one hand gently and slid the strap of her sundress off her shoulder and undid the top few buttons of the heart-shaped bodice so that the swell of her breasts gleamed like ivory where the dress fell away. He watched the satin smooth curves he had exposed rise and fall to the tune of her accelerated breathing intently for a long moment. Then he lifted his eyes to hers and she trembled again down the whole length of her, because she knew what he was going to do—knew too that she would let him because she didn't have the will power to resist, didn't want to have it.

'Anna?' he muttered, his lips barely moving.

'Yes . . .?' she whispered uncertainly.

'This is what you've been thinking about every time you've worn a swimming costume in my presence, isn't it? Every time you couldn't wait to get your everlasting towelling dress on?'

'I . . .' She looked up at him tormentedly.

'Well, I have,' he murmured, and slid his fingers beneath her dress. 'I've often thought about undressing you somewhere in the sunlight or the moonlight or lamplight, and laying you down and touching you with my hands and my lips—exciting you as I think I could.'

His gaze rested on her partly open lips, then moved to her wide eyes and the fluctuating colour in her cheeks; he moved her a little away from him and undid two more buttons and very gently slid the other strap off her shoulder, exposing her breasts completely.

She took a tortured breath but could not stop herself

from looking down. And it seemed as if the impact was doubled, to see and to feel his lean, strong fingers touching her nipples delicately, then moving away to cup each breast with a caressing gentleness, and to see each rosy bud harden in a response that she felt with a shuddering intensity through to the pit of her stomach.

A flood of colour poured into her cheeks and she looked away—anything rather than have to look into those grey-green eyes and see the triumph and perhaps the mockery in them.

But when he made her turn her head to him with his fingers beneath her chin, there was no triumph, no mockery, only an expression she couldn't fathom. He said softly, 'Don't . . . look like that, Anna.' He traced the outline of her mouth with one finger. 'It's not a crime to respond like that. In fact for a man and a woman to excite each other in this way is like nothing else that ever happens to you, and it's a pity to spoil it with feelings of guilt and shame . . . or something you can't forget, won't let yourself forget.'

'What . . . what if those feelings come afterwards?' she queried unhappily after a long hesitation.

His eyes narrowed and he looked at her piercingly as if he could see right through to her soul. 'All right,' he said at last, and sat her up against the wall, buttoning her dress up and slipping the straps back into position. 'We'll leave it be.'

But perversely those words seemed to cut her to the quick and to her horror she felt hot tears well and trickle down her cheeks. 'I . . .' she said despairingly, and lifted her eyes to the ceiling in a gesture of helplessness.

'You don't have to say anything, Anna.' His voice was steady and even compassionate as it had been earlier in the day.

'Yes . . . yes, I do,' she said with an effort, and brushed her hair back from her flushed, tear-streaked face. 'I have to try to explain.' She looked at him. But in the very act of beginning to tell him how she had misled him originally, she paused, and discovered suddenly that she couldn't do it. But why? she

wondered shakenly. Is it because I'm using that lie like
a coat of armour? Is that why I went along with it in the
first place because I realised subconsciously even then
that I was going to need some protection against him?
Against a terrible attraction that's turned into something
more? Perhaps turned into the very thing he mistrusts
most?

'Go on,' he said quietly.

She licked her lips. 'I wish I had the courage to go to
bed with you,' she said in a low husky voice. 'But I
don't. It . . . it's something to do with the way I'm made
I think. Nor do I have the . . . whatever it takes to
marry you, knowing you don't love me so much as
want m-me.' Her voice shook, but she went on
resolutely as he moved restlessly, 'And like me and
respect me as I do you.'

Richard didn't say anything, just watched her
carefully as she tried to think clearly because although
she couldn't tell him the whole truth, it seemed
desperately important to get across to him what was
still the truth she felt in her heart. 'I think *you* must be
right—this time. I must be as insanely romantic as the
rest of them after all. I do want someone to fall madly
in love with me and I probably will fall madly in love
myself one day with all the trimmings I was so scathing
about.' Only I'm terribly afraid that might have
happened already, she added to her heart.

They stared at each other for a long time, then he
smiled at her with a heartbreaking gentleness and
touched her cheek lightly. 'He'll be a lucky man, Anna,
when you find him. You can tell him that from me.'

'Richard,' she began, the tears falling more rapidly
now, 'I'm sorry . . .'

He thought for a moment with his head bent. Then
he looked up and said with a curious wryness, 'Perhaps
not as sorry as I am.'

'That . . . that's the nicest thing you've ever said to
me,' she answered tremulously. 'I . . . I'm not sure if I
deserve it.'

'Oh yes.' He stood up in one lithe movement and she
jumped. 'No, don't you move, Anna.' He grinned down

at her. 'We've still got a few things to work out. And I reckon we could both do with a bit of this.' He pulled open a cupboard and withdrew a bottle and poured some of its contents into two battered old tin mugs. Then he switched the overhead lights off and came back to sit down beside her.

It took a moment or two for her eyes to adjust, but it wasn't really dark. There was a bright swathe of moonlight coming through the open slipway doors. Another Yandilla moon, she thought.

'Here, it's brandy,' he said offering her one of the mugs. 'We keep it down here for medicinal purposes.'

'That—sounds like a good idea,' said Anna, accepting the mug.

'Yes.' He glinted a smile across at her. 'Letty doesn't approve, however.'

'Oh?'

'No. Probably because on the odd occasion Samson and I have abused its medicinal qualities. Letty is a zealous teetotaller. So is Samson, but every now and then he gets melancholy.'

'Letty has good reason not to—from what she was telling me, about Samson's father.'

'So I believe. Do you know, she's a tower of strength, Letty. She was to my mother, she is to Phil and to me and Chrissy. The only person she doesn't exert too much influence over is Samson. Otherwise she'd have had him married years ago and had a whole tribe of grandchildren!'

'That's often the way with mothers and sons, isn't it?' remarked Anna. 'But talking of Samson, you *think* he's melancholy, then he surprises you and you know he's not melancholy at all but secretly ... I don't know, more in tune than most people.'

'How right you are!' he said with a glinting look of amusement 'Feel better?' he added abruptly.

'I ... I guess so.' She sniffed and licked her lips.

'Have some of your brandy.'

She obeyed, and was grateful for the strengthening warmth that slid down her throat.

'To get back to the subject of Phil, how long does she think she'll be away, did she think?'

'Six weeks to two months,' said Anna.

'That's not . . . so long.'

'No,' Anna agreed quietly. She stared down at the mug in her hands, then looked up to see him looking thoughtfully into space. 'I . . .' he said at last, 'feel rather guilty about Phil as it is.'

'I don't think you should—apart from this,' Anna said. 'She loves Chrissy. I don't think it's been any burden to her to . . . be here for her.'

Richard's eyes came back to rest on her face. 'No,' he said slowly. 'And certainly, every time I've tried to tell her she needn't bury herself on Yandilla for Chrissy's sake, she's got rather hurt. But all the same, on account of Chrissy, I think she deliberately shut the door on something that could have blossomed into a . . . beautiful friendship, let's say.'

Anna's lips parted and her eyes became alert. 'Do you . . . do you mean Colonel Jackson?' she said slowly.

He looked surprised. 'Has she said something to you? The one time I tried to talk to her about it she told me I was imagining things and that she was far too old to be indulging in that sort of thing.'

'No, no, she hasn't said anything to me. But I saw the Colonel looking at her that night at the barbecue and . . . and it popped into my mind that he was in love with her. But she didn't—I mean, she didn't give any indication that she even knew about it. So I thought *I* must be imagining it.'

'Yes, well,' he said, 'I rather allowed myself to be lulled into the same kind of thinking. She and my uncle were one of the happiest couples you could find. But every now and then I can't help thinking that Phil and the Colonel would be perfect for each other. Yet I haven't wanted to push anything in case she was genuinely not interested.'

'What does Letty think?' asked Anna.

He smiled slowly. 'Do you know, I never thought to ask her! How foolish of me not to think of consulting the oracle!'

She smiled back at him, understanding perfectly. Then they both sobered and he said abruptly, 'We can't hope to solve that problem overnight, but would you consider staying while she goes overseas?'

'I . . .'

'You needn't be afraid of me, Anna. What's past is past now,' he said levelly, and stared at her searchingly.

'There's still Chrissy, though,' she whispered. 'We agreed that the longer I stayed, the harder it's going to be.'

'Yes. But I don't suppose six weeks or even two months is going to make such a difference. We might even be able to . . . prepare the ground a little. I did tell her at the beginning that you wouldn't be here for ever.'

Anna winced inwardly and thought of the child who had somehow managed to touch her heartstrings, and was shaken by a sudden thought—will I ever be able to leave here? Will I honestly ever have the strength to walk out on Chrissy and . . . Isn't it better to go now before the trap closes completely? I saw the trap, she thought despairingly, yet I kept on walking into it. I couldn't help it—I don't think I wanted to . . .

'Anna?'

She lifted her head and sighed. 'All right. I too owe Phil something. She's been so kind and she's so concerned. I . . . some days I feel as if she's my aunt as well. So I'll stay.'

'Thank you,' he said very quietly.

'Phil,' Anna said determinedly, 'you're going and that's that!'

It was eight o'clock in the morning and bright sunlight was streaming into the kitchen where Anna was helping Letty clear away breakfast while Sunshine started on the bedrooms.

'But I don't understand!' Phil said bewilderedly. 'I really don't! *Yesterday* . . .'

'Yesterday was yesterday,' Anna said idly. 'Gone and done with.'

Phil frowned. 'It's all very well to say that now,' she protested agitatedly, 'but if you recall . . . and anyway, we'd have to consult Richard. I mean . . .' She twisted her hands together awkwardly, and seemed to have some trouble continuing.

Anna looked at her affectionately. 'I've already consulted Richard, Phil.'

Phil's mouth dropped open. 'You have?' she said weakly at last.

'Mmm.'

'And what . . .?'

'We agreed to . . . disagree about some things, but we found ourselves in total agreement that you're going to London if we have to deliver you there personally!' She laughed at Phil's look of astonishment. Then she said softly, 'Trust me, Phil. It's going to be all right—and promise me you'll go with a clear mind and a happy heart, because Chrissy will be just fine with me. And of course Letty. Won't she Letty?'

'. . . Sure will,' said Letty after a moment, and began to stack the dishwasher energetically. 'I don't understand what all the fuss is about!'

Anna suffered a moment's remorse as she suddenly remembered that Letty for once wasn't privy to everything that had happened. Unless—Phil's told her? she thought. But no, I doubt it. And maybe I will tell her one day, because it doesn't seem right somehow to have secrets from Letty and I wouldn't want her to think badly of me . . .

CHAPTER EIGHT

'Do you think Phil's missing us, Anna?' asked Chrissy one hot and rainy day about ten days later.

'I guess so, honey.' Anna ruffled Chrissy's hair. 'You missing her?'

'Yes,' Chrissy said ruefully. 'And I worry about her sometimes. She told me she had to change planes in Rome. What if she gets on to the wrong plane? And what if she loses her glasses? She's always losing them around here and she can't read or write without them.'

'I think she might manage better on her own than we give her credit for, love,' said Anna. 'And I bet in a few days' time we'll get a fat letter from her. Tell you what, since we're thinking of her let's write to her.'

'Oh yes,' Chrissy said enthusiastically. 'I'll do it in my best running writing.'

It took Chrissy about an hour to perfect her letter to Phil. Then they took it in to Richard to get the address.

'Well, ladies,' he said, surveying them with mock gravity across an untidy, paper-laden desk, 'what can I do for you?'

Chrissy giggled and ran round to climb on to his lap. 'Anna's a lady, Daddy. I'm only a little girl.'

'I just hope you'll grow up to be as nice a lady as Anna is,' he said seriously.

'So do I. I've been trying terribly hard ever since Anna came to be just like her! Haven't you noticed?'

Anna stirred and went faintly pink and looked wryly into two pairs of grey-green eyes. 'Thank you both kindly,' she said with a mock curtsey. 'But I think Chrissy Gillespie is very nice just being Chrissy Gillespie. Don't you think so, Mr Gillespie?' she queried seriously.

'You're right, Miss Horton,' he replied but with a smile tugging at the corners of his lips. 'In fact I think she's going to be a real heartbreaker.'

'That doesn't sound very nice!' Chrissy protested. 'Anyway, I think you two are teasing me.'

'When do I ever do that?' Richard Gillespie said to his daughter, feigning offended surprise.

'All the time,' she said lovingly. 'Except when you get cross with me. But you haven't been cross with me for ages—and do you know why?'

'I'm agog,' he drawled. 'No, why?'

'Because I've been following Anna's example and trying to be good and ladylike, of course, silly,' she answered, and patted his face tenderly. 'Letty reckons I'm reformed since Anna came!'

'Letty should know,' he said a touch dryly, but he shot a laughing look at Anna.

But later that night when Chrissy was in bed and Anna was sitting on the verandah outside her room mending one of Chrissy's nightgowns with tiny, delicate stitches, he came to sit beside her.

'Anna . . .' He stopped and grimaced as the mosquito coil she had lit billowed its acrid smoke in his direction.

She stitched conscientiously for a few minutes. Then she looked up to see his eyes resting on her. 'What is it?' she asked. 'You were going to . . . ask me something?'

'Only . . . how things were going. Not that I need to ask on Chrissy's behalf. But—on your behalf?' He looked at her questioningly.

'I'm fine, thank you,' she said steadily enough and with a faintly surprised grin that she thought she managed very well. But inwardly she trembled and wondered if he could possibly have noticed what she herself had only become aware of in the last couple of days. That the fact that she had had trouble sleeping lately was beginning to show in the form of faint shadows beneath her eyes. And that she had had to move the buttons on a couple of skirts because they had become too loose . . .

'If you say so,' he said after a moment. 'But if there was something bothering you, I'd like to think you at least . . . trusted me enough to tell me. Is it—the thought of leaving Chrissy?' he added, his eyes narrowed watchfully.

'No . . . I mean, of course I worry about that, but . . . well, often these things have a habit of working themselves out anyway.' She smiled slightly.

'Then there's nothing else, Anna?'

'No, not that I can think of. Have I been looking worried? I didn't mean to! I'll take more care in future,' she said with a laugh, trying desperately to make light of the whole matter.

'All right,' he said after a moment. 'I'm glad to hear it.' He stretched and yawned. 'Well, I think I might make it an early night. Samson and I have an expedition tomorrow to Cardwell and Hinchinbrook. Two American scientists I met on my last trip are in Queensland to study our mangroves.' He grimaced. 'You know what that means, don't you—being eaten alive by sandflies. Goodnight, Anna.' He stood up.

'Goodnight. I'll think of you tomorrow, among the sandflies,' she added cheerfully, and they exchanged rueful smiles.

But as she watched his tall figure disappear round the corner of the verandah, she felt her heart contracting as if it was being squeezed and she thought despairingly, I could never tell you what's bothering me. How could I? How could I tell you I'm so afraid I spoke no less than the truth that night in the boatshed when I said I would probably fall madly in love one day. But that ironically, since saying those fateful words it's been almost as if they were the magic password, a kind of open sesame but to the door of my heart. Because I can no longer pretend to myself that I don't know what I feel for you, Richard. I know now . . .

But how do I know? she asked herself exasperatedly and with a shimmer of tears in her eyes.

Because nothing else could hurt this much, Anna, she told herself, and not for the first time. And nothing less could make the prospect of leaving this place seem as if it would be a kind of death—as if your source of life was being cut off. And nothing else surely would make you wonder if you shouldn't after all have accepted his offer of marriage even when you know you've been assessed and . . . could almost have come up on a computer!

She sighed and laid her head against the back of the chair with her eyes closed. How did this happen to me? she mused. How could one man, without even *trying*— or at least only to prove a point initially—make me so conscious of him that I can't even sleep any more? What is it about him? Perhaps if I can work it all out, I might have some chance of lessening this thing.

But she found her mind was flooded with images of Richard that didn't help to work anything out. Richard teasing Chrissy, Richard and Phil sharing a joke, Richard meekly accepting Letty's strictures but with his eyes laughing devilishly at her, Richard and Samson together—friends with a bond so strong, Richard telling her about the reef, and letting her see how painfully he cared for Chrissy. So many Richards, and not the least,

Richard kissing her, holding her, even being angry with her, justly and unjustly.

'It's been like a revelation,' she whispered. 'Oh, what a fool I've been! So many things I've said ... if only I hadn't, I might not be feeling so bad now.

'But then again,' she whispered, and licked the salty tears from her lips, 'the fact that I feel a bit foolish isn't the worst part of it, is it? The worst part is that he doesn't feel the way I do. That's by far the worst part.'

The days continued very hot, although not as hot on the mainland. And the rain went away and stayed away for nearly two weeks which almost constituted a drought in that part of the world. And life on Yandilla ran its quiet course, but there was a difference for Anna.

A sense of strain had her firmly in its grip now, for the most part that she should unwittingly give herself away. And she found she had a curiously new feeling of vulnerability not only towards Richard, but to so many little things, almost as if she had lived her whole life with most of her senses partly blinkered. The beauty of the butterflies she and Chrissy were cataloguing seemed to affect her more deeply, and the orchids they found hurt her to look upon them. It was as if the world had broadened or that her sensibilities had been heightened, to make her feel that way.

It *has* to be love, she thought one day. Is this what love does to you?

It was the day after she had asked herself this question that she bumped into Mike Carmody. In a conscious effort to start cutting the ties that bound her to Yandilla, she had started to take more interest in visiting the mainland and on this occasion had gone over with Samson to do some shopping for Letty and herself. Samson had driven her and Chrissy to Tully, left them to spend a few pleasurable hours wandering through the not so extensive shops Tully had to offer, but when you haven't been shopping for months they were more than adequate, she found. Then Samson had reappeared and he and Chrissy had gone on ahead to the car, laden down with packages, while Anna slipped into a chemist for something she had forgotten.

She came out and cannoned into him.

'Well, well,' he drawled as he restored some of her packages to her. 'If it isn't Anna!'

'Mike!' She looked up at him with wide, troubled eyes and a trace of pink coming to her cheeks. Because she had never answered his note, although she had thought of doing so, only to find she didn't quite know what to say. 'I ... I'm sorry,' she stammered. 'You must think me very rude.'

'Then you did get my letter?'

'Yes ...'

'Oh, *I* see,' he said after a moment. 'They've barred you from having anything to do with me, haven't they? I'm surprised you let yourself be pushed around like that. I thought you had more spirit,' he added with a defiant look.

'Mike, it's difficult,' she said awkwardly.

'Is it? I thought you only worked there. I didn't think Richard Gillespie owned you. Perhaps I'm wrong, though? You wouldn't be the first sheila who's fallen for him. He's got a lot going for him. But one day you might find out he can be a right bastard too.'

Anna gasped, and would have turned and run from him, but he put a hand on her arm and held her fast. 'Not so fast, Anna!' he cautioned. 'You see, I've spent the past few months carrying a vision of you around in my mind that's been mighty hard to shift. I know that's not your fault, but then the fact that the Yandilla mob treat me like a leper shouldn't have to extend to you either. Believe me, Anna, if I could undo some of the things I did, I would. But if it's any consolation to Richard Gillespie, that's going to be my burden for the rest of my life. That I can't. That I was a thoughtless stupid fool and I'll always have to live with the knowledge of it.'

Anna was arrested by the bitterness in his voice and his eyes. 'Oh, Mike,' she said at last, 'if it's any consolation to you, they don't all want to treat you—like that. They—Phil anyway understands ...'

'But he doesn't?' He stared at her searchingly.

'No. I don't know, it's none of my business,' she said confusedly. 'Do you ... really expect him to?' she added uncertainly.

He dropped his hand from her arm. 'Nope,' he said laconically. 'But if it's none of your business, why won't he let you have anything to do with me? He won't, will he?' His brown eyes, that she had once seen so open and bright, were now dark and brooding.

Anna hesitated. '... No,' she said very quietly.

'So you think he has the right to dictate to you like that?'

'Mike ...'

'Or is it that since you've found out the whole dark story, *you* don't want to have anything to do with me, Anna?'

'It's not that,' she said desperately, feeling a flood of compassion for him.

'Then prove it,' he said simply.

'I ... you don't understand, Mike,' she said helplessly.

'No? I think I do,' he said at last. 'Well, then I guess I won't be seeing you again, Anna. Goodbye.' He turned away abruptly.

Anna watched him walk away and shivered suddenly, as if the day had gone inexplicably cold.

Six weeks went by, and still Phil made no mention in her letters of coming home. For that matter, she didn't make much mention of the television series she was helping to script either, but wrote a lot about London and the great time she was having revisiting favourite spots. Richard remarked once that her butterfly brain was at its most evident in her letters, but added that she had always been loath to mention her work.

Anna winced as she thought of the lurking grin in his eyes as he had said this, and she thought, I hope Phil comes home soon, because I don't think I can stand much more of this, living side by side but always trying to hide what I'm thinking and feeling. Always afraid I'll break down one day and go to him and tell him that I

feel like a flower withering because I can't get the
thought of his mouth on mine or his hands on my body
out of my mind—that I need those things to keep me
alive. But most of all I need him to love me. Oh yes, the
sooner Phil comes home the better. But what about
Chrissy? Chrissy needs me . . .

'I wonder when Phil will be home, Letty?' she said later
that same morning. They were sharing a coffee break at
the kitchen table.

'Darned if I know,' Letty replied absently. She was
flipping idly through a calendar. 'Hey, look at this!' she
exclaimed. 'Chrissy has an appointment for a dental
check-up in Innisfail tomorra and I'd clean forgot!
Want to come, Anna? We usually make a day of it.
Samson takes us over, then he drives us up.'

'Yes. Thank you,' Anna said slowly, and frowned.
'Letty, just now you sounded as,' she moved her hands,
'as if Phil might never come home . . .'

Letty pursed her lips and hung the calendar up
carefully. 'She'll come home, Anna,' she said at last. 'I
wouldn't count on it being too soon, though.'

Anna stared at her. 'I don't understand,' she said
with a curious feeling at the pit of her stomach.

'Don't you?' asked Letty with a wise little smile. 'It's
simple. Phil doesn't want you to leave here until you're
very sure about it. That's why she went overseas when
she did, although she isn't due in London for that TV
thing yet even.'

'But *why*?' Anna's eyes were wide and disbelieving.

'Why don't we want you to leave here? I don't either,
Anna. Look, there's an old legend on Thursday Island.
There's a funny kinda tree there called the wongai tree,
and they reckon if you eat the fruit of it you'll always
go back to Thursday Island some day. Well, there isn't
no wongai tree on Yandilla, but I reckon for you, if you
leave here there'll always be something calling you
back. And it'll always hurt like hell if you can't come
back.'

There was a tense little silence, at least on Anna's side
it was tense. Then she said hoarsely, 'Letty, you and

Phil are as bad as Chrissy.' She stood up and moved over to the sink to look out of the window. But she turned away almost immediately because she could see, through a gap in the shrubbery, Richard and Chrissy on the beach skimming stones into the sea.

'Are we?' Letty's voice was gentle. 'Honey, do you think I can't see you eating your heart out for him?'

Anna caught her breath, but relaxed slightly, although it was shortlived, as Letty went on with a little shrug, 'I can't understand why he doesn't see it, but then men can be so blind. Now you just tell me it's not true, Anna. That you don't ache for Mr Richard.'

Anna put her hands up to her face and just stood there for a minute. Then Letty got up and put her arm around her and she burst into tears and sobbed into Letty's shoulder.

'There, sweetheart,' Letty said soothingly. 'You want to tell me about it?'

'Yes. I . . . he doesn't love me, Letty. Oh, he likes me and thinks I'd be good for Chrissy, but he doesn't love me. I don't think he even believes in love any more. But even if he did, I don't think it would be me. I . . . I just have the misfortune to be a good governess who might make a good wife because I'm all the things—*she* wasn't. Chrissy's mother.'

'You seem mighty sure of all this,' Letty said quietly.

'Of course I'm sure,' Anna wept. 'You see everything, Letty, and I think you must know he asked me to marry him. And that I said no! But can you see that it's made the slightest difference to him?' She raised her flushed face to stare into Letty's eyes. 'Can you? I can't,' she said bitterly. 'But you can see what it's done to me.'

'Here.' Letty pulled a hanky from her pocket and handed it to Anna. 'Sit down. I'll make us some more coffee.' She glanced out of the window. 'Don't worry, they're still down at the beach. What you might not have taken into account, Anna, is two things,' she went on a few minutes later as she set the coffee on the table. 'Does it make you love him any less because he don't love you?'

'Not . . . no, but . . .'

'Okay, so you're gonna have to live with it whatever happens. Aren't I right?'

'Letty . . .'

'Hang on, we gotta sort this all out. Is that right or isn't it?'

Anna sighed. Then she said with a mixture of bleakness and anger, 'I don't know.'

'Don't you?' Letty looked at her with an eagle eye.

'Very well, I do,' Anna said at last. 'What does that prove?'

'That you're gonna be miserable too if you go! Maybe more miserable.'

'I wish it was that simple. I wish I had a set of scales that could measure it up. But that's not the point, Letty.'

'What is the point?'

'What's the point of *staying* if I'm going to be miserable? And eaten up with despair. What good is that going to do anyone?'

'Honey, you don't know that you will be! So we all have dreams over the moon that don't come true. But not many of us get as close to them as you could. Look, I've seen you two together and while he might tell you he don't believe in love, he gets along pretty damn well with you!'

'Sometimes.'

Letty snorted. 'Most of the time. And you ain't ever gonna find a man you get along well with *all* the time, believe me,' she said, slipping into a less grammatical form of English than she normally spoke. 'But the other thing is, he might have some cause to *believe* he won't fall in love again. She—Miss Julie, she gave him a rough time. For that matter I reckon they gave each other a rough time. But she couldn't change no more than he could, and when whatever it was between them burnt itself out it left behind one helluva mess. So he has some cause to be bitter, and if she were alive, she might too. Bitter and wary and hurt. But I'll tell you something, Anna, there's no man or woman alive who can say for sure they won't fall in love again . . . or perhaps for the first time, in his case. Who's to say? But if you don't believe that, take Phil and the Colonel. There's two people who thought it could never happen to them. Both of them had happy marriages, although the Colonel lost his wife young and I wouldn't be surprised if he hadn't looked at another woman till his eyes lit on Phil. Mind you, she's about as stubborn about it as you are. But at least she has cause. She don't want to leave Chrissy.'

'So ... that is true,' Anna said slowly.

'True as I stand here!'

'But to get ... to get back to Richard,' said Anna, and blinked away a fresh set of tears. 'Who's to say I'll be the one he falls in love with?'

'For one thing, you'll be the one on the spot.'

Anna shivered. 'I ... I just can't think straight,' she said tearfully. 'And you're right about being on the spot, Letty. Phil ... shouldn't have done this.'

'Well, can I tell you why she did? Because she was pretty damn sure Richard was more than a little in love with you already, only he won't ... can't, whatever, admit it!'

'Well, I'm afraid that's where I have to differ,' Anna said tautly after a moment. 'In fact I'd like to have a bet with you, when I go ... *if* between the two of you I ever manage to make it, he won't lift a finger to stop me. You see if I'm not right. So I can't agree with Phil.'

'And that's what you can't live with, Anna?'

'No, I can't.'

'That might only be a small thing compared to the things you could share.'

Anna was saved from answering by the sound of footsteps down the passageway and Letty took a look at her face and said, 'Slip out the other door, love. I'll tell 'em you've got a headache and gone to lie down. I'll watch Chrissy.

Anna did lie down for a couple of hours. Then she forced herself to reappear as if she was quite restored.

But the next morning, the accumulated strain told and she woke up with a blinding headache, the likes of which she hadn't seen since being prone to them for a few months after her parents had died. And she knew that the last thing she felt like doing was making the trip to Innisfail.

Letty and Chrissy were both concerned and quite ready to cancel the trip, but Anna wouldn't hear of it. 'I'll be fine,' she said weakly. 'Honestly I will.'

'Well, if you're sure,' said Letty. 'I'd leave Sunshine with you, but she hasn't been off for ages and she wants to do some shopping ... I'm coming!' she called stridently to Samson, who could be heard pacing the verandah impatiently. 'But anyway,' she brightened, 'Mr Richard will be here. He just went off for an hour or two to look for some specimens. So you'll be right!' Letty beamed, and Anna winced inwardly but agreed.

And after they had gone she tottered back to bed, and maybe because the house was so quiet or simply because she felt so emotionally exhausted, she fell asleep and slept for hours, and woke feeling more genuinely refreshed than she had for some time and with the headache gone.

But there was no sign of Richard when she went into the kitchen to make herself some lunch, and she frowned faintly and then decided he must be down at the boatshed. But a walk down to the boatshed after lunch proved that he wasn't, and she came to the conclusion that he had gone off the island again because the small but powerful shark cat was not at its moorings, which meant two boats, including the one that Samson had used to get to the mainland this morning, were missing from Yandilla.

'Which also means I'm the only living soul here at the moment,' she said out loud as she walked round the beach back towards the house. 'Unless you take into account all the possums and wallabies and so on.'

The afternoon was very hot and still, and even just strolling along, the humidity left one drenched in sweat. But she noticed a massive build-up of cloud out to sea and thought thankfully that at least some rain was on the way.

But as the afternoon wore on she found herself grappling with a strange trickle of apprehension. There was still no sign of Richard and an eerie wind had got up to blow in short ferocious gusts that slammed doors and then subsided, only to rise again. And it began to rain, but intermittently too and as if the raindrops were being flung at the windows.

Then she was struck by a sudden thought and ran to turn the transistor radio on in the kitchen—only to gasp in disbelief as she heard what sounded like an air-raid warning siren being broadcast and then the steady tones of the station announcer reading a cyclone warning alert for areas from Cairns to St Lawrence.

Anna stared at the radio and swallowed several times. Then she realised that the same steady voice was dispensing information on just how to batten down for a cyclone ... Secure all loose objects around the house, because winds of that ferocity could turn even relatively harmless objects like metal garbage bins into lethal weapons ... Leave some windows open on the side of the house not in the path of the wind to reduce pressure. Remember that bathrooms were often more solidly constructed and offered more protection ... stock up on batteries for torches and transistor radios and, above all, stay tuned to your radio.

None of this was new to Anna. Having been born and bred in Queensland she'd heard it all before. But as Richard had said only a few nights ago, very few cyclones vented the full force of their fury as far south as Brisbane. What stunned her was to think that she was quite alone on Yandilla and right in the path of one.

'I don't believe this,' she whispered—and jumped about a foot into the air at the sound of a sharp crack and a dull thud, then ran outside to see to her horror that a branch from an overhanging mango tree had broken off the tree and fallen across the telephone wires, uprooting them from their connection against the verandah roof.

Now I'm cut off, she thought. But no, the boatshed might still be connected. Let me think carefully ... The line comes by submarine cable from the mainland—yes, and for the most part is underground on the island until it gets to the house, so it might . . . but no, she realised almost immediately, you can switch a call through to the boatshed from here, but you can't get one directly there . . . oh God! So I am cut off, because it all works off this line!

The telephone confirmed this by being quite dead when she tried it. All the same, I'll go down to the boatshed and see, she thought, maybe there's a radio transmitter . . . But first I'll batten down as much as I can up here.

The trip down to the boatshed was a weird experience. Depending on what direction she was going in she was alternately being pushed along by the wind or fighting to take each step, and all the time she was fighting for breath as the wind seemed to gain momentum and the rain started to fall with a stinging vehemence, and as the light faded she could see coconuts being bounced off the palms like missiles and her heart contracted with fear for two reasons, because it was three hours before the full force of the cyclone was due to hit, so what would it be like then? And because, unless by some miracle Richard was in the boatshed, he must be out somewhere in this . . .

But he wasn't in the boatshed and the phone didn't work, and there was a two-way radio, but it was lying on one of the benches in pieces as if it was being repaired. In fact the only piece of good news she found was that the cutter, the third and last part of the Yandilla fleet, was up in its cradle and under cover and not moored in the water. Not that it was of any immediate help to her, because she knew she had no chance of getting it into the water, even if she could sail it which she knew she couldn't. But at least it had less chance of being damaged or sunk. Then she realised that at least something else was in her favour. The heavy double doors of the boatshed, which didn't fit very well in any case, were faced away from the wind—at the moment at least, so it seemed a fairly safe place to stay.

Not that she felt she had much choice, because she didn't think she was capable of making the return trip to the house, beside the fact that it obviously would be a dangerous thing to do.

'In any case,' she muttered to herself, 'this is the best place to be, because this is where anyone who does come will come to. If anyone comes. Oh!' Her eyes dilated as she thought of Letty and Samson. 'Surely they wouldn't attempt to cross in this? But at least they know I'm here. Although they might think I'm safe with Richard ... oh God! Where is he? He must know I'm here on my own. But he hasn't come back, which can only mean he's out there somewhere, caught in this awful wind ...'

The next three hours were the longest she had ever experienced. The wind grew steadily in intensity until it was shrieking and howling dementedly, clearly to be heard over and above the torrential rain that was hammering on the roof. And the roof was her worst worry, because while the walls seemed to be standing firmly enough the roof was creaking and she was terribly afraid it was going to lift off or come crashing down on top of her.

She crept under one of the strongest-looking laboratory benches and tried to close her ears and began to pray as she'd never prayed in her life before, and to cry and sing ... anything to keep at bay her terrible fear of the savage, maniacal wind and the other even more terrible fear that was gripping her heart.

When the lull came, she didn't realise it at first, but finally it was borne into her that the wind had died somewhat and she dared to crawl out from under the bench, only to wonder if it wasn't the eye of the cyclone passing overhead and that soon the wind would blow again but in the opposite direction.

Then when the lull had lasted for a good half an hour and she was just beginning to breathe more easily, a tremendous gust slammed the boathouse doors open inwards and she knew her worst fears were realised. But at the same time, or perhaps only moments before she heard another sound, a curious grating like tearing metal on concrete, and she reached for the torch as a blast of rain blew all over her, and thought she was dreaming because the beam of light picked up the figure of a man staggering up the slipway in the driving rain.

'Richard . . .?' Her lips moved, but no sound came.

But he turned to the source of the beam of light that had picked him up and switched on his own torch. Then he covered the last few steps towards her at a run and swung her up into his arms. 'Anna! Thank God . . .'

'Oh, Richard,' she sobbed, 'I thought you were dead!'

'No, but we might both be if we don't move fast. Come . . .'

'Was it only the eye?'

'I think so . . . listen, just do as I say now.'

She did, with no clear idea of what she was doing except that she was being bundled into a cupboard that was fairly big and that she tripped over a pile of what felt like canvas and that Richard followed her in and pulled the heavy wooden door closed behind them. But it wasn't a cupboard, she realised as she came up against the back wall and felt that it was stone. Then Richard switched his torch on again and she looked around to see that it was a store room of sorts and that he couldn't stand upright in it because the ceiling was so low, and that it was narrow but quite long and that the canvas was a pile of tarpaulins and sails.

'It used to be a cool-room,' he said, 'so the walls are stone and doubly thick. We'll just have to hope the door holds . . .' He stopped abruptly as a new tearing sound came through the seams and cracks of the door and there was a tremendous crash, and Anna flew into his arms, trembling with fear.

'That . . . that was the roof going,' he said into her ear.

'I kn-know,' she stammered. 'I've been expecting it to go . . . Oh!' She shuddered as there were more horrible tearing sounds and the wind shrieked and he held her hard against him.

They stood like that for an age, breathing as one, waiting for the wooden door to split into matchwood and for the awful wind to fill every crevice of the old cool room and break it up. But the door held and he moved at last as if to let her go.

'Don't!' she pleaded. 'I mean . . . not just yet.'

'I'm not going to, but we might as well be

comfortable. Come . . . there,' he said a moment or two later when he was sitting on the pile of canvas with her in his lap. 'How's that?'

'. . . Fine,' she whispered.

'You must have been very frightened on your own.'

'I . . . was. I was singing . . . how silly!'

'No. I didn't know you were here, you know.' Richard touched her cheek.

She frowned. 'Didn't you? But . . .'

'No,' he said again. 'I thought you'd gone with the others. I went out to look for specimens this morning and the outboard packed up. So I drifted mostly and ended up on Bedrock—where I spent the morning with Colonel Jackson and his strange assortment of boarders trying to fix my motor. They persuaded me to stay for lunch, which I did thinking there was no one on Yandilla anyway.'

Anna expelled a shaken breath. 'I thought you must have come home and gone out again. It . . . never occurred to me you didn't know I was here, although I suppose it should have. Then . . . how did you know I was here after all?'

'When I heard the cyclone warning I was all set to leave and come home, but Colonel Jackson pointed out that seeing as it was moving in pretty fast and there was no one on Yandilla, it might be wiser to stay there. That seemed to make sense—until we got a frantic call on Bedrock from Samson and Letty. By that time the wind was well and truly blowing and they'd been trying to raise Yandilla for some time . . .'

'A branch of that mango tree fell across the line,' she explained.

'Ah! Well, anyway, in the slight confusion I said not to worry just to look after themselves. In fact I was intensely relieved to hear from them and to know that they were in the care of a State Emergency Service team and not driving down from Innisfail unaware . . . But then Letty said, tell Anna Chrissy sends her love. They thought you must be with me on Bedrock. Well, of course, that let the cat out of the bag, thank goodness. But by then the wind was so strong that although we got the boat launched three times, it just got steadily blown back on to the beach and it wasn't until the eye came over . . . but you know the rest.'

'I thought . . . I thought you were out there.' Anna swallowed painfully. She turned her head into his shoulder and said in a muffled voice, 'Are they really safe? Chrissy and . . .'

'Yes. But very worried, I've no doubt.'

She bit her lip as she thought of Chrissy. Richard felt the tremor that shook her as she pictured the child waiting and worrying, and his arms moved round her, drawing her closer. And together with the sounds of terrible devastation going on around them, it all became too much for her and she started to cry.

'Don't, Anna,' he said into her damp hair, but she couldn't stop until he lifted her face very gently from his shoulder and began to kiss her tears and then her lips, but very gently, as if he was kissing a distraught child.

But very soon it changed into something deeper. She couldn't resist the urge to touch his face with trembling fingers and there was no urgency about it, no stunned surprise on her part, just something slow and beautiful and so profound she couldn't explain it, except to think dazedly that she had never in her life got so intrinsically close to anyone. And when it ended, she fell asleep in his arms, as much exhausted by this new facet of her relationship with him—as if this intensely physical act had moved it outside a purely physical plane somehow—as by the trauma of the cyclone.

Richard held her in his arms while she slept, careful not to wake her and stared fixedly into the pitch darkness.

CHAPTER NINE

BUT the next morning, when they eased themselves out of the old cool-room and stared round disbelievingly at what was left of the boathouse—a few twisted girders, and Anna turned to him in the patchy sunlight and tried to thank him for risking his life to come back and save hers, Richard only shrugged and said lightly, 'Any time, Anna. By the way, what . . . happened last night between us, I think should be struck from the record.'

She stared at him with parted lips.

He shrugged. 'After all, in those circumstances,' he said wryly, 'I don't think anyone should be made to account for their actions. Do you?'

'I . . . no,' she said with an effort. 'No.' And was surprised that she could speak at all because her heart seemed to freeze into a lump of stone in her breast. But she made a further effort. She turned away so that he wouldn't be able to see what was in her eyes, and said with a genuine unsteadiness, 'It's just . . . been blown away. I can't believe it. The cutter too, all your specimens . . . oh! The house!'

'Anna . . .' There was an odd note of urgency in his voice, but whatever he had been about to say was lost as they heard a faint shout and both swung round to see the only remaining member of the Yandilla fleet bearing down on what was left of the boatshed jetty.

It was a tumultuous reunion. Chrissy was beside herself as she hugged her father and Anna repeatedly, laughing and crying but dangerously close to a sort of nervous hysteria. And Letty hugged them both, although more restrainedly outwardly, yet with an inner thankfulness that needed no words. Sunshine too was visibly moved and shedding happy tears of relief, and for the first time Anna saw Samson smile a wide white smile that threatened to crack his face.

Then another shout was heard and they all turned to see Colonel Jackson's cabin cruiser puttering in, but this time his oddly assorted crew were singing, 'Onward, Christian s-o-l-d-i-e-r-s, marching as to war . . .'

'Oh, God,' Richard muttered, 'this might turn out to be quite a day!'

Yes, Anna thought later—much later, when she was getting ready for bed. Quite a day . . .

By a miracle, or perhaps not, because it was the oldest, most solidly constructed building on Yandilla, the house had escaped with very little damage. A lot of water had come in, three windows had been broken, but structurally it had remained sound, although some of the verandah furniture had been discovered quite far away, one chair even lodged in a tall tree.

'I forgot,' Anna had said, conscience-stricken. 'I brought the garbage in and all the pot plants . . .'

'Honey,' Letty had said soothingly, 'you did well. Don't worry about it.'

But Phil's studio had suffered the same fate as the boathouse. It was a wreck and the garden was strewn with debris.

'But I tell you,' the pilot of the Emergency Services helicopter which had arrived on a routine check of all the islands said, 'you're bloody lucky! There are some poor folks who've lost every thing they possess.'

Yes, Anna thought, as she brushed her hair, we were lucky.

She stopped brushing as Chrissy stirred but settled. In the end it had been the only way to get her to sleep. Not Richard, not Letty had been able to soothe her overwrought imagination as dark had closed in and the tension of two days had finally claimed the child as Anna had seen it would. The only thing that had comforted her was to be rocked to sleep in Anna's bed with the promise that she could stay there all night.

Anna got up from the dressing table and moved over to the bed and knelt beside it. She slid her hand into Chrissy's and murmured, 'I'm here, baby.'

Chrissy's hand closed over hers and she relaxed, and Anna marvelled as she had once before at the long shadows her lashes made on her cheeks.

Then she turned her head as the bedroom door opened with no invitation and Richard stood there.

For a moment they stared at each other and Anna felt her heart turn over in a way that told her it was not dead but painfully alive, as she took in everything about him that tormented her so. His tall, powerful body, his intelligent grey-green eyes, his thick fair hair, his well cut mouth . . . She turned her head away and thought in despair, I must have imagined what happened last night. Perhaps he's right, it . . . was the circumstances. Otherwise he would have felt it too, surely? It seemed— to me anyway—to be so . . . special . . .

'Anna,' he said quietly.

She took a breath. 'Yes?' she whispered.

'Is she all right? Chrissy?'

Anna looked down at Chrissy, now sleeping peacefully again, and gently released her hand. She stood up and moved away from the bed, suddenly conscious but strangely uncaring that she wore only a slender white satin nightgown.

'Yes. She's fine.'

'Thanks to you,' he said abruptly.

Anna shrugged. 'A little, perhaps.'

'No. A lot. Anna . . .'

'Don't,' she interrupted.

'You don't know what I'm going to say.'

'I think I do,' she whispered. 'You're going to thank me for . . . coping with Chrissy tonight, but it's not something I want to be thanked for. It's . . . my job.'

'Is it?' he said, his eyes searching her face.

They stared at each other until she licked her lips and said with a strange reluctance, 'Yes, of course.'

'Yes, of course,' he repeated, and smiled bleakly. 'But I'd still like to be able to thank you. Sleep well, my dear,' he added, and went out, closing the door softly.

It was a long time before Anna got to sleep. Even

with Chrissy curled up in her arms like a kitten, breathing easily, the turmoil in her mind refused to be quelled. But one thought kept returning above all else—when I thought he was dead, I wanted to die too. And not even what he said this morning can change that. So what do I do? I can't go on like this, I just can't. But then there's Chrissy ... Round and round it all went, until her tired brain gave up and she slept.

By midday the next day a lot had been done to restore Yandilla. The garden had been cleared with the help of Colonel Jackson's crew again, the phone restored and a lot of the debris from Phil's studio carted away. And two insurance assessors had come to estimate damage to boats and property and a building contractor had inspected the remains of the boatshed.

And after lunch, when all the activity had quietened down a bit, Anna knocked nervously on the study door and entered as bidden.

'Yes, Anna?' Richard said briefly, looking up from his desk.

'Are you very busy?'

He looked at her penetratingly, taking in the shadows beneath her eyes that she'd tried to hide with make-up which she didn't usually wear. His gaze flicked down her rapidly and something about her brought a slight frown to his eyes. She wondered what it could be, because she was only wearing a soft pink blouse and a full cotton skirt with green and pink stripes on it—an outfit he had seen a dozen times before.

'No. Sit down,' he said finally.

Anna sat and gripped her hands in her lap and wondered how to say what she'd come to say. Perhaps the best way was just to take the plunge.

'Richard ... do you still want to marry me?'

There, the fateful words are out, she thought, staring down at her hands and wondering briefly if it was her imagination or if the world had gone very still. She forced herself to look up, to see him studying her intently with narrowed eyes.

'You surprise me, Anna,' he said at last. 'What's

made you change your mind? Even as late as last night you were determined to make it clear to me that this was a job and nothing more.'

A faint tinge of colour came to her cheeks, but she said surprisingly steadily, 'Chrissy, mainly. It's hard to put into words how I feel about her. But I can say that I just don't think I could leave her.'

'Is that all?'

'No,' she said slowly. 'There are other things. I feel ... curiously as if I belong here. It's like being part of a family, something I've missed. Another thing is that having experienced ... I don't know, I guess the kind of security of being surrounded by Letty and Chrissy and Phil and Samson has made me realise that I don't want to be heading off for the wild blue yonder any more. I ... seem to have got that out of my system.'

'I see.' There was a strange, tense little silence during which his eyes roamed over her expressionlessly until she bit her lip and said huskily, 'But you might have changed your mind. Of course I'd understand if you had.' She looked down at her hands in a misery of hot confusion and wished desperately that she had never spoken.

'No, I haven't changed my mind,' he said quietly, and her lashes flew up at some note in his voice that she couldn't decipher.

'But ... you don't think it's such a good idea any more?' she whispered uncertainly.

He smiled slightly. 'Are you asking that, or hoping it, Anna? But no,' he went on without giving her a chance to reply, 'I still think it's a very good idea—with one proviso. If it's going to make you look a picture of misery, and lose weight as you have done lately, and a lot of sleep, then maybe it isn't such a good idea. But on every other count, I haven't changed my mind since we last discussed it.'

'How ... did you know?' she asked unhappily.

'I'm not blind, Anna,' Richard said dryly. 'What *has* made you change your mind?' he asked directly, and looked at her enquiringly. 'Only those things you mentioned? Chrissy and so on?'

Oh God, she thought, don't do this to me. How can I tell you that in the final analysis, it was *you*! Even though I tried to pretend to myself it was Chrissy—and it is—but it's also you ... Perhaps I should tell you? But no, that wouldn't be fair to either of us. Because that would make it a lopsided relationship. She shivered inwardly and thought, no, I can't do that to myself.

She stood up and walked over to the french windows, staring out over the garden for a moment and trying to take a grip on herself. Then she turned back to him. 'I have been unsettled lately. And unhappy and confused. One half of me has been saying that the only sensible thing to do is leave Yandilla while the other half,' she grimaced ruefully, 'seems to want to stay. And not only on account of Chrissy,' she said honestly. 'I can't,' she looked away, 'I find I can't help wondering what it would be like to be married to you, although I'm sometimes still not sure ... about that. But,' she raised her eyes to his, 'I think what cast the deciding vote was the night before last when you came back in the cyclone. I ... it made me feel ... as if I had an anchor. And,' she went on quietly, 'when I thought about it, it seemed to me as if out of all the things I've thought and said, that was one solid fact, and it might be worth as much as all the rest in any case.' And that's the truth, she realised with some surprise. At least part of it. The other part of it is that you hurt me unbearably the next morning when you said what you did, but that's my affair, isn't it? And just something I'll have to guard against. Besides, as Letty said, there might be things to more than compensate for that kind of foolish hurt.

'O.K.,' he said. 'If you're sure, so be it. I think you've made a wise choice, Anna. From my point of view I know you have, and from your point of view I'd only like to say I'll do everything in my power to make sure you don't regret it.'

He stood up and came over to her and tipped her chin up with his fingers. 'Would you like to kiss me to seal the bargain?'

She closed her eyes briefly and for a startling, blinding instant, wished she could say no. But that's what it's all about, isn't it, Anna? she thought. You can't say no to this, can you?

Then she could think no more as his lips descended on hers.

The next two weeks passed in a whirl of activity and something of a daze for Anna. Chrissy's joy had been unbounded, and her touching declaration to Anna had brought tears to her eyes.

'I prayed for this, you know, Anna,' she said, her hauntingly look-alike eyes shining. 'Daddy told me I mustn't even think about it and I tried hard not to, but all the while I couldn't help just hoping a little bit and keeping my fingers crossed. And saying a prayer *every* night! You couldn't call that interfering, could you?'

'Not really, sweetheart.'

'And I couldn't help feeling rather m-mortified,' she said experimentally, 'to think what my meddling could have done!'

'What meddling? Oh—you mean . . .?'

'Yes! But it's taught me a lesson! To think that I could have married Daddy off to one of those others and missed out on you. I shall never meddle again. I'll just leave it all up to God in future,' Chrissy said dramatically. Then, being Chrissy, she got straight to the heart of something she was wondering about. 'How long does it take to have a baby, Anna? I'd love to have a baby brother or sister.'

'That's not something you can predict, Chrissy,' her father said, coming up unexpectedly and shooting Anna a wry glance as she coloured faintly. 'We'll just have to wait and see.'

'Oh! Oh well,' Chrissy said philosophically, 'I don't really mind waiting. I'm so happy as it is . . .'

Letty was also happy, it seemed. 'You did right, honey,' she said. 'But there, I knew you would.'

'Did you, Letty?' Anna said curiously. Then she added quietly, 'I hope I have done the right thing.'

But Letty didn't reply, just smiled wisely as if to say, wait and see . . .

Then Phil created a diversion by arriving home out of the blue two days later.

'Phil,' Richard said exasperatedly, 'I've been trying to contact you in London to let you know we're all right. And all the time you've been on the plane home!'

'Of course I was on the plane home!' Phil said tartly. 'As soon as I heard about the cyclone I hopped on the first plane. They did tell me at Australia House that there were no fatalities, but I wanted to make sure for myself. You've no idea what it's like sitting around waiting for news!'

'But you must have known I'd get on to you as soon as possible. And what about your series?'

'Oh, that!' Phil said airily, going faintly pink about the ears. 'I'll tell you about that some time.'

'Aunt Phil! Aunt Phil! Guess what? Daddy and Anna are going to get married!' Chrissy cried, hurling herself at Phil and adding to the confusion considerably.

'They . . . are?' Phil said weakly, looking at Anna and Richard in turn and then at Letty.

'Sure are,' said Letty.

'Well . . . what a surprise,' said Phil, and turned away from a distinctly—oh yes?—look she discerned in Anna's eyes. But she turned back almost immediately. 'Then it's a jolly good thing I did come home after all, Richard,' she said militantly. 'If you thought you were going to get away with a wedding without me, you were much mistaken!' And she stuck out her chin in an aggressive gesture that was so unlike her, everyone burst out laughing.

'Dear Phil,' Richard said finally, and put an arm round her. 'It wasn't that at all. And I'm very glad you're home. I should have hated to get married without your presence. But I just thought . . .'

'Well, don't you think any more,' Phil said fondly, and blinked away a tear. 'I wouldn't miss this for anything!'

'Anna?' Phil said several days later when they had sunk down exhaustedly in their Townsville hotel room. 'You're very quiet. Wasn't this trip to Townsville to shop for your trousseau a good idea after all?'

Anna looked across at her affectionately. 'It was a

lovely idea, Phil,' she said quietly. 'Most of your ideas are.'

'Then . . . it's the idea of me paying for it all that you don't like?' Phil said hesitantly.

Anna got up suddenly and knelt beside the older woman's chair. 'No. It's a wonderful gift, and I love you for it, Phil.'

'What is it, then, pet?'

'I think . . . I think,' Anna said tremulously, 'it's a good old-fashioned dose of bridal jitters.'

'Anna,' Phil said gravely, 'please tell me, because I'm a little tormented about it, shouldn't Letty and I have interfered the way we did?'

'Probably not,' said Anna with a glint of humour. 'But I'm glad you did. You see, at least I know that you . . . approve of me and like me. And that means a great deal to me.'

Phil put out a hand and touched her hair. 'You mean a great deal to us, my dear. That's why I'm a bit conscience-stricken, do you see?'

Anna took a deep breath, 'Phil,' she said steadily but with a shimmer of tears in her eyes, 'I'm marrying Richard because I can no longer pretend to myself that I don't love him. And that's not anything to do with you or Letty, except that you've made it easier.'

'And—Richard?' Phil queried.

'Will go out of his way to make me happy and secure,' Anna said slowly. 'If I didn't believe that I wouldn't be doing this. But not so much because I'm me as because I'll be a suitable . . . wife who he can trust.'

'Is that going to be enough for you, Anna?'

'Yes, Phil. More than enough,' Anna said huskily but firmly. 'And I'll get over these jitters, you see. I guess being a virgin bride at my old age is enough to give anyone the jitters,' she added wryly, but thought wincingly, that's the heart of the matter, isn't it, Anna? You still haven't told him, can't seem to find the right time or the right words, but soon it will be too late. Will it matter very much, though? And it's not always such an earth-shattering thing, if you can believe what you read.

'Anna?'

She looked up at Phil. 'Sorry . . .'

'I was only going to say, if that's what's worrying you, I was a virgin bride at the grand old age of twenty-six. And even in those days we weren't quite so prudish about these things as we like to make out we were now. So I was quite convinced I was some kind of a freak. But in the end I was very glad I'd saved it up . . . Dear me, did I say that? It sounds awful when you say it like that. But you know what I mean.'

'Yes, Phil,' Anna murmured with a loving little smile.

One week later she was married to Richard Gillespie in the garden of Yandilla homestead.

She wore a frothy cocktail-length dress that wasn't quite blue and wasn't quite grey and was romantic enough even to satisfy Chrissy, who had had visions at one time of seeing Anna in something like the Princess of Wales had worn. Her dark hair was uncovered and it gleamed almost blue black and lay smooth and naturally curved to her shoulders. She also wore a pair of diamond studs in her ears that had been Richard's present to her, together with a diamond engagement ring that wasn't large but was exquisitely cut so that every facet of it sparked a blue, unmistakable fire. And she was to carry a bouquet of orchids, tiny white, star-like ones that Samson had picked himself and Letty had wrought beautifully into two bouquets—one for Anna and a smaller one for Chrissy.

'You look—I've never seen anyone look as pretty as you do, Anna,' Chrissy said with tears in her eyes.

'Nor I you, sweetheart,' Anna answered with a lump in her throat as she adjusted her bow and smoothed her long fair hair. 'Chrissy, we won't be gone for very long. Will you mind?'

'Oh no! Letty explained to me about honeymoons. And Phil's here and she says the Colonel has some treats in store for us. I wonder what they are?'

'Special treats for a special little girl, I suspect.'

But strangely, it was Mrs Robertson who spent the last few minutes with Anna before she was married.

Her arrival on Yandilla had come as a complete surprise to Anna the day before. Richard had escorted her up to the household and announced, 'I have a very special guest, Anna.'

'Oh! Mrs Robertson ... Oh!'

'Anna!'

And now, in those last few minutes before the service began, Mrs Robertson said with a funny little smile, 'I have to tell you, Anna, Bob Wetherby sends his regards—and said to tell you he hasn't ever seen me struck dumb before, but I was when your Richard rang.'

Anna had to smile. 'It is hard to imagine, isn't it? If it hadn't been for your Mrs Lawson, I'd never have come here.'

Mrs Robertson settled her enormous, flowery hat more securely and suddenly her bright, bird-like eyes were a little misty as she surveyed Anna. 'It's only what you deserve, though, love. It couldn't have happened to a nicer person! And the very next time anyone tells me I'm an interfering old busybody—Bob Wetherby, for example—I'll tell him, nothing ventured, nothing gained, and look what happened to Anna!'

'Mrs Robertson, I love you,' said Anna, a little mistily herself.

'Well, you just promise me one thing, love. Be happy—sometimes it takes a bit of working at when it isn't all so new any more, but it's worth it.'

'I'll ... work at it, I promise.' They hugged each other warmly.

It was the Colonel who gave her away. And it was his flock who formed the greater part of the congregation. In fact the minister who performed the service looked faintly incredulous as he surveyed them.

But the Colonel said in a quiet aside to Anna as they came down the verandah steps, 'They will behave, my dear. Don't worry about that.'

'I rather like them when they don't, Colonel.'

'Funny you should say that, so do I. Nevertheless a

wedding is a wedding! Not something you do every day!'

No, she thought. Thank God!

But despite its strange origins and strange assortment of guests is was somehow a solemn occasion. Phil and Letty cried openly and Samson, who was best man, cleared his throat after those final words had been pronounced and said, 'Richard and Anna, you two best take care of each other like the man said. 'Cause you're mighty precious to us all.'

The congregation had answered, 'Hear, hear!' and then begun to sing beautifully and obviously rehearsed, 'All things bright and beautiful, all creatures great and small! All things wise and wonderful . . .'

Richard and Anna looked at each other fully for the first time, Richard with eyebrows slightly raised, and she said, 'Th-that sounds like Chrissy's choice. It's her favourite.'

'The Lord God made them all . . . it was,' Phil sang.

Richard turned and Chrissy flew into his arms, while Anna looked at the two fair heads so close together and felt her nervous tension drain away as a kind of peace claimed her.

'Anna.'

Anna turned away from the window of another hotel bedroom, this time overlooking the lights of Sydney, and took a deep breath.

'Yes?' she whispered.

'Come here,' Richard said gently.

She obeyed mutely. 'You're tired,' he murmured, and touched her pale face with two fingers. 'And all wound up.'

She could only nod helplessly after a moment. For it was all too true. Her state of peaceful euphoria had lasted through the long day, the drive to Townsville and the long flight to Sydney. It had seen her through dinner at a premier Sydney restaurant, and then quite suddenly it had deserted her when the door of their suite had closed on the rest of the world and Richard had taken off his jacket and thrown it over the back of a chair and pulled off his tie. She had looked at him and in a moment of panic seen a tall, attractive stranger whom she was expected to go to bed with shortly—and discovered to her horror that that was the last thing she wanted to do because incredibly she was as fearful about it as some silly teenager.

And even now, showered and changed into one of her new nightgowns, she felt no better about it.

'There's no need to be,' he said, his grey-green eyes searching her face. 'We don't have to rush anything. We have all the time in the world.'

'I . . . I'm sorry,' she said with a catch in her voice. 'You must think I'm awfully silly . . .'

A shadow of a smile crept into his eyes. 'Not silly,' he said very quietly. 'Quite wise, in fact. Come.' He took her hand and led her to the enormous bed and pulled aside the lavender silk sheet. 'Lie down.'

She did, and he pulled the sheet up and sat down beside her. 'Some things are better left until they happen ... spontaneously.' He pushed a wayward strand of hair behind her ear as if she was Chrissy. 'So why don't you go to sleep and stop worrying. Then tomorrow—well, that's another day. Goodnight, my dear,' he said, and kissed her wrist. 'Sleep well.'

The surprising thing was that she did.

And when she woke with the faint half-light of dawn coming through the uncurtained windows, she lay quietly for a few minutes, then felt a movement beside her and turned with her heart in her mouth to see Richard propped up on one elbow, watching her.

'Have you been awake long?' she whispered.

He reached out a hand and cupped her cheek. 'A little longer than you, Mrs Gillespie. I'm an early riser. How do you feel?'

'Fine.'

'You look ... more beautiful than you usually do,' he said gravely, and his hand slid down to her shoulder.

So do you, she thought as her gaze slid involuntarily to his wide, bare shoulders. She smiled, her lips just faintly unsteady, 'You have a nice line in early morning lies, Mr Gillespie,' she murmured. 'I'm sure I look a mess.'

His eyebrows rose and he shot her a wicked look that made her tremble. 'All right,' he said, 'put it this way. Your hair is gorgeously rumpled, your skin faintly flushed, your eyes still calm and dreamy and you have an unguarded air of *déshabillé* about you that makes me long to complete the process.' He lay back with his head beside hers on the pillow. 'Would you mind very much if I did?' he asked, his eyes suddenly completely sober.

'Not . . . not when you ask so nicely,' she responded, suddenly filled with a quivering tenderness as she thought of how understanding he had been last night when he need not have been. When many men wouldn't have been in the circumstances. And she took a deep breath and thought, it's now or never. Perhaps I could still tell him? But no, it seems cowardly somehow to do it now . . .

She slid her fingers through his, then lifted his hand to her mouth and kissed it.

She thought later, dimly, that she was doing well. But almost immediately she realised that she personally was not all that responsible for what she was doing. Because Richard was slowly and expertly arousing her to a pitch of fevered desire that was wringing responses from her that she had no need to mime in any way. And that somehow, his hands that were so sure, and his lips, were doing things to her body that were unmercifully releasing the floodgates of longing she had been so carefully and for so long keeping tightly leashed.

Then, in spite of herself, she tensed as he took her, and her body convulsed with a tearing pain. Richard lifted his head and felt the tremors that racked her; he held her hard against him and said with a kind of despair, 'You haven't ever done this before, have you, Anna?'

'I . . . no . . .'

'Why did you lie?'

'I don't know,' she whispered tearfully. 'But you mustn't blame yourself. I seem to make such a habit of doing foolish things. And I thought you might not necessarily ever have to know . . .'

'Oh, Anna,' he sighed into her hair, still holding her as the pain began to subside. 'It's all too late to change it now.'

'I don't want to. Please don't stop ... It would have happened anyway.'

'Perhaps,' he said with an effort. 'Although there are ways to lessen it if you *know*.'

'Richard,' she wept, 'don't make me feel worse.'

'All right—don't cry,' he said quietly. 'Relax, if you can, and we'll start all over again.'

He began to kiss her body slowly, and all over again she fell prey to the exquisite beauty of his touch on her until finally she was transported to a kind of heaven with her senses reeling and that tearing pain only a shadowy memory.

They lay in each other's arms for a long time afterwards. Then Richard put her away from him and stared down at her. 'You should have told me, Anna,' he said sombrely. 'Why did you let me think that?'

She sighed tremulously. 'I was—I don't know, when you assumed what you did that day, I was angry and I thought, *let* him think that if he wants to ...'

'So you haven't had an unhappy love affair? Or didn't it get to the going to bed stage?' His eyes searched hers.

'No, I've never been in love,' she whispered.

'Then—O.K. I can understand what happened that first day. But why didn't you tell me later?'

Why? How can I tell you why? Her eyelashes fluttered and were beaded with tears. 'Because I felt an incredible fool,' she said huskily. 'I think that's why. But was it so important? Unless,' her lashes flew up and her eyes widened painfully, 'unless you wanted someone experienced? Not gauche and fumbling ...' She closed her eyes and felt herself shrivelling like a fallen leaf. 'I never thought of that. Men do, they say,' she added shakily.

'Who says?' he asked, his voice suddenly strangely dry.

'Well,' she moved helplessly, 'I've read it.'

'You shouldn't always believe what you read, Anna,'

he said ironically. 'Did you also read somewhere that virgins can pass themselves off as experienced women? Did you read up about that?' His eyes bored into hers.

She coloured and turned her head away, wishing miserably that she could die. 'I'm sorry,' she whispered. 'I see now that it's quite natural you would have wanted someone more . . . more . . .'

'I didn't say that,' he interrupted.

'But if you'd known—I think you're trying to tell me that if you'd known, you wouldn't have married me. Yet I honestly didn't think it would make much difference. I mean, the other things stand, don't they? All the other reasons for us getting married?'

'Oh yes.'

She stared up at him with her heart beating like some dead, muffled drum. 'But you wouldn't have, would you? If you'd known . . .?'

'No.'

The single syllable cut her to the quick. 'W-won't you tell me why, at least?' she stammered.

Richard looked over towards the window where the dawn was losing its early rose colour to a shimmering, pale blue. 'Because I thought, with the basis of some experience to work on,' his eyes came back to her face and they were bleak, 'you'd be able to make a reasoned, rational judgement when I asked you to marry me.'

'I did that in the end,' Anna whispered. 'I worked out that what you said made sense. In fact, that what you said were my original thoughts on the subject. And that really I could spend my life looking for love never to find it or to find that it wasn't the real thing after all and then I'd regret turning my back on things that do mean a great deal to me. Like . . . Chrissy and Yandilla and in a sense, you.' Liar, Anna, something rose up inside her to taunt her.

But at the same time she knew too, with a deeply hurting honesty, that she could no more tell him the truth than she had ever been able to. Less able to now, in fact.

'And what do you know now, Anna?' he asked with a

haunting gentleness. 'Was it worth it to take such a gamble?'

'I . . . that depends on you,' she said unhappily.

'Ah! There you've unconsciously put it in a nutshell, my lovely deceiver,' he said with a wry twist to his lips. 'If you knew anything about me, you'd know that I didn't want to be burdened with a virgin bride because that's a situation I'm not best equipped to deal with. I thought we were two people who'd suffered some . . . disillusionment which had left us ready to deal in realities. I *don't* think anybody's first lover, whatever the outcome, should have to be someone like that—like me, a rather coldblooded, cynical realist. But I have to hand it to you, Anna. I've heard of this particular deception being practised the other way around . . . hell!' he said with a sudden savagery and his eyes dark. 'Don't look like that. I'm *sorry!*'

He pulled her into his arms. 'Forget what I said,' he murmured, holding her close as her body shook in a paroxysm of despair. 'We'll make it work somehow.'

And a little later, when she had subsided exhausted against him, he tilted her chin up gently and smudged the tears on her lashes and said, not quite smiling, 'Who knows, I might turn into a Prince Charming for you after all. You're beautiful enough to bewitch me, and despite what you read, I found your . . . inexperience charming. So much so, I suspect that'll be the least of our problems.' But the last part of his sentence was said inaudibly to Anna, and he stared across the top of her head at nothing in particular but with a curious look of pain in his eyes.

CHAPTER TEN

IF there was one word she could apply to her honeymoon, Anna often thought afterwards, it would have to be 'unforgettable'.

Yet while that was true enough, it didn't express so

many things. The heights and the depths, the laughter that sometimes hid tears, the uncertainty that she couldn't always hide, the sensation that she'd once suspected—that to be his lover would be like flying too high, or the fact that love could grow as hers did. Nor did it express the fact that only once during those two weeks did the things said on the first morning of their marriage surface again and that for all the rest of the time he seemed determined to try to wipe them out. And he was so successful, she found that she could often pretend that Richard Gillespie didn't regret having married Anna Horton.

They did everything they couldn't do on Yandilla—went to the theatre, art galleries, antique auctions. They shopped for things the cyclone had damaged in the house, and more besides.

'It's your home now, Anna,' Richard told her. 'It should reflect your personality.'

'But I like it the way it is!'

'I didn't think there was a woman alive who could resist that kind of invitation,' he said, looking at her quizzically.

'That's because you don't think much of women,' she retorted before she could stop herself. But she managed to grin at him almost immediately as if she was only teasing. And because she had so nearly fallen into the trap she knew she must avoid at all costs, she allowed herself to be partly persuaded. They bought some paintings and china that she especially liked, some silver cutlery that he had monogrammed with their initials, and a beautifully crafted mahogany rolltop desk—the kind which had fascinated her ever since she could remember—for her own personal use. They also shopped for Chrissy and spent some time and some hilarity trying to find presents for Letty and Sunshine, Samson and Phil.

They went to the races and to the cricket. Richard had managed to get tickets for the third day of an Australia versus England test match at the Sydney Cricket Ground.

Anna, who was not a particular cricket fan, said after

a few hours with a lurking smile, 'If I'd known you were such a cricket fan, I might not have married you.'

'I thought you must have guessed,' he replied innocently.

'How should I have guessed?'

'Why do you think we came to Sydney for our honeymoon? This week particularly?'

'Oh ... you! No, seriously . . .'

'Seriously, Anna,' he said, laughing at her expression, 'why don't we leave them to it? I can think of something I'd much rather be doing, after all.'

She stared at him with her lips parted. 'You don't mean . . .?' And her cheeks grew pink at the way he was looking at her. 'But it's only two o'clock in the afternoon!'

'That's a very good hour for what I have in mind,' he said with his lips quirking. 'When most other sober citizens are diligently pursuing their lawful pursuits, it adds a certain spice to it. Besides, the cricket is awfully dull.'

'Well!' she exclaimed indignantly.

'And besides all that,' he said, and lifted a hand to trace the outline of her mouth with one finger, 'I haven't seen you without your clothes for hours now. That's too long.' He didn't attempt to lower his voice.

'*Richard*,' she whispered, and looked around uneasily, to see a few people staring at them amusedly. 'Oh! Let's get out of here,' she muttered, with her colour fluctuating deliciously.

They did, and he made love to her laughingly in the sunlit bedroom of their suite and teased her about being so awfully prim and proper. Then they slept until it was dark, showered together and went out on the town and didn't get back to the hotel until three in the morning.

'See what I mean about making love in the afternoon?' said Richard, his eyes glinting devilishly as he removed her wrap and shoes and swung her up into his arms to sit down with her in his lap on the settee. 'It leaves the night free for other things.'

Anna, who was still drifting on a cloud of the bewitching music they'd been dancing to, cast him a sudden suspicious glance from beneath her lashes. 'Like what?'

'This,' he said gravely, and started to kiss her.

'Isn't that what we were doing this afternoon?' she asked a few minutes later.

'Is it?'

'Richard, don't tease me,' she begged, 'or I'll . . .'

'Or you'll what, Mrs Gillespie?' he asked politely.

'Oh, really give you something to tease me about,' she threatened, laughing as she said it but even closer to tears, because her love for him was threatening to overwhelm her and sweep her away to the extent that she would lose all caution.

'Hey,' he said gently, taking her face in his hands, 'what's this? Am I going too fast for you, Anna?'

'No . . . oh no!' she said tremulously.

He looked at her searchingly. 'All the same, you're a very new bride.'

'Not that new . . .'

His lips twitched. 'All of a week old. Perhaps we should have a moratorium—say, until this time tomorrow. I won't touch you or kiss you or mention anything in public about how beautiful you are without your clothes . . . and I'll take cold showers at hourly intervals. How does that sound?'

'Terrible! Oh, Richard, you are an idiot sometimes!' But she felt herself relaxing all the same and she snuggled up closer to him. 'I never dreamt you could be like this when I first met you.'

'That's because I was very cross with you,' he said idly, and stroked her hair.

'Yes, you were.' She sighed suddenly.

'What is it?'

'Nothing . . .'

He stroked her hair. 'Do you feel sleepy?'

'Mmm . . .'

'Go to sleep, then, Anna.'

'Here?'

'Why not?' He swung his legs up on to the settee and settled them both comfortably.

'Are you serious?' she asked drowsily.

But he didn't answer. Just kept stroking her hair until she fell asleep.

But the façade did slip once. It happened the night they were to go to the opera, and Anna had no intimation of what was coming as she got ready, taking her time about it and making sure she looked just right.

She bathed, using an expensive and fragrant bath oil, then smoothed a matching body lotion all over so that her skin glowed with the sheen of silk. And she put on a matching set of French satin and lace underwear and carefully drew on a pair of sheer fine tights. Then came the dress, a thing of almost living beauty, she had thought when she and Phil had chosen it. Nor had it changed since she had tried it on in the shop, she saw as she studied her reflection in the long mirror. The coral chiffon was still the same vibrant colour, the pleated low-cut bodice that was supported by narrow, halter-neck ties still fitted perfectly, hugging her figure and emphasising the slenderness of her waist, and the skirt was still soft and clinging despite its yards upon yards of material. Gold sandals with very high heels completed the outfit.

She moved back to the dressing table and sat down to put the final touches to her appearance. She had put her hair up and the moisture from her bath had added just a touch of waywardness to it, but the effect was rather nice. In fact, she couldn't help feeling pleased with the whole effect as she applied perfume from a delicate cut-glass bottle to her wrists—a matching fragrance again. Her translucent lipstick and her nail varnish toned with the coral of her dress, a pale grey eyeshadow seemed to make her eyes look enormous and the mascara she had used sparingly made her lashes look even longer. And Richard's diamond earrings shone in her ears . . .

Her dark lashes lifted suddenly as another reflection joined hers in the mirror—Richard.

He had been waiting in the lounge of the suite for her, and even though she had seen him briefly in his evening clothes before he had left the bedroom to watch the news, something about him made her catch her breath. But it wasn't only that evening clothes suited his fair good looks very well—that the dark jacket of his dinner suit and the starched whiteness of his shirt sat as well on him as jeans and a bush shirt—it was something else too . . . a strange air of remoteness, as if this was some tall stranger and not the person who so often teased her and now played such an intimate part in her life.

'Have I taken ages?' she asked self-consciously. 'I'm ready now.'

But she didn't stand up. Because there seemed to be something magnetic keeping his eyes riveted to hers in the mirror.

Then at last he said, 'It was worth waiting for. You look sensational, Anna.'

'Thank you.'

'Yes,' his grey-green gaze roamed her reflection meditatively, 'too beautiful to take out, I'm afraid,' he added with a strangely twisted smile.

She stared at the mirror with parted lips as his hands came up and he undid the halter-neck tie at the back of her neck. Her eyes widened as he very slowly, lingeringly pushed the bodice of her dress down so that her breasts were revealed, cupped in the lacy strapless bra she wore.

She moved then, a tiny almost defensive movement that he stilled with his hands on her shoulders. Then he looked down and slid his fingers down her back and opened the zip at the back of her dress, then he undid the clasp of her bra and slipped the wisp of beige lace and satin off and laid it on the dressing table.

'I prefer you without one,' he said quietly.

Anna swallowed suddenly as she gazed at the images in the mirror. The softly lamplit room, Richard behind her, his head bent as he looked down at her . . . and herself, naked to the waist with her breasts gleaming like ivory and rose. And as she watched, he put his hands on her shoulders again and moved them slowly downwards.

She shivered slightly then, conscious of a confused

mixture of emotions—a strange feeling of expectancy tinged with a desperate vulnerability. Because somehow the sight of him standing behind her looking austere and remote, yet doing what he was doing, made her feel like an expensive piece of merchandise, to be appreciated at whim—or discarded in the same way like a lovely but lifeless stone statue.

Is this a moment of truth? she wondered with a sickening lurch of her heart. Is that how he really sees me?

But there was nothing lifeless about the way her breasts swelled beneath his hands. And a bright wave of colour stained her cheeks and she said foolishly, 'We'll be late . . .'

He looked up at last and his eyes captured hers in the mirror and he smiled slightly, a cool, chiselled movement of his lips that didn't quite reach his eyes. 'What's the point of going if I'll be spending the whole evening wanting to do this, Anna?'

'You . . . you could do it when we got home,' she said haltingly and uncertainly.

'I might not have the will-power to wait that long,' he drawled ironically.

She bit her lip, not knowing whether to believe him or not. But surely he couldn't be serious? She said awkwardly, 'I think you're teasing me again.'

An undisguised spark of amusement touched his eyes. 'Then I'll have to show you otherwise, won't I, my much-misused Anna?'

She winced inwardly because the irony was still there and it hurt. And she looked at him in the mirror with eyes that were dark and troubled and lips that were not quite steady.

'What's wrong?' he asked softly. 'Isn't this after all what you set out to achieve—in fact what all women set out to achieve when they take a lot of trouble with their appearance? That some man will be moved to undress them and make love to them? Well, you've achieved that, Anna, here and now, so isn't it a little pointless to waste time on the rest of the charade?'

Anna paled and with jerky, unco-ordinated movements, freed herself and stood up, pulling her dress up clumsily as she did. '*No*,' she whispered, appalled. 'If that's what you think . . .'

'It's what I know,' he interrupted dryly, and leisurely reached for her. 'I'm not *complaining* about it—just acknowledging it. Does that upset you? It shouldn't, because you could say the joke's on me.'

If she was pale before, she went white now. Because for the first time since he had taken her in a kind of ignorance and said that he wouldn't have married her if he'd known, he was showing her the side of him she had begun secretly to hope did not exist any longer. That part of him that viewed women so cynically—and perhaps what hurt most, she realised anguishedly, he was showing her too, that he had no cause to revise his opinions.

'Well, it does upset me,' she said raggedly. 'How would you like it if I told you I wasn't interested in spending any time with you other than in bed?'

His lips twitched and his eyes glinted devilishly and he started to speak, but she was so sure it was going to be something mocking and clever that she would have no answer for, a spontaneous spark of anger ignited within her, fusing all her hurt and love and uncertainty into a blazing rejection of his sentiments. Her arm flew out to slap him, but he caught her wrist in a grip that threatened to crush her bones.

'Don't do that,' he warned grimly, and with no further ado picked her up and tossed her on to the bed and sat down beside her, effectively imprisoning her with an arm on either side of her. 'It's quite a while since you've been angry with me, Anna,' he added.

'It's quite a while since you've been your usual objectionable self,' she retorted bitterly, close to tears of despair.

'I wouldn't have thought it was objectionable to pay you a compliment,' he said coolly.

'That . . . what you said wasn't a compliment. It was more like a shot fired in anger,' she answered tightly, and turned her head away defiantly.

'And I wonder what you would say this is,' he murmured, and despite every futile effort she made, finished undressing her carefully and somehow objectively until she was crying, tears of frustration and humiliation.

Then when he had finished and her clothes were lying in a heap on the floor, he stood up and started to take his own clothes off, but his eyes never left hers.

And when she said in a husky, goaded voice, 'If you think I'm enjoying this or feeling complimented, you're wrong!' he merely smiled slightly and said, 'We'll see.'

She did see not much later. She saw that her anger and hurt weren't proof against what he did to her, slowly and inexorably. She saw that while she could stop herself touching him, she couldn't stop herself trembling as his hands moved from her breasts to her waist to her thighs, stroking, cupping, exploring. She saw her puny defences go up in smoke, one by one.

But most of all, she saw why. That it was no good consoling herself as she had tried to once before, with the thought that he was sufficiently attractive and experienced to wring a response from her despite her better judgement.

No, she thought dimly. If I really didn't want him to be doing this to me, I could stop him because I'd be frozen with contempt and dislike and revulsion. But I'm not. I'd like to think I was, but I'm not ... And why? Because Richard Gillespie fascinates me and torments me and makes me feel more alive than I thought possible even when I think I hate him. And if I think I hate him now, it's because he, of all men, is the only one I want in so many ways—and can't have in so many ways. I want his companionship, his admiration, his respect ... his love. I don't only want to be someone he enjoys taking to bed. Oh God, she thought torturedly, I thought I could live with it, but I don't know if I can! Not this ...

And a terrible sense of longing intermingled with frustration took possession of her heart, much as the hurt anger had consumed her earlier, and even though she knew tauntingly that she was handing him this particular round game, set and match, she suddenly didn't care.

She came alive beneath his wandering lips and

pushed her fingers through his thick fair hair and arched her body towards him in an unmistakable invitation. As she did so she ran her hands down his back, skimming over his smooth skin, then stopping every now and then with a firm but gentle pressure and with her fingers wide-spread. And when that seemed to please him, she began to kiss his body and trail her tongue along the strong lines of his throat and the smooth tanned skin of his shoulders, all the time touching him more and more intimately and caressingly and moving beneath him as her own pleasure and excitement seemed to increase with each movement she made. She grew even more daring, to the astonishment of one tiny corner of her mind, which was all that was left of her that was not totally absorbed in what she was doing. She eased herself slightly away from him and reached out to switch off the bedside lamp so that the only light coming into the room was through the doorway leading into the lounge, and sat up on her heels beside him, proudly so that every curve of her body from the swell of her breasts to the slenderness of her waist and the rounded sweep of her hips was outlined in a golden glow against the shaft of light coming in. She stayed as still as a statue, offering herself for Richard's inspection demurely yet tantalising, with her lips parted and her breathing not very steady and her nipples telling their own tale, hardening in anticipation of what his touch could do to them, of the pleasure he could inflict on her by just touching them.

They stayed like that for what seemed an age, with his narrowed gaze roaming over her as he lay with his head resting on one hand. Then he stretched out the other hand and plucked at each swelling, throbbing peak, and Anna watched his fingers for a moment. Then she closed her eyes and tilted her head back, and tremors of exquisite torment racked her until she could stand it no longer, and her head sank forward and her dark hair, which had tumbled down, shadowed her face like a silky curtain.

Richard's hand left her body abruptly and he sat up with a suddenly tortured breath and her lashes fluttered

upwards uncertainly and she saw, in the intent way his
eyes were devouring her and in the muscle that jerked in
his jaw and the way he was breathing, that she had stirred
him for the first time, she thought, to a pitch of such sheer
naked desire for her that there was no place for any gentle
mockery or teasing provocativeness or even anything
protective, as there had always been in his lovemaking, in
deference, she assumed, to the fact that she was a
newcomer to it and he didn't want to hurt her again or
frighten her. There was nothing of that now, just
something white-hot and elemental between them that
had him as relentlessly in its grip as it had her.

But the thought stumbled into her mind that she
should be getting some satisfaction from this fact, yet
curiously she wasn't. Because she was quite suddenly
just a little afraid . . .

Then it was too late for fear as he started to kiss her
breasts and run his hands from her waist to her thighs,
and she moaned despairingly and pressed his fair head
closer and began to say his name over and over,
pleadingly and gaspingly and with an aching sense of
love that she couldn't disguise. Until finally, when she
thought she must faint from the savage beauty of his
lovemaking, they reached a pinnacle of spinning
intensity together, which made every other time she had
experienced it seem pale by comparison, and she clung
to him helplessly as they eventually floated down slowly
from it, and she murmured anguishedly, 'Hold me . . .
oh, please, don't let me go . . .'

'I'm . . . not letting you go, Anna,' he said huskily
into her hair and as if it was an effort for him to speak.
Then he held her hard until their bodies were still at last
and she fell instantly and deeply asleep in his arms.

A pale, marshmallow pink dawn greeted her eyes hours
later through wide-swept curtains. Her first waking
thought was that she had closed the curtains last night
when she was getting dressed to go . . .

She bit her lip and a tide of colour rose up from the
base of her throat to stain her cheeks as the events of
the previous evening washed over in a living tide.

She lay for a long time with her eyes closed, remembering and feeling almost as shaken now as she had then. Until gradually it dawned on her that she was alone in the bed—in the room, probably in the suite, because she could hear no sound of Richard. And she was sadly glad—if that's possible, she thought—because she didn't feel in any condition to face him.

In fact, she mused, she felt as if she had been dropped from a great height and she was still lying sprawled with a sort of twisted, abandoned grace.

'Abandoned,' she whispered, 'that's a good choice of words in more ways than one. Not only do I feel literally abandoned at this moment, I feel totally abandoned in the wanton sense of the word. Languid, not sure if I have the strength or the energy or the will to move, but curiously fulfilled.' She grimaced ruefully and turned over—and couldn't quite stifle the small sound of pain that rose to her lips as the movement hurt her aching breasts.

'Anna . . .'

She jerked convulsively and turned back to see Richard standing beside the bed staring sombrely down at her. He was dressed in jeans and a fine wool sweater that matched his eyes and his hair was ruffled as if the wind had been tugging at it.

She trembled. 'I didn't know you were there.'

'I haven't been—for long,' he said quietly, and sat down beside her. 'Are you all right?'

'Oh yes . . . yes,' she stammered.

He studied her piercingly for a long moment with his lips set and pale. Then he said abruptly, 'It didn't sound like it just now.' And he prised the sheet from her fingers which were unconsciusly grasping it tightly, and drew it away from her.

'Richard,' she whispered uncertainly, 'I'm all right.'

He closed his eyes briefly. 'You also bruise more easily than most people, or I was far too rough last night. I'm sorry, Anna,' he said tiredly, and laid the sheet back carefully and looked away.

She wondered if he didn't want her to see the pity and compassion in his eyes and realised that she didn't, that it would hurt her far more than a few bruises.

She put out a hand and touched one of his. 'Don't be sorry,' she said softly. 'I was there too, remember? And I'm not sorry. How could I be? You told me once that when a man and a woman ... affect each other like that, it can be like nothing else that's ever happened to you. I know what you meant now. And,' her voice cracked slightly, but there was something painfully honest in her eyes as she went on, 'whatever else is ... not quite right between us, I could only feel poorer for not having experienced that.'

His eyes had come back to rest on her face as soon as she had touched his hand. But as she stopped speaking he looked away again and it seemed to her as if he winced inwardly, and she wondered why. Wondered if she'd said the wrong thing.

When he spoke, at last, his voice was uneven and his fingers not quite steady as he fitted them through her own. 'Anna, what is—not quite right between us is the fact that you deserve *more* ... because you're so courageous, so beautiful, so ...'

'Don't,' she said involuntarily. 'Please don't. I'm not really.'

He smiled slightly, a smile that was more an expression of pain. 'Yes, you are. And it's breaking your heart that I can't give you more, isn't it? Can only give you the kind of treatment I meted out last night over the simple matter of going to the opera. I should be shot for what I said,' he added.

Anna felt as if her heart had stopped beating. He knows, she thought hazily through a sudden tensing of all her muscles.

But his next words made her wonder.

'That's—what I was worried about, you see,' he said, and traced a meaningless pattern on her hand with one finger. 'When it happens to you for the first time,' he looked up and captured her compelling gaze, 'it's hard not to be,' he hesitated, 'not to be all-encompassed by it. Do you have any idea what I'm talking about?

Oh yes, she thought unhappily, I do. Only that

happened to me first, long before last night. But even though you don't know that, you do obviously know something of what I feel now. Which is not so surprising, she thought with a sudden flickering of her nerve ends as she recalled the way she had acted. But how to put it into perspective, your kind of perspective which doesn't believe in it?

She looked up at the ceiling briefly, then back at him.

'Yes,' she said gravely, 'I do see. But although I'm,' she grimaced, 'running true to type—as romantic as the rest of them—there are other things that . . . that more than compensate. For one thing, at least we can talk about it. And the way we've been for so much of the time has . . . has meant a great deal to me. It's more than enough.'

She stared up at him with her heart now thudding painfully and was suddenly conscious that she meant every word she'd said and that her mouth had gone dry in case he rejected it, because it hit her suddenly, with almost the same force the cyclone had, that it was as much him as his love that she needed. Even in his cynicism, which was in any case slightly counterbalanced by the fact that he did care enough to try to make her understand.

'Richard,' she said on a sudden breath, 'I don't mind that it's not perfect. I knew . . . it couldn't ever be. But I think we can make the best of it.'

'God,' he muttered barely audibly, and gathered her into his arms, 'if you only knew what a low, rotten kind of heel it makes me feel to hear you using my own arguments and philosophies!'

'No!' she pulled away from him. 'No, you don't understand!'

'Yes, I do,' he said, roughly. 'More than you know. I understand that I'm a bloody sight luckier than I deserve to be. And I just have to hope it stays that way. *Don't* . . . don't cry,' he added with a gentle bitterness, and kissed her eyelids. 'If there's one thing I wish, it's that I *could* be your Prince Charming,' he said huskily. 'Because you deserve no less.'

They stayed like that for an age until Anna was able

to get a grip on herself. Then he held her away and said seriously, 'Did I hurt you very much last night? How do you feel?'

'I . . . I'm not sure,' she said huskily—and added with her lips quirking, 'Depends what you have in mind. I don't feel like doing anything too strenuous, like sightseeing or . . .'

His eyes softened. 'That wasn't what I had in mind.'

'Richard,' she said breathlessly.

'I like the way you say that.' His voice was perfectly grave.

'. . . Richard . . .'

'Yes, Anna?' But she could see the teasing smile at the back of his eyes and he took pity on her confusion. 'No,' he said with a grin, 'that wasn't what I had in mind either. Not yet awhile, my beautiful bride. What I did think of doing was something not in the least strenuous. I thought you might like to soak in a warm bath while I order a special breakfast, which you can have in bed.'

'Sounds like a good idea!'

But her eyes widened when she was back in bed and breakfast was wheeled in accompanied by a bottle of champagne in an ice-bucket, and she had to laugh. 'Letty wouldn't approve,' she murmured as he loosened the cork and poured two glasses and brought one over to her.

'Then let's not tell her,' he said with a wicked glint in his eye. 'Mind you,' he added as he put the cork back into the bottle, 'I don't think it would be a good idea to drink it all. We'll keep some for later. By the way, perhaps I should warn you. I fully intend from now on to feed you on oysters and asparagus . . . maybe a little powdered rhino horn—and myself, of course.'

Anna grimaced. 'Whatever for?'

'Because they're all supposed to be great foods for lovers, and in case I haven't mentioned it before, my lovely Anna,' he said with his eyes warm, 'you're a sensational lover. So much so, I'm going to have great difficulty keeping my hands off you at all times. Which means we both have to keep our . . . strength up.'

'Richard,' she said trying hard not to giggle, 'if you dare feed meanything powdered . . . anyway, you might only end up making me get fat!'

'Would it matter if we got fat together?' he enquired.

'I think it might defeat your whole purpose,' she said, laughing.

'Ah, I see what you mean . . .'

'No, you don't,' she answered, still laughing but feeling almost faint with love for him. 'You're just teasing me—yet again.'

His face sobered suddenly. 'Maybe about the one, but not the other, Anna. You were—last night you were everything any man could wish for.'

'I . . . I'm glad,' she whispered. But only because it was you, she added to herself. And if I was, it was only because it was you and what you do to me.

'Eat your breakfast,' he said a moment later. 'You can sleep all day if you want to.'

She didn't sleep all day, but after breakfast she did feel sleepy and relaxed, perhaps due to the glass of champagne, and she did sleep for a couple of hours, to wake with a curious sense of physical well-being and a feeling of peace in her heart. And she thought, how many people do have it quite perfect anyway?

The rest of the two weeks passed uneventfully.

At least, if you could call the mere fact of being married to Richard Gillespie uneventful, Anna mused once. But at least she felt they had come to a kind of understanding, greater than any they had had before. And if she felt wistful now and then, she resolutely put the feeling away from her.

But all too soon the fortnight came to an end and she found herself possessed by another feeling—one of nervousness, which was very hard to explain. Why should she be nervous about going back to Yandilla? Particularly now that she'd crossed the biggest hurdle of her life, let alone one connected with Yandilla.

But the day they flew home it dawned on her what the reason for her attack of nerves was—in fact that there were two reasons. The first one, which was

probably going to be a problem always, was the fact
that everyone there seemed to be able to read her like
an open book. She grimaced ruefully but decided it was
something she had to learn to live with and not as
worrying as the second reason.

She glanced at Richard and wondered why she had
never thought of it before. Perhaps because we've been
away from Yandilla, on new ground, so to speak? she
thought. But there must be memories for him at home,
she mused. Memories of Chrissy's mother. And she
wondered in a sudden startled flash if it was any
particular memory which had made him the way he was
the night they didn't get to the opera—and felt a little
flicker of outright fear prickle her skin unreasonably.
But all it means really, she tried to reassure herself, is
that I'll have to be on my guard. Which I am anyway.

And she deliberately made herself relax.

CHAPTER ELEVEN

ABOUT two months later Anna stopped what she was
doing one day and thought wryly back to her fanciful
fears. For in fact it had been a joyful homecoming.
Chrissy, predictably, had been ecstatic, but then Phil and
Letty had been hardly less so, and Samson had looked
at them both and shrugged and said, 'Hey, man!
Whatever you two are doing with each other, it seems
to be agreeing with you! Never did go much on the idea
of marriage myself, but I reckon I might give the matter
a second thought after all!'

Richard had laughed and Anna had blushed, while
Chrissy had hugged her adoringly and said brightly, 'I
think it's just a simply super idea. It also seems to be
c . . .' She stopped and clapped a hand to her mouth,
but went on in a moment, 'We've moved you and
Daddy into the biggest bedroom, Anna, come and see!'
She'd tugged at Anna's hand and would not be denied.

But later that night when the house was quiet, Anna

had looked around the biggest bedroom and felt a return of some nervous tension.

And when Richard had come in quietly and closed the door behind him, she had jumped slightly and his eyebrows had risen. He had come across the room and taken her in his arms and asked quietly, 'What's wrong?'

She had tried to smile. 'Oh, nothing. Just tired.'

He had frowned down at her, then looked around the room. 'Anna,' he had said slowly, 'I've never used this room before. My mother was still alive the—last time I got married, and although she offered to, in fact tried to insist on moving out, I wouldn't let her. It didn't seem right, to me, to move her for the little time she had left. Nor, eventually, did it seem right somehow to bring to this room, which had known a lot of love, the kind of . . . disharmony Julie and I shared. So there are no ghosts for you to worry about, here, except the nicest ones. You'd have liked my mother, I think. And I know she'd have liked you.'

For a moment Anna had been unable to speak, torn between anger at herself for being so transparent that the one subject she wanted to avoid had cropped up, and almost dizzy at the thought that he didn't mind sharing this room with her. Then she had said gruffly, 'Thanks.'

'A pleasure,' he had said gravely, and picked her up and laid her on the wide double bed. 'That's in lieu of carrying you over the doorstep, by the way. I'm surprised Chrissy let me forget that. But talking of Chrissy and the rest of our family,' he had gone on as he had lain down beside her and started to unbutton her blouse, 'did you by any chance get the same impression I got? That they were big with news?'

'I—now you come to mention it, yes.'

'Want to have a bet with me? What their news is?'

'Now you come to mention it, no. Because it's got to be—another wedding in the family, say?'

'Right again, Anna. Who would you say the parties involved were?'

'Well, seeing that Samson has only just begun to give the idea as a whole some thought, and seeing that Letty doesn't have a beau to my knowledge, I reckon it has to be Phil and the Colonel,' she had answered, and laughed softly. 'Do you think the Reverend will take kindly to another Yandilla wedding?'

'Don't see why he shouldn't. I think they're very nice, Yandilla weddings.'

'All the same, let's not let on we've worked it out!'

They hadn't, and Anna smiled to herself as she recalled Richard's expression when Phil had dropped her bombshell the next evening when Chrissy was in bed and out of earshot.

'You're ... what did you say, Phil?' he demanded incredulously as they sat on the verandah.

Phil went pink. 'I said, I'm going away with the Colonel. We're ... going to have an affair. And if it turns out well we'll get married.'

'Phil, you can't be serious!'

'Richard,' Phil said awkwardly, 'I'm sorry to shock you, but I think I'm old enough to work out what's best for me. And I'm certainly old enough not to be stampeded into anything. I ... well, I'd like to be very sure. Besides, I thought that was the accepted way of going about things these days.'

Richard stared at her and then swore fluently, and Phil went pinker with alarm.

It was Letty who intervened at that stage. 'She's right, and swearing never helped anyone, Mr Richard,' she said sternly. 'Because'm you done everything by the book, it don't say the rest of us is bound to, and I reckon Phil's earnt the right to do things the way she pleases. After all, it's not as if she hops off every few months with a different bloke, now is it?'

Richard regarded Letty narrowly, but she was in no way intimidated. Not even when he said, 'So you say, Letty, but the only time your grammar ever deserts you is when you're deeply disturbed about something! And don't try to ...!'

'Of course I'm disturbed!' Letty cried, and fixed him with a belligerent glance. 'I'm disturbed 'cause they been eyeing each other, Phil and the Colonel, over this damn stretch of water,' she gestured widely, 'for years! And at last they've reached some kind of a decision. I tell you, that's a mighty step forward, but all you want to do is muck it up! And while I'm normally all for doing things by the book, I reckon there can be some exceptions! Mind you, I'm glad you didn't make no exception for Anna here, don't think I'm not, and I'd have told you pretty damn quick what I thought of you if you had! But for Phil, you be advised by me, you just be happy for her!' She leant forward agressively.

'I don't need you or anyone else to tell me how I feel about Phil, Letty,' he said grimly, and stared back at her angrily.

Anna found herself intervening at this point as Phil muttered distractedly, 'Oh dear, oh dear!'

'Richard, Letty, I think you're both right,' she said soothingly, and could have laughed as she became the recipient of two sets of smouldering glances. 'You're both disturbed because you're so fond of Phil. But,' she went on calmly, 'I don't think it's our place to tell Phil she's either right or wrong.' She glanced suddenly and meaningfully at Letty. 'There are some things it's best not to meddle with,' she finished quietly.

Letty looked away and betrayed the first aura of discomfort Anna had ever detected in her. But something oddly acute entered Richard's eyes as he studied Anna and then Letty.

'Oh, I see,' he said at last, and Anna tensed.

'No, you don't,' Phil answered. 'You really don't, Richard.'

'I think I do,' he said slowly with a strange twist to his lips and a sudden clear, piercing look at Anna. 'Not that it matters, it's just strange that I should have been so blind . . .'

'Well, I have to confess I tried to hide it,' Phil said helplessly. 'But we have been . . . eyeing each other—I suppose that's as good a way of putting it as any other—for some time. So if you're thinking I've suddenly gone mad and am trying to re-live my youth or anything like that, Richard, it just *isn't* like that. It's been growing and it's nothing light or as if I'm embarking on a last flirtatious fling. Oh, how can I explain it!' She stared at him anxiously, seemingly unaware that they were talking at cross purposes at that precise moment.

But Anna was aware of it and it brought her an oddly apprehensive feeling. Letty, too, was looking at Richard with a strange expression in her eyes.

'All right,' he said abruptly. 'Perhaps Anna is right. What—or rather how—are you going to do it?'

'Well,' Phil said awkwardly, 'we're going to London for a couple of months because ...' She stopped uncertainly.

'Ah yes,' he said. 'Your television series. That seems to be dragging on, doesn't it?'

'Well,' said Phil, and shot a flustered look at Anna, 'to tell you the truth I ... got the dates mixed up. You know how awfully stupid I can be at times?'

There was silence while Richard studied Phil, this time meditatively and searchingly. Then he surprised them all by saying only, 'And what have you told Chrissy?'

'That ... that,' Phil said tearfully, 'that the Colonel and I like each other very much and that we're going to go overseas for a holiday and that one day we might get married. I must say Chrissy had no reservations whatsoever,' she added. 'And she's too young to understand or even think of the morals of it. Besides, in my heart, I just don't feel as if I'm compromising my morals. Nor that it's anyone's business if I do.'

Richard's face softened suddenly. 'Oh, Phil,' he said quite gently, 'it's not that. I guess—it did just take me by surprise. But then you're often a surprising lady, which is one of the reasons I love you as a person and an aunt.'

'Richard,' Phil said tremulously.

Anna and Letty faded away discreetly then and didn't hear any more. But in the kitchen, they stopped and looked at each other, and Anna said, 'Letty?'

'Don't you bother your head about it, Anna. Men just don't like to think they aren't godlike creatures who don't need a discreet shove in the right direction sometimes.'

Anna had to smile, albeit reluctantly.

'Anyway,' Letty said softly, 'were Phil and I wrong? I know you don't hold with meddling, but didn't it work out right for you? I only got to see the way you look at him . . .'

Anna flushed faintly. She said with a little sigh, 'Yes, it worked out right for me, Letty.'

'Then what's to worry about?'

Anna came back from her reminiscences with a little grimace. Letty had been right again. After that night Richard had never given any indication that he resented what Phil and Letty had done. In fact he'd never even mentioned it, and that nameless apprehension she had felt had subsided.

And once Phil and the Colonel had left, life had settled into a smooth, easy-flowing pattern, one that had seen Chrissy blossom and lose much of that occasionally fine-drawn highly-strung air.

This alone had delighted Anna and she was able to further contribute to it by putting into operation something she had thought of often. She enrolled Chrissy with the School-of-the-Air, which had its northern headquarters in Cairns. The results had been well worth it because for the first time in her life Chrissy was in contact with other children, and even though it was only via a special two-way radio transmitter set, she blossomed even more because of it and made a special friend, a little girl called Louise, of her own age, who as it happened lived on an island in the same area as Yandilla. Which meant that one day they would be able to see each other.

As for herself, there were no more sleepless nights, no more tortured confusion. Instead of that, a marriage that, for all it was not quite perfect, was more than fulfilling for her in those days. A blend of friendship and laughter that was not particularly loverlike in public—in that Richard wasn't particularly demonstrative in front of the others, more as if they were good friends; and something that wasn't quite the same behind the closed doors of the biggest bedroom. Nor was the less public side of their relationship reserved for the nights, Anna discovered. Because sometimes, at the oddest times, she would look up and find him watching her with a look in his grey-green eyes that made her tremble inwardly.

The first time it happened she was confused and not sure if she was reading it right. It was late morning and she was polishing her new silver cutlery, while Chrissy was sitting at the kitchen table labouring over a composition she had been given as homework in an earlier session of the School-of-the-Air.

Richard came in through the back door. He and Samson had been out in one of the boats since early morning. He smiled at Anna, ruffled Chrissy's hair and pointed out a spelling error to her, then turned to get himself a cool drink. Anna went back to polishing the silver, but she looked up for some reason to see him leaning against the sink, watching her. Then he had turned away and walked out of the kitchen.

It was then that she found she couldn't get on with what she was doing, because she was filled with a strange restlessness and a clamouring of pulses that his look had aroused. And eventually she asked Letty to take care of Chrissy for a while and helped them to pack a picnic lunch to take down to share with Samson and Sunshine. But as she watched them walk down to the rebuilt boatshed, she was filled with a flood of uncertainty and her nails bit into her palms as she wondered if she wasn't making an awful fool of herself.

All the same, she went into the bedroom and stood in the middle of the room with her head bent and her fists still clenched.

But after a very little while Richard came. He closed the door and stood leaning back against it with his arms folded, not saying anything.

Until finally he spoke very quietly. 'Take your clothes off, Anna.'

She found, though, in spite of the way she felt, that one small part of her was rebelling against the fact that he could do this to her with just a look. And it was that part that enabled her to grasp one tiny straw of face-saving initiative.

She lifted her head and said just as quietly, 'Why don't you take them off?'

His eyes narrowed and glinted and the air between them was suddenly taut and threaded with a tinge of hostility.

'All right . . .'

He undressed her there in the middle of the sun-dappled bedroom, sliding her dress off slowly, his eyes never leaving hers and his lips moving in a slight, cool smile as her skin shivered wherever his fingers touched it.

Then he moved back and that grey-green gaze roamed her body leisurely. But a last remaining shred of that odd spirit of rebellion kept her head up proudly and her eyes faintly challenging.

But he had only smiled slightly again and said huskily, 'You're very beautiful, Anna. But I think I've told you that before. Come.' He held out his hand and she took it after a slight hesitation and he led her to the bed. 'Lie down.'

She obeyed and lay quietly, her hair spread across the coral pink pillowslip like dark silk. Richard stared down at her for a long heart-stopping moment. Then he started to undress and she watched, her eyes grave, and the only indication of what the sight of his tall, powerful body was doing to her was a fluttering of the delicate skin in the hollow at the base of her throat.

And when he finished, she sighed and murmured, 'You're beautiful too . . .'

After that it was no contest at all. She gloried in the things he did to her and the knowledge, later, when she lay with her head on his shoulder, that she had pleased him.

But in the gentle aftermath of their lovemaking, he said against the corner of her mouth, 'Didn't you like the idea of me making love to you in the middle of the day, Anna?'

She hesitated, then thought, why not be honest? 'Yes and no,' she whispered, and her lips curved into a smile.

'Oh?'

'Mmm. I don't always like the idea that I'm going to keel over like a pack of cards every time you look at me. You've done it before, at the cricket.'

She felt a jolt of laughter shake his body and he said, still smiling, 'Why don't you think of it this way, then? *You* don't even have to look at me to put these ideas in my mind. Just the sight of you polishing silver has the oddest effect on me sometimes.'

She smiled back at him, but said almost immediately with a touch of guilt, 'What would they think if they knew? I mean . . .'

'If you mean Letty and Samson, they probably exchanged knowing looks over Chrissy's head and had a quiet chuckle.'

'Oh!' Anna blushed.

'And in their heart of hearts,' he went on lazily, tracing the colour in her cheeks, 'envied us. By the way, I don't know how we keep getting back to this subject—there must be something in the air—but I've noticed Samson watching Sunshine when he thinks no one is watching him.'

'Really? Oh, definitely something in the air!' Anna teased gently. But she sobered suddenly. 'If you're right, though, how can that be? They're related.'

'I doubt that. The number of nieces Letty has had here over the years is prodigious. At the closest Sunshine is probably the niece of a niece of an old friend. Blood ties are not the only ones that matter to them. Also, I suspect Letty imports them to Yandilla at such an astonishing rate for more reasons than one.'

'Letty,' said Anna after a moment as this sank in, 'is . . .' She stopped abruptly. In a class of her own so far as being an indefatigable matchmaker, she'd been going to say, before she'd almost bitten her tongue off.

'Letty is . . .?' he queried.

'Well, you said yourself she'd love to have grandchildren,' she said lamely.

'So I did,' he remarked pensively. 'Anna?'

Oh no, she thought. Here it comes!

'Yes?'

'If you don't get up out of this bed very soon, I might start getting those odd ideas again.' His arms moved round her gently. 'How does that thought affect you?'

'Do you really want to know?' she said slowly, filled with relief and a sense of love that was almost too great for her heart to hold.

'Uh-huh . . .'

'I think, and I told you this once before,' her lips trembled in a smile, 'that there should be a law about men like you, Richard Gillespie! Especially at *this* time of day!'

And she fled the bed laughing as he reached for her and then subsided, laughing himself.

Yes, Anna mused on that day about two months after they had arrived home on Yandilla from their honeymoon and she'd found herself in a mood of reminiscent daydreaming, only a fool would complain about this marriage.

And even if it can't last in this same way, even if it must inevitably lose some of its fire, at least I'll have these memories to hold on to, these days when it was easy to pretend I was truly loved . . .

But it was only a couple of days later that the whole fabric of her pretence was ripped apart and she was faced with the bare truth. Richard did not love her, and no memories were enough to compensate for it.

It all began with a perfectly harmless shopping expedition.

The weather had cooled down, not that it could be called cold, precisely, but there was a new zip in the air at night time and in the early morning and less humidity and Anna found herself correspondingly, feeling energetic, creative and brisk.

And for a time, two days exactly, she found plenty of outlet for this state of mind. She rearranged the furniture in several rooms, went through all Chrissy's clothes, sorting out the ones that no longer fitted, she re-potted all the pot plants on the verandah—but it was when she started on the kitchen that Letty intervened.

'You pregnant?' she enquired when she found Anna rearranging all the kitchen cupboards one morning.

Anna stopped what she was doing rather suddenly. 'No. Why?'

'Well, I did those cupboards out only a few weeks ago. Oh, I'm not saying I mind you doing them! Except you helped me do 'em, which made me wonder. See, being pregnant takes different people in different ways. Some lie about while others get the urge to do things.'

Anna half smiled. 'Well, I don't think I am.'

Letty looked at her affectionately. 'That could change overnight, pet,' she said.

'Letty!' Anna replied with a grin, but at the same time feeling a sudden deep longing.

'Well, it can!'

'O.K., it can,' Anna acknowledged. 'But at the moment I think I'm only suffering from a reverse spring-cleaning syndrome. I think it's the nip in the air, in other words.'

'Ah! So happens I am too. Always do at this time of the year. But between the two of us this house is so damn clean, there isn't anything left to do. Why don't we try our hand at something else?'

'Like what? Do you have anything in mind?'

'Yes. Batik.'

'Batik? But do you know how?'

'Reckon I do,' said Letty. 'There's a woman on T.I., she comes from Java and she was showing me how she did it last time I was up there. See, you paint part of the material with wax, then you dye it. I thought if we got the hang of it we could even teach it to the Colonel's crew when he comes back. Don't think they're into batik yet, and there's a market for sarongs and things like that. What do you think? Like to try it?'

'Love to,' Anna said promptly.

And so it was arranged that Anna should make a trip over to the mainland to purchase what they needed. Chrissy was to go with her, but at the last minute she remembered that one of her School-of-the-Air class-mates was having a birthday and a rather special lesson had been planned.

Anna set off with Samson and Letty's list and was soon driving Richard's car, which was kept on the mainland, into Tully. She had declined Samson's offer to drive her and arranged to meet him at the jetty that afternoon.

All the same, as she climbed into the low-slung car, she experienced a touch of nerves. It was so obviously expensive she would feel awful if she had damaged it. Not that Richard had had any qualms about her driving it, obviously, because he had kissed her goodbye with a lurking smile and simply handed her the keys.

But after a few miles and an encounter with a large, strange-looking bird on the road, which had illustrated to her that the brakes worked very well, she relaxed.

'That must have been a cassowary,' she told herself. 'Wait till I tell Chrissy!'

Then she found herself thinking of the first time she had been in this car and how it seemed almost like a life time away.

But the return trip, after a successful shopping expedition, turned quite suddenly into a nightmare. On a deserted stretch of winding, narrow road about five miles out from Mission Beach, one of the tyres blew with a deafening bang and the car slewed across the road and came to rest facing in the opposite direction with the other rear wheel resting in a fairly deep cane-irrigation ditch.

Anna climbed out shakily with her heart pounding violently, glad to be alive but horrified at the damage she might have done. Yet an inspection of the car reassured her somewhat. There seemed not to be a mark on it. However, it dawned on her that even if she did get the tyre changed, there was going to be the distinct possibility that the car would be bogged in the muddy ditch. She looked around, wondering if it wouldn't be easier to go for help rather than attempt anything herself, but knew it could be a long walk and her best hope was for a passing motorist either to give her a lift or give her a hand. But how long will I have to wait? she thought to a sigh of despair that immediately changed to cry of joy as a large Land Rover hove into view like an answer to a prayer. It stopped in response

to her frantic signalling and Anna ran forward
thankfully—only to find herself staring up into a pair of
sardonically amused brown eyes.

'Well, well, if it isn't Mrs Gillespie,' Mike Carmody
drawled. 'Much as I dislike ignoring damsels in distress,
perhaps I should drive on?'

'Oh ... Mike,' she said awkwardly, 'please don't. I
really need help.'

He glanced over the top of her head at the car,
consideringly. 'You're not running away from Richard,
by any chance, are you, Anna?'

'No, of course not! Why would you think that? Oh, I
see,' she went on hastily as his eyes changed, and felt
her face colour. 'No, in fact I'm going in the opposite
direction, to Mission Beach, but I had a blow-out and
skidded. The thing is, though, I'm due there in about
twenty minutes and if I don't turn up Samson will start
to worry ...'

Mike looked at her. 'So you married him, Anna? That
didn't altogether surprise me. But it's ironic, don't you
think, this habit he and I have of fancying the same sheila.
More ironic that he's always the one married to them.'

'Mike, please,' she begged. 'You and I barely knew
each other.'

He laughed. 'Yeah—he made damned sure of that.'
Then he shrugged. 'What the hell! Let's see what we can
do.' He opened the door and stepped out.

'Oh, thank you, Mike!' she breathed.

'Will you tell him who came to your rescue, Anna?'
he asked with a mocking look, but when she coloured,
he relented. 'Forget I said that.' He grimaced. 'Okay,
you've got yourself into a right mess, lady! Lucky I've
got a towbar and some rope ...'

It took them nearly an hour to get the car
roadworthy again—at least it took Mike nearly an
hour, for there was not much Anna could do to help.
Then he suggested that he follow her to make sure she
got to Mission Beach safely, seeing he was going there
himself anyway.

But she had no further mishaps and garaged the car
with a sigh of relief but still worried that she was over

an hour and a half late. But the garage Richard rented was in sight of the jetty, and she locked the door carefully and turned to find Mike stepping out of his Land Rover.

'Mike, I can't thank you enough,' she said quietly. 'You're a real friend.'

'For you, Anna, any time,' he answered, and leant forward to kiss her on the lips. 'No, don't say it,' he warned, his eyes glinting devilishly. 'I've been dying to do that just once. Perhaps I'll be cured now . . . See you, Anna.'

He turned away and she started to hurry towards the jetty, her eyes searching for the Yandilla launch. It was there, she saw with some relief, and broke into a run as the person lounging on the jetty beside it straightened.

But it wasn't Samson she all but collided with. It was Richard.

And her apologies and explanations died on her lips as she realised that he was looking at her coldly, almost murderously.

'Richard . . .?' she whispered. And although she had not the slightest need to feel guilty, she looked round and realised instantly that he would have seen her and Mike, and a hot colour flooded into her cheeks. 'I . . . can explain,' she stammered.

'Don't bother. You just did,' he muttered through his teeth, his eyes on her hot cheeks. 'Get aboard,' he added grimly.

'No . . .'

'Don't argue, Anna,' he said violently, and picked her up bodily and put her in the boat, then climbed in after her.

'No . . . I mean, no I haven't explained anything! You've just jumped to a conclusion quite ridiculously and . . .' She gasped as the motor tore viciously to life and the boat surged forward away from the jetty, and she collapsed on to a bench in an undignified heap, dropping all her parcels.

Suddenly she was as angry as he was. 'I hate you, Richard Gillespie!' she cried furiously as she scrambled up and as he uninterestedly steered the boat in the direction of the sunset. 'I hate you!'

He only shrugged then and said, 'We'll see. You might think you hate me now, but you'll find you have good cause to really hate me if I ever catch you within a mile of Mike Carmody again.'

'If . . .' Anna struggled to speak through a red mist of rage, 'if I didn't know you better, I'd be tempted to think you were insanely jealous of Mike. But where there's no love, how can there be jealousy?'

But she took a precipitous step backwards as he cut the engine and reached for her, to dump her unceremoniously into one of the padded fishing chairs, where he imprisoned her by leaning over her with a hand on each arm. And in spite of her rage she couldn't help cowering back at what she saw in his eyes.

'You're right, Anna,' he said softly but with so much threatening menace, she shivered. 'There's no jealousy, only this—Mike did me an incredible disservice once, and as a result of it, I have this curious but nevertheless very strong aversion to him. And I don't care to have anything to do with him, let alone share any of my possessions with him. If I had a dog that would include it, and it includes you. So, if from being such a determined virgin, you've now begun to think longingly of all the years and all the men you missed out on, we might be able to come to some arrangement, but if it's Mike Carmody you particularly want, forget it, because I don't even share my cast-offs with him, and we shall just have to get along as best we can.'

Anna's jaw sagged and her eyes widened incredulously under this cruel onslaught. And something died in her heart, in fact she wondered dazedly if she had a heart left at all, because a frozen, alien object seemed to have taken its place in her breast.

'Do we understand each other now, Anna?' he said gently—the kind of gentleness, she thought, that would cut ice.

She swallowed and said hoarsely, in a voice quite unlike her own, 'Yes . . . oh yes.'

'Good.' He straightened up. 'Then perhaps we can get home.'

Home, she thought wildly. How can I go home to Yandilla with him, like this? How can I ... carry on as if nothing's happened? How?

CHAPTER TWELVE

YET she did carry on as if nothing untoward had happened, although she never knew how she did it. She helped Letty get started on the batik, mothered Chrissy as usual—no, not as usual, even more caringly and warmly if anything, because she couldn't bear to think of Chrissy sensing that anything was amiss with her bright, perfect world that had endured for such a short time. She even managed to act normally towards Richard in public, although it was a different matter behind the closed door of the biggest bedroom. They still shared a bed, there was no way they could not without arousing at least Letty's suspicions, but he didn't try to touch her and only came into the room when she was already in bed, and he was gone when she woke in the morning.

For two weeks Anna carried on the charade. Then she snapped.

The breaking up process happened one night when Richard came into the bedroom for the first time in two weeks before she was in bed.

She was sitting at the dressing table brushing her hair and she was already dressed for bed in a white broderie anglaise nightgown that had been part of Phil's wedding present. It had a low-cut, square neckline with a ruched bodice and tiny puffed sleeves and red ribbons threaded round the sleeves. She was also wearing white satin mules trimmed with swansdown that complemented her tanned, bare legs visible from just below the knee where the nightgown ended. But as she brushed steadily, she was not thinking of how she looked. She was thinking of something quite different, and she jumped when the door opened and Richard walked in and closed it behind him.

They stared at each other in the mirror for about a minute, then she looked away but didn't say anything.

'Anna?' His voice was contained and quiet.

'What is it?'

'Look at me, Anna.'

Why should I? she wondered. So that you can pin me again like some helpless butterfly? All the same, her lashes lifted and even as distressed and wounded as she felt, she couldn't deny with an inward tremor, the impact just his presence had on her.

But she forced herself to say calmly enough, 'Yes?'

His eyes narrowed and searched her face. Then he said abruptly, 'You don't look well.'

'I'm fine,' she answered quietly. 'Is that—what you wanted to say to me?'

'No ...' He hesitated briefly. 'I've only just noticed it. Are you sure?'

'Quite sure,' she said steadily. 'I think I have the kind of looks that go off when I'm not ...' She stopped and bit her lip.

'When you're not happy?' he supplied after a pause.

'Probably,' she agreed dryly.

'Then perhaps I can restore you,' he commented.

'. . . Oh?'

'Yes. Samson used the car today,' he went on with no further preamble. 'It's the first time it's been used since you took it to Tully that day. And when he discovered the blown-out tyre in the boot, and told me about it with quite some surprise, it wasn't hard for me to deduce what must have happened. And so I've come to say I'm sorry for the things I ... inferred that day.'

Anna stared at him in the mirror with her lips slightly parted, but he merely returned her look dispassionately. She blinked confusedly and thought shakenly, no, you're not. You're just as angry as you were then. You're only trying to put a better face on it because ... because ... why? Are you trying to tell me we made a bargain and the time's come for me to hold my end up again? Or something like that ...?

She licked her lips. 'That's all right,' she said huskily, and started to brush her hair again, not looking at him.

But Richard leant over swiftly and removed the brush from her fingers. 'You didn't say that very convincingly, Anna,' he remarked.

Her uplifted hand sank into her lap and she literally felt the breaking up process begin within her, like an over-taut rubber band giving way at last.

'Is that so strange?' she answered bitterly. 'I wasn't particularly convinced by what you said. I don't think you're sorry at all!'

'Then why did you tell me it was all right?' Richard asked sardonically.

She swung round on the stool, her eyes suddenly bright with anger. 'Because I have no option!'

He smiled unpleasantly. 'Poor Anna,' he said with a steely mockery. 'You've had a rough time since you came to Yandilla, haven't you?'

'I . . . what do you mean?' she demanded.

'Well, this business of options, for one thing. I'm not quite sure why I didn't realise it at the time, but it's since become plain to me that Letty and Phil jockeyed you into a position where you thought you had no option too. *Didn't* they?'

Two things flashed across her mind at that point. That he was trying to force some sort of a confrontation with her and that it went even deeper than what had happened the day she'd gone to Tully. And secondly, that she had been right to worry about his reaction to the discovery of Phil and Letty's connivance, after all . . . But what does it matter? she thought suddenly. What does anything matter any more?

'Oh no,' she said tautly, that flame of anger burning steadily. 'No one jockeyed me into anything. I made my own mistakes, Richard.'

'Go on.' Their eyes clashed.

'What more is there to say?'

'Oh, I thought you might be going to add something like—I made my own bed and now I have to lie in it,' he murmured, his lips twisting ironically.

She gasped. 'If you think I'll ever willingly share a bed with you again,' she shot at him, 'you're very much mistaken!'

'I wonder about that,' Richard said coolly, his eyes mocking her. 'You were a quick learner, Anna. You even surprised me. And seeing that you're not going to have anyone else to share your bed until, and if it ever suits me, I wouldn't make sweeping statements of that nature if I were you.'

She stumbled up with but one thought in mind, to attack him with her fists, anything . . .

All she succeeded in doing, though, was to end up clamped in his arms, her breath coming in tearing sobs of frustration and just about every other futile emotion she could think of.

He held her like that until her puny struggles ceased. Then he picked her up and laid her on the bed and stood looking down at her detachedly. 'Yes,' he said finally, 'you might find it's not as easy as you think to return to a life of celibacy, my passionate lady-wife. And when you're ready to admit that, let me know, won't you? I might put you out of your misery.'

He turned and walked out of the room without a backward glance.

Anna stared up at the ceiling with stark eyes for a long time, consumed with an unequalled sense of torment and despair. And when she finally fell asleep, it was with one thought in her mind—I have to get away from here . . .

The next morning not even her best friend would have told her that she looked well. She had dark smudges like bruises beneath her eyes which intensified the pallor of her face. But curiously, while she was wondering what to say when anyone taxed her with it, she found she had no need to say anything.

Because Letty, who was the first person she encountered after she had got up, took one look at her and exclaimed, 'Oh, you poor thing! Another of those headaches like the one you had the day the cyclone hit!

Now you just get straight back to bed. And don't you worry about getting Chrissy to her friend—I'll take her.'

Anna bit her lip. She had forgotten in her turmoil that Chrissy had been invited to spend the next couple of nights with her new little friend, Louise. But she found herself thinking dazedly, if I really want to go, this might be the best opportunity I'll get—if Richard's out . . . But I don't know that. All I know is that he didn't come back to this room last night.

But it was Letty who solved this too. 'Now,' she said, sailing into the bedroom a little before ten o'clock, 'everything's arranged. Samson's gonna take me and Chrissy across to her friend—not quite sure when we'll be back, after lunch, probably. Samson tells me Mr Richard went out to the Reef at the crack of dawn and won't be back till lunchtime, but I guess you know that? But just in case you're worried another cyclone is gonna sneak up on you, it's too late for them now, and in any case, Sunshine's here.'

'I'm not worried about that,' Anna said with a weak smile.

'Good. Then maybe you can have a nice long sleep. You sure look as if you could do with it!'

Anna stared up into Letty's eyes and wondered how much she had guessed. But all she could see was a warm look of sympathy.

Then Chrissy tiptoed into the room and came to lay her head beside Anna's on the pillow. 'Should I stay and look after you, Anna?' she asked softly.

'No, darling,' Anna whispered with some difficulty. 'I'll be fine. Are you sure you've packed everything you want to show Louise?'

'She's packed enough to stay a month,' said Letty with a grin. 'Drat, there's Samson pacing about like a caged tiger!'

And so with a flurry of goodbyes they left, but not before Chrissy gave Anna a last warm, fierce little hug. And Anna turned her head into the pillow and wept as she hadn't been able to last night. But even as she thought brokenheartedly of what it would do to Chrissy to come back and find her gone, she felt that in the long run it would do much more harm to have to watch her new mother disintegrate at the hands of her father.

'And that's what I'll surely do if I stay,' she murmured. 'Even although I'm going to have his baby . . oh God! How ironic it's all been. I *was* pregnant and didn't know it that day Letty asked me. But I can't any longer not admit it. Especially after feeling distinctly nauseous these past few mornings. But what am I going to do? I have some money saved, though it's not a fortune . . . but I'll cope somehow. I'll just *have* to. And if I'm going to do it, now's the time . . . And I won't be quite alone.'

She made her preparations stealthily so as not to alert Sunshine, whom she could hear singing round the house. Not that there was much to prepare. It was simply a matter of pulling her two bags down from the top cupboard and packing them with her old clothes. Then she waited until she heard the back screen door close, and knew from long experience that Sunshine would be occupied in the laundry for some time, because that was her inevitable routine every day, and she went swiftly into Richard's study to make a phone call with surprisingly steady hands and voice.

At least, until the bright young voice on the other end of the line said still with a tinge of surprise, 'Yes, Mrs Gillespie. As a matter of fact the *Lotus Lady* is making the run now, but I could contact her on the radio and get her to call into Yandilla . . . let's see, it's only a supply run, so she would get there in about a half to three quarters of an hour's time. Is it a package you'd like to consign?'

It was then that Anna's nerve deserted her momentarily. 'Er . . .' She closed her eyes as she thought of the *Lotus Lady* and Mike Carmody. 'Yes,' she said breathlessly. 'Is . . . is Mr Carmody making the run?'

'No. He's away for a few days, Mrs Gillespie.'

'Oh. Well, look, I'm not quite sure if I'll have it ready in time . . .' Anna! she chided herself. What's this? You know you can't back out now.

But the voice at the other end of the line solved yet another dilemma for her, unwittingly. 'That's no problem, Mrs Gillespie. If you get it ready in time, just leave it at the end of the jetty. That's the arrangement we have, anyway. And if not, perhaps you'd care to give me a ring and we can make some other arrangement. But it's no problem for the *Lotus Lady* to check.'

'All right. Thank you very much.' Anna put the phone down with now shaking hands. Someone is going to get a shock when they discover what the Yandilla consignment is, she thought. But at least it won't be Mike, it'll be a stranger, so I won't have to make explanations. Not that there won't be a lot of speculation still . . .

She stood with her head bowed, in the middle of this room which had seen her make some momentous decisions. But as her resolution began to falter she heard his words again—if I had a dog, that would include it, and it includes you—I might put you out of your misery. And when you're ready to admit that . . . 'No!' she whispered on a gasping, trembling breath. 'No. I can't stay. I just can't.'

But it was so ridiculously easy to leave, that too seemed to rise up and taunt her for some strange reason. She could hear Sunshine singing distantly in the laundry as she went back to her room to collect her bags.

And all I have to do is go, she thought. If I leave the door closed, Sunshine won't even come in for fear of waking me. She looked around the room through a mist of tears and foolishly tidied up a few odds and ends as if that could eradicate the awful disharmony that had after all come to this bedroom. Then she licked the salty tears from her lips and picked up her bags and walked out.

She was half way down to the deep-water jetty when she tripped over a root of a tree. It was not a heavy fall, but as she tried to save herself she was conscious of a sudden flash of fear that she would never normally have experienced for such a mild tumble. Nor was the fear for her, she realised, but for the tiny, precious seed of life she carried within her. And as she sat on the path, examining this new dimension of her which until only so recently had not even been a certainty, a great tide of emotion rose up within her, making it difficult even to breathe. But one thought hammered at her brain insistently, refusing to be denied.

'I can't go,' she said out loud, with tears streaming down her face. 'How foolish I was to think I could,' she marvelled. 'Because for better, for worse, I made Yandilla a part of me that I can't tear out. I can't do it to Chrissy, I can't do it to this baby, but most of all I can't do it to myself. I just can't bear to think of living without any of them, even Richard. Especially Richard,' she acknowledged, and shivered as a shaft of pain pierced her heart. 'How can he do this to me?' she whispered. 'How can he make me hate him but love him at the same time? Love him so that I *can't* leave him. How is it possible?'

She sighed deeply and sat with her chin on her knees. Then she got up carefully and looked around. She pushed her two bags into a clump of bushes and started to walk again, but not towards the jetty.

About twenty minutes later she heard the asthmatic siren of the *Lotus Lady* toot twice, yet she kept walking steadily along the beach in the opposite direction. But not long afterwards she began to feel inexpressably weary and she sat down beneath the slanting branches of a strangler fig. The sand was warm and soft and the light breeze ruffled the leaves above her gently, and she lay back. Then she turned over with her head buried in her arms and fell asleep.

She only slept for an hour—to her relief. And she thought that with a bit of luck, she might even get back to the house without Sunshine discovering she had ever left it. 'Or anyone else, for that matter,' she muttered. 'But no one else should be back yet.'

It wasn't until she reached the front verandah and had her hand on the screen door that opened into the long central passageway of the house that she remembered her bags. She grimaced and half-turned to

go back for them, when Sunshine erupted into the
passageway from the bedroom, stopped dead at the
sight of Anna, stared incredulously for a moment, then
burst into tears, at the same time waving a hand
distractedly at the doorway through which she had
come. Then before Anna could say a word, she turned
and fled towards the kitchen.

There's been an accident! was Anna's first reaction as
she stumbled down the passageway. But the sight that
greeted her eyes as she came abreast of the bedroom
took her breath away. Because it was not the tidy room
she had left. In fact it looked as if it had been
ransacked. There were clothes strewn everywhere and
cupboards open and drawers hanging out.

And with his back to her, standing at the window,
Richard.

Anna made a small, unintelligible sound. He turned
slowly and she saw that his face was pale and rigid and
his eyes dark and violent. So violent, she took a step
backwards and put out a hand helplessly as if to ward
off the worst of his anger.

But it didn't come, at least not physically. When he
spoke, though, it was there unmistakably. 'I don't know
why you came back, Anna. But it's just as well you did,
because it saved me the bother of fetching you back,
which I wouldn't have done too politely. In fact,' he
said, speaking clearly and distinctly, 'I might as well
warn you not ever to do it again unless you wish to be
treated less than . . . civilly.' And there was something
so hard in his eyes, she shivered and paled.

'Do you understand, Anna?'

'I . . . no!' she cried brokenly. 'I don't! You . . .
we . . .'

'Then I'll explain it to you,' he said remorselessly. 'I
don't quite know how you did it. But you did—you
bewitched me to the extent that I can't live without you.
And seeing it was you yourself,' he said harshly, 'who
once had such faith in a grand, hit-you-on-the-head
passion like this, seeing it's *you* who did it, you're going
to have to live with it whether you like it or not!'

'Richard . . .' she whispered incredulously.

He smiled unpleasantly. 'Didn't you know? Didn't you even begin to suspect? I thought it must be obvious ... what a fool I was making of myself.'

Anna licked her lips, more totally confused than she'd ever been. 'I ... wished it and hoped it,' she said tremulously.

'Did you?' he asked curtly. 'I wonder why? So you could say I told you so?'

'*No*,' she breathed, her distress showing plainly.

'But you didn't do anything about it,' he shot at her savagely.

'How could I?' she said helplessly. 'You've been so ... lately, so ...'

'Yet I'd have thought, if you cared at all, some time in the last two weeks you could have tried to tell me how wrong I'd been. You had the proof.'

Anna's eyes widened. 'Is that why you were still so angry?'

His eyes blazed with a bitter light of self-mockery that answered her question as effectively as words.

'I ... I ...' she stammered, feeling her heart beginning to beat somewhere up in her throat.

'But that's beside the point now, isn't it? And perhaps I wasn't so wrong after all. Mike must have been delighted to discover yet another Yandilla wife needing rescuing from my clutches.' He looked at her sardonically.

'No! Richard, I didn't ... I came back.'

'Did you forget something?' he asked cruelly. 'Did you persuade Mike to bring the *Lotus Lady* back? Oh yes, between us, Sunshine and I were quite able to work out what had happened when you weren't to be found anywhere and your two bags and your own clothes and your tape recorder weren't here. And when she remembered hearing the boat toot twice, for no apparent reason, I rang their office. They said you'd wanted to consign a package. But I knew better. It was yourself, wasn't it?'

'Yes,' she conceded distractedly, and took a wavering breath as she saw his mouth tighten. 'I did plan to go. But I couldn't do it. I never set foot on the *Lotus Lady* and Mike isn't on her—I've no idea where he is! Nor do I want to . . . You can check—they'll tell you!'

For the first time a hint of doubt showed in Richard's eyes. 'Then where have you been? And where are your things?'

Anna looked around the dishevelled bedroom and swallowed. 'When I found I couldn't go, I went for a walk along the beach and . . . I fell asleep. My bags are stowed under a bush. I forgot about them.'

'If,' his voice was laced with pain suddenly, 'if you got that far, how come you couldn't do it? No, don't tell me. It was because of Chrissy, wasn't it?'

'Yes. Partly.'

They stared at each other and her heart contracted at the look of weariness in his eyes. As if he was drained now of all emotion.

'It's always been because of Chrissy, hasn't it, Anna?' He spoke unevenly and very quietly. 'That's why Letty and Phil got through to you with their machinations—I know that now.' His lips twisted in a bitter little smile. 'But I used Chrissy too, you know. In days gone past when I was still telling myself I could take you or leave you . . . even then I was banking on the fact that Chrissy would hold you here . . .'

'Well, you were wrong,' she said, searching his face and seeing what she had despaired of ever seeing. And the shock of it brought tears to her eyes that brimmed over foolishly and wet her cheeks.

'Was I? How was I wrong, Anna? Tell me,' he said huskily, his eyes roaming her face. 'I could make you— I've thought of it . . . You see, I've learnt too. I know how to make love to you just the way you like it. I know what makes you quiver and tremble. I know the secret, most sensitive parts of your beautiful body—I know every inch of you in a way I could never forget. Is that what you won't tell me? That you can't live without the way we make love to each other?'

'No,' she whispered, finding her throat strangely constricted. But then the words seemed to tumble out of their own accord, shakily and not very coherently. 'It's so much more. It's like an ocean that I can't begin to

describe. That's why I tried to go. I thought I couldn't
live like this any more, loving you and knowing—
thinking you couldn't ever love me, didn't even trust
me. I just couldn't stand the hurt any longer. And I
thought I could do it, because, you see, I'm going to
have your baby . . .' She stopped as he took a suddenly
tortured, understanding breath. 'I thought—I thought
I'd have that at least, something to live for, something
of yours that I could care about even if you didn't care
about me. But I couldn't do it, because I need you on
any terms, it seems.'

'When did you know about the baby?' His voice
shook and his hands were clenched as if to stop himself
from touching her.

'Only a few days ago, for sure.'

'And that's why you've been looking so pale—oh
God!' He closed his eyes briefly. 'How could I have
been so stupid and so blind?'

'Richard,' she whispered, and reached out to lay a
hand on his arm, 'I love you.'

'Why?' he said roughly. 'I'd understand it better if
you said you hated me. Don't you know that I've been
fighting you, and this, ever since I first laid eyes on you,
covered in dust but still so beautiful and spirited and
desirable?'

'I fought it for a while too,' Anna said softly.
'Remember? That—that was the real reason I let you go
on thinking I wasn't a virgin. I—it—I know it sounds
stupid, but it made me feel less . . . vulnerable,
somehow. But the night of the cyclone, when I thought
you must be dead, I felt like dying too. And I knew
then that I couldn't go on pretending to myself any
longer that I didn't love you.'

His eyes searched her face and one hand came up
involuntarily to cover hers. 'Is that . . . what made you
decide to marry me?' he asked huskily. 'Not, Chrissy,
not what Phil and Letty did?'

'Yes. But to love you is to love Chrissy too.'

'Anna . . .'

'Oh, Richard, hold me,' she whispered.

He did. He kissed her hair and her eyelids and her

throat as if he could never get enough of her. Then he picked her up in his arms and carried her to the bed. He returned to the door with a wry grimace and closed it, then he came back and lay down beside her and took her in his arms again. 'Sunshine thinks I've gone mad,' he said wryly.

'Why?' Anna pushed her fingers through his hair.

'Well, I told her, amongst other things, that I'd get you back if it was the last thing I did and I'd make you love me if it was the last thing I did too. I also told her she shouldn't be put in charge of a dog and if, when I did get you back, Letty couldn't keep her meddling fingers out of it, they'd all find themselves back on Thursday Island faster than you could say Jack Robinson. Just another manifestation of my insanity! Anna, my darling,' his voice was deep and unsteady, 'I still can't quite believe this.' He touched her face gently.

'Didn't you ever suspect—either?' she whispered, and kissed his wandering fingers.

'Yes—at least I wondered. When I found out I'd taken your virginity, almost casually, I wondered then. And I realised, looking back, that I should have known you were a virgin, but the mills of my mind grind exceedingly slow, I'm afraid,' he said grimly. 'And I was still not prepared to admit what I was feeling—still trying to tell myself that what I felt for you was a particularly strong attraction that then became coupled with a sense of guilt—you were so lovely, so eager to please, so easy to please . . .'

Anna trembled in his arms, but he drew her hard against him. 'Now, I know I loved that, more than you'll ever know,' he said very quietly. 'But *then*, in my heart I was still fighting you, Anna. Fighting the way you were growing more and more into my heart every day, every hour, it seemed. The night we were to go to the opera was one time I tried to buck against it.'

She moved her head so she could see into his eyes.

'Yes,' he traced the outline of her mouth with one finger. 'I thought, cope with this, Anna Horton, see what you can make of this. See if that—serene, virginal willingness can cope with these dark depths of my soul.

I was doing battle with you in earnest that night, Anna. Did you know?'

His eyes roamed her face and there was something so tender in them she trembled anew.

'Not that it matters,' he murmured. 'You routed me completely that night. You loved me in a way that was so honest, so generous, so—special, it was like nothing I'd ever known before.'

'Only because it was you. And because I loved you so much and couldn't tell you . . .'

He winced. 'I'm sorry, so sorry. But that's when it began to dawn on me that I was fighting a losing battle. That's when things began to change and I found that instead of being preoccupied with my feelings, more and more I was beginning to think of yours. And I began to hope. But when you're in the twisted, paranoid frame of mind I'd been in for so long, it doesn't take much to dash your hopes. And the first setback mine received was to discover that Letty and Phil had been putting pressure on you too. I thought then, maybe you did only tell me the truth when you said you'd marry me.'

'I nearly did,' she confessed.

He held her close for a long time. Then he said on a curiously tortured note, 'All those things I said, all the things I thought—can you ever forgive me?'

'Of course,' she whispered, and kissed his hand again with trembling lips.

'You shouldn't. How come you do?'

'Because I know what you went through before . . .'

'Yes, Julie,' said Richard with a tiny frown of pain between his eyes. 'I lived in torment with her memory for too long. But now . . . I only wish there was some way I could make my peace with her. Does that sound strange to you?'

'Oh no,' she whispered. 'It makes me very happy.'

He stroked her hair and watched her with eyes that were loving and calm at last. 'And Mike,' he said, but moved his head negatively almost immediately. 'No, not Mike,' he added very quietly.

She looked at him, her eyes a little troubled.

'Oh, in my heart, yes, because I know now what he might have been going through with Julie. I've had the evidence of my own insanity where you're concerned,' he said with a slight smile, 'to understand. But if he admires you, and I think he does, then we're destined to be two people never to see eye to eye.'

'He . . . he . . . but I never thought of him like that. How could I?' Anna said tearfully. 'Since that day you nearly ran over me I haven't had a thought to spare . . .'

'Anna, sweetheart, don't cry,' he murmured remorsefully, and kissed her tears.

'Kiss me properly, then I won't,' she said with a trembling little smile. 'Although sometimes you do it so beautifully that makes me want to cry too.'

He did. And a little later, he undressed her and stared down at her searchingly, taking in every detail of her body. Until he lifted his head at last and said huskily, 'I can't see any changes.'

'It's too soon. But in a few months' time there'll be more . . . so much of me, in fact, you might not like what you see any more,' she teased gently.

'I wouldn't count on that,' he commented. 'I suspect I shall be just as proprietorial as I am now, if not more so. And jealous and proud and filled with a sense of my own importance as I watch you grow big with my baby. I'll probably be impossible to live with. Will you mind?'

She laughed softly. 'I suspect not.'

But Richard sobered and as he bent his head to kiss her breasts, he murmured, 'It's been so long, Anna.'

'Two weeks.'

'That's two weeks too long. Is it any wonder I was a raging lunatic?'

'Ah,' she said breathlessly, 'so that's the answer? I'll remember that the next time you get cross with me!'

'I don't think there'll be a next time,' he said between kisses.

'That might be a pity.'

'Why?'

'I've just worked out the way to deal with it,' she answered, her eyes dancing impishly.

Richard lifted his head. 'Tell me.'

'Oh—I thought I might try my hand at seducing you for a change but if you say . . .' She wasn't allowed to finish.

'Forget what I said,' he interrupted with the most wicked glint in his eyes. 'And why wait until I'm cross to do it? I . . .'

'I know all about *you*,' Anna said primly but with her eyes alight with love and laughter. 'You're one of those unprincipled men who is no respecter of ladies or conventions, and believes in making love at the oddest times.'

'Hell,' he said with a grin, 'don't tell me it's lunchtime again! Tell you what—I'll show you how reformed I am. I shall desist . . .'

'Don't you dare! Besides, I've got used to it now,' she said airily.

Richard's eyes danced. 'You do realise Letty and Samson and Sunshine are probably all in quite a state by now, wondering what's going on? Don't you think at least we should . . .'

'Later,' she said softly, and ran her hands along his shoulders, caressingly. 'Anyway, Letty will have worked it all out by now. She's always one step ahead of me.'

'And me,' he said wryly. 'Anna,' he went on, suddenly completely serious, 'will you say it again? And keep saying it while you . . . do what you're doing?' he added with an effort. 'Then I might believe it's not just a dream.'

'I love you, Richard. I love you, I . . .'